Vanessa Gordon lives in Surrey and has spent many years working as a concert manager, musicians' agent and live music supplier. She visits Greece as often as possible.

The Martin Day mystery series is set on Naxos, the largest island in the Cyclades, Greece. It is an island of contrasts. The modern port of Chora is crowned by a Venetian kastro which is surrounded by an interesting old town. You can find uninhabited central hills, the highest mountain in the Cyclades, attractive fishing villages, popular beaches, and archaeological sites. There are historic towers and welcoming tavernas, collectable art and ceramics. Naxos has produced some of the finest marble in Greece since ancient times. Now, Martin Day has moved in.

The Search for Artemis

Artemis

A Naxos mystery *with Martin Day*

Vanessa Gordon

Published by Pomeg Books 2021 www.pomeg.co.uk

Cover photograph and map © Alan Gordon

Cover image: Paros, Cyclades

ISBN: 978-1-8384533-1-2

Pomeg Books is an imprint of
Dolman Scott Ltd
www.dolmanscott.co.uk

To Mary Chipperfield with love

Warm thanks to Christine Wilding and Alan Gordon for proofreading and to Cristine Mackie for her useful insights.

I am grateful to Zois Kouris (Hellenic Centre), Efthymios Stamos and Koula Crawley-Moore for their guidance regarding the Greek language.

Thank you, Genevieve Nielsen, for sharing your expertise regarding the firing of pottery.

My special thanks to Robert Pitt, who has shared with me his knowledge of Greece and been an excellent companion on many Greek journeys.

To Alan and Alastair, thank you for everything.

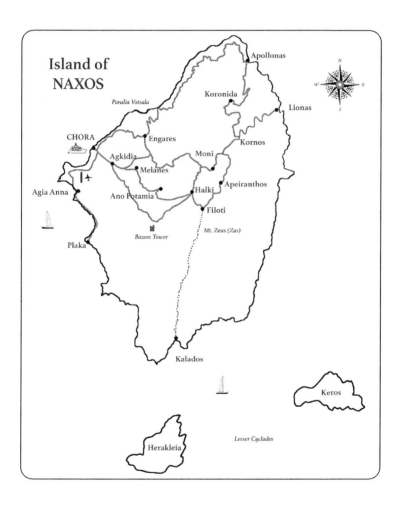

Island of
NAXOS

Apollonas

Paralia Votsala

Koronida

Lionas

CHORA

Engares

Kornos

Agkidia

Moni

Melanes

Apeiranthos

Agia Anna

Ano Potamia

Halki

Filoti

Mt. Zeus (Zas)

Bazeos Tower

Plaka

Kalados

Keros

Herakleia

Lesser Cyclades

A NOTE ABOUT GREEK WORDS

Readers without a knowledge of Greek might like to know about one or two things that they will notice in the book.

'Kyrie' and 'Kyria' are forms of address like monsieur and madame. 'Mou' means 'my', often used after a name as a term of affection.
'Agapi mou' means 'my dear'.
'Pappou' means Grandpa.
'Kali Orexi' means 'Bon Appétit!'
'Kalos Irthatay!' means 'Welcome!'
'Stin yia sas!' means "Good health!', a toast.
'Oriste!' is a common way to answer the phone.
Zas is Greek for Zeus

Greek names sometimes have changed endings in the vocative, which is when the person is directly addressed. This is why you will see Thanasis become Thanasi, Vasilios become Vasili, and other examples, when the characters are being spoken to directly.

Greek place names can be found in different spellings in the Latin alphabet; spellings most likely to help with pronunciation are used in this book.

The main town of Naxos is called Chora (or Naxos). You pronounce the ch in Chora as in the Scottish 'loch'. Similarly, Halki (also written Chalki) begins with that sound.

Peppino's "Mingia!"
Translations differ, but this is a common exclamation in Sicily and probably should be given in asterisks.

1

An earthquake woke Edward Childe in the night. He woke with a sense of loss and foreboding. The sweat dried cold beneath his pyjamas. It was pitch dark, silent and still. Then he heard a noise, a car driving past on the Cambridge street outside.

He opened his eyes properly, fighting a nameless despair. Clearly there hadn't been an earthquake. He limped to the bathroom; his legs had begun to stiffen up at night around his seventy-sixth birthday. He wasn't too concerned, because his mind still worked and that was all that mattered to Edward. He got back into bed and switched off the light.

The July night was very warm and before long Edward felt too hot. It reminded him of Greece, where people slept under a single sheet throughout the summer. Edward shifted his left leg to the cool side of the bed and gently guided his thoughts away from Artemis, who had been summoned to his mind by thoughts of hot Greek summers. He tried for the last time to remember the dream that had woken him. He had a lingering feeling of dread.

He was unsuccessful, and instead invited Artemis back into his mind. Artemis was like a favourite book, one which you have loved since childhood. For the last sixty years, ever since the day she had disappeared from his bed on a hot August night in Greece, memories of Artemis had been his pleasure and his solace.

Edward thought about the letter which had arrived yesterday from Athens. It was from somebody called Angelika, who wrote that she was Artemis's granddaughter and that she had recently learned of Edward's part in her grandmother's life through reading her diaries. Artemis, she informed him, had sadly died a few years before, but Angelika had searched for Edward, finally found him, and wanted to meet him.

Edward Childe was an optimist. He gave no more thought to the demons of the night that assail even elderly professors. He fell asleep pondering what Angelika, the lady who had beckoned to him as if from his youth, might look like.

Like Artemis, he hoped.

2

Martin Day, freelance archaeologist and now the owner of a house on the island of Naxos, was woken by the already powerful heat of the August morning. Realising that the air-conditioning was off, he reached out and found the remote, listened for the system to whirr into life, and waited for the energy to get out of bed. He remembered he was alone in the house for the first time in months. His friend Helen had taken the ferry to the mainland yesterday, to catch a flight from Athens to London. He was sorry, of course, that she had a funeral to attend, but his beautiful Greek house was too quiet now without her. Day felt more sad than he had expected.

Day made for the shower, sweeping his bathrobe off the chair without breaking step. The floorboards creaked and the iron swayed on the board, reminding him to switch it on. One day he must iron more than a single shirt at a time.

The shower began to banish his gloominess and his thoughts turned to the future. One guest out, one guest in. Today somebody potentially very interesting was arriving, Edward Childe, Emeritus Professor of History, King's College, Cambridge. Quite a title, impressive in itself, yet that was not what really excited Day. This Edward Childe, who was about eighty, wanted to discuss a professional collaboration.

Day was in two minds about the new proposal. It was like London buses: no bus for hours then several come at once. He was still in the middle of a major piece of work, a biography of Nikos Elias, an archaeologist from Naxos who had died about twenty years ago and who had found an underground tomb dating back to the Bronze Age. In theory, Day didn't have time for Edward Childe and his new project. The Elias book would keep Day's agent happy, and Day was not by nature inclined to work harder than strictly necessary. However, neither was he a man to turn down something potentially spectacular, as Edward Childe's idea promised to be, without giving it a great deal of thought.

Thinking along these lines, Day lingered in the shower and forgot to pay attention to his use of water. As it trickled over him he thought of Deppi, enjoying the glow of guilty pleasure it gave him to think of her. He loved to recall her devotion to her little boy, Nestoras. He loved imagining her standing on the prow of her husband's yacht, black hair flying in the wind, spray cooling her as she held on to some rope or other. Day knew nothing about boats. Ah well, a cat can look at a queen, he thought, and briskly turned off the shower.

Day was always desperate for his first coffee. He filled the cafetière and left it steeping while he dressed. Edward Childe was not due till after lunch, so Day had time to work on the biography before he arrived. He decided against driving across the island to the Elias house to work in his office there. He took his coffee and laptop to the balcony instead. Looking out across the Filoti valley, he was struck again by Helen's absence. Over the last three months they had often chatted round this old table under the cane awning. She would notice things, with her novelist's eye, in which he had taken no interest until she had arrived. From now on, Day would have to look for himself. He scanned the opposite hills for the blue beehives she had liked, the shepherd with his dogs that she had watched every day, and the mule she had noticed tethered in the shade of a solitary tree. He could see the beehives. That was something, at least.

Day checked his mobile. There was a message from Helen saying she was safely home in Hampstead, and one from Edward Childe confirming he would arrive in Filoti as near two o'clock as possible. Forcing himself not to open Facebook, Day closed his phone and opened his computer to work.

Flushed with coffee as he was, the morning felt very warm. August was a little cooler here than July, tempting Athenians to come to Naxos to escape the stifling heat of the city, but Day found thirty-eight degrees very hot even so. He sensed the heat rising in invisible waves from the valley, as if trapped there and seeking an escape route across the balcony and through his living room. If it was this hot in the middle of the morning, what would it be like when Edward Childe arrived? He hoped the elderly professor was prepared.

Day opened his work at the place where he had left off the previous night, and within minutes was completely absorbed in Nikos Elias's discoveries off the west coast of Naxos.

***

So engrossed was Day in his work that he gave no thought to eating lunch. A text from Edward Childe informed him that his visitor expected to be in Filoti in ten minutes. Day sent a reply and put away his laptop. He looked round the main room of his Greek house with a mixture of pride and despair. He had done so well buying this place, it was the best thing he could have done with the inheritance from his father, and after only four months as its new owner he was still very much in love with it. However, despite its charms it was certainly not tidy. Books everywhere, hats thrown on chairs, glasses waiting to be washed up by the sink. Too late now. He heard a car in the road outside. Smoothing his blonde hair with one hand he unlatched the front door with the other and placed a smile on his face.

The elderly man who paid off the taxi and turned towards Day was most certainly an English gentleman - both English and a gentleman. Day chided himself for such an old-fashioned reaction and struggled to understand what he was registering, as Edward Childe lifted his small bag and walked towards the house. It was simply that if Edward had been wearing a tweed three-piece suit, which thankfully he was not, he could not have looked more of 'an Englishman of a certain generation'.

Within minutes, as he held out his hand to Edward, Day amended this impression. His visitor was wearing cool beige slacks, a short-sleeved white cotton shirt and quite respectable deck shoes without socks. He was clearly accustomed to the Greek summer, and almost 'on trend'. He was of medium height, much shorter than Day, and maybe in his late seventies. Day regretted not having checked his visitor out online. Despite his age, the professor had dark hair, maybe thinning a little. What struck you about Edward Childe was the kindness of his face. He was smiling, of course, but it was more than that.

"Professor Day! Delightful to finally meet you!" began Edward cheerfully, shaking hands. "I'm sorry I'm a little late. So hard to get the time right in Greece."

Day laughed, not at his guest but at himself. In so few words his visitor had already teased him. Day had been dubbed 'Professor' on a certain American history series which he had presented a year ago, and unlike Edward Childe had not earned the title in any university.

"Welcome! The pleasure is mine. Do come in."

He led the way into the cool of the front room, where Edward Childe threw his small bag on the floor behind the door and rubbed his hands together enthusiastically, looking round the place with admiration and almost sniffing the air.

"You have a beautiful house here, and your choice of Filoti is excellent. I've always been fond of this village. Oh, I can smell the fresh island air even inside the house. Oregano and the sea, isn't it?"

"Something like that, yes. Come through, Edward. Let's sit on the balcony. Can I get you a glass of water? A little lunch? Glass of wine?"

"If it's no trouble, all of those sound wonderful, Martin."

In the galley kitchen at the far end of the living room, Day prepared some local cheese, some pieces of Italian ham which he particularly liked, and some rocket dressed with olive oil and sea salt. He had no bread in the house; he would have to visit the supermarket soon. There were a few crackers in a tin, usually eaten with his evening aperitif, but he threw a few on the plate next to the cheese. Two generous glasses of white wine and a bottle of water. Done.

Edward Childe was already settled on the balcony. As he talked to Day he devoted an intense and appreciative scrutiny to the fields and hills which filled the view from where he sat. When Day put the tray on the table, Edward nodded happily. They raised their glasses of wine with a camaraderie which had everything to do with men who both enjoy their pleasures.

"I really like your house, Martin. It has space and air. You must find it excellent for your concentration."

"Very much so, when I work here. I often have to work in the Elias house, over on the coast near Engares, because all the documents and artefacts are kept there. You know about my current project?"

"I've heard about it from my publisher, Jonathan, at Browne and Moore. Not much escapes Jonathan. You're preparing a book on the late Nikos Elias, I believe? I was told there's a newly discovered Mycenaean burial site, which Elias apparently found some years ago but kept to himself, and you re-discovered earlier this year?"

"That's right. I propose to bore you with all the details later, over dinner. But tell me, what are you doing these days, Edward?"

Edward Childe laughed contentedly, his gaze shifting from Day to the farther side of the valley, where a man was leading a mule across the landscape towards the outskirts of the village.

"I bounce from one project to the next as if I were still a young man, Martin. It's the only way to live when you get to my age, believe me. What are you - about forty? I'm eighty-one, would you credit it? Only when I hit eighty did I have to admit I was really quite pushing it. What do they say in Greece? 'A heart that loves is always young'. Such a wise people, the Greeks. I love my work. There's so much I still want to do."

"It's certainly doing the trick. You don't look a day over seventy!"

"Well said!" Edward chuckled happily, and Day knew he had hit the right note. As he neared his fortieth birthday, he rarely felt young enough these days to make a joke about age. He passed his guest the plate of cheese and tossed the rocket in the dressing.

"Bon appétit!" said Edward, about to tuck in. "I should say, 'Kali Orexi', should I not? Many thanks, I forgot to eat today apart from a Marks & Spencer sandwich on the aeroplane."

"The view's better here, despite the heat. Kali orexi!"

As they ate, Day reflected that he felt so at ease with this eminent historian that they might have known each other for twenty years. Edward had the trick of landing in your pool and making minimal ripples. Such ripples as did emanate from him were an adornment rather than a disturbance. Day shook his head. He wondered how his elderly guest had already affected him like this.

"Thank you, Martin," said Edward, closing his knife and fork politely. "A delicious lunch, at the right time and in a beautiful place."

"Would you like to unpack, maybe have a rest and a shower, and then you can tell me all about the new venture? I'm looking forward to hearing the details."

Day refilled Edward's glass of water from the bottle in the fridge, retrieved his bag from the table by the front door and showed him to the guest room. He was relieved that he had remembered to prepare the room the previous night. This had been Helen's bedroom for three months, and it felt slightly strange to give it to somebody else. At least it was tidy.

He opened the thin white curtain, the window and the shutters, and let in the scented air from the valley. Edward smiled when he saw his private balcony with traditional wooden chair, and declared it was charming. Day grinned.

"Your bathroom's just over there. Clean towel behind the door. Remote for the aircon is here on the table, but it should be on the right setting already. I'm off for a bit of a siesta. See you later, about six?"

"Perfect. Thank you again, Martin."

***

Day set his alarm, and after a deep sleep unbroken by dreams he took another shower and ironed a second shirt. After careful thought he left the air conditioning on in his bedroom. He arrived in the living room to see Edward happily enjoying the view from the balcony as if he had not moved since lunch. Completely at ease, he seemed unaffected by the heat and in an excellent mood.

"Ah, Martin. Did you have a good rest?"

"I did, thank you. Did you?"

"Yes, a good hour or so. Most restorative."

"Tea?"

"How English! Yes, please. Can I help?"

"No, you just chill out. Ha! A poor choice of phrase. I'll bring some cold water too."

***

"So, Martin, how much have you heard about this idea of mine?" said Edward. "I take it your agent contacted you after hearing from Jonathan at Browne and Moore?"

"Yes, my agent in London, Maurice Atkinson. He's very good. He told me something about your proposal. It's probably best if you tell me everything yourself, Edward. I liked what I heard from Maurice, it sounded more than exciting enough to whet my appetite, but this is your brainchild. Why not start at the beginning, and we'll carry on over dinner? There's an excellent local taverna I thought we should visit tonight."

"What a treat! Very well, then, I'll tell you. For the last forty years or so I've been collecting original writings and art by nineteenth-century English travellers to Greece. I think it's what they call an 'idiosyncratic' collection. Some of the travellers are quite well-known figures, for example I have an Edward Lear watercolour and some letters written by Mabel Bent. Other travellers aren't well known but their work is tremendous. I've never done anything about pulling the collection together or doing something worthwhile with it, and that's a great pity.

"My idea is that an item from the collection could introduce each location, or episode, in a series of accessible documentary programmes. The subject of the series will be my particular love, marble. I've always been fascinated by marble, and I'm far from alone in that. I suppose it's no surprise that my greatest love is for ancient marble, but I also admire modern marble sculpture, and since my retirement I've indulged in finding out about the Greek marble artists who working today. In my art collection I have some paintings which show ancient marble buildings and sculptures from various parts of Greece.

"I thought it would be nice to combine my collection, the subject of ancient marble, the lives of the ancient sculptors, and an introduction to modern marble artists in Greece. You and I would travel all over Greece following in the footsteps of the travellers in my collection, examining the use of marble, past and present. It could make a stunning series of programmes, I think … and my hope is that you would present it. What do you think?"

"I think it's extremely interesting. How many episodes do you envisage?"

"Ten at least. We can do a lot of linkage between past and present, some in-depth work on living artists, with interviews and so on, and tie in some of the items in my collection. A lot of the things have never been seen before."

Edward took a contented sip of his tea before turning to Day with the enthusiasm of a schoolboy.

"I thought we'd start by involving a friend of mine who lives and works here on Naxos. In fact, I've taken the liberty of arranging for you and me to go to his workshop tomorrow, if that suits you, Martin? He's absolutely fantastic, one of the leading marble artists in Greece, if not Europe. Over dinner I'll tell you all about him. If you don't want to be involved in the project after you've met Konstantinos Saris, so be it. But I think you'll be captivated."

3

Out of respect for his guest's age, Day resisted the temptation to offer him the gin and tonic before dinner that would be Day's usual habit. They finished their tea, closed up the house and began to walk into Filoti to the taverna. They drew a few stares from the locals, the tall, blonde Englishman and the wiry old professor who was old enough to be his grandfather. Edward talked about his life in Cambridge as they sauntered along the road. After retiring fifteen years ago from his position as Professor of Ancient History at King's, he had continued to live on his own in one of Cambridge's tall, elegant townhouses in a quiet road near Jesus College. He had never married or had a longterm partner, but he was very content with his life. He maintained a close association with his old college, and often met former colleagues at High Table and annual events. He had never stopped working, and still spent much of his time in the library.

Day envisaged the overwhelming beauty of King's College while his eyes fell on the small houses of Filoti and sun-bleached cars full of dents and scratches parked up on the cracked pavements. Old people sitting on ancient chairs by their front doors were chatting across the street in the now gentle heat of evening. Different worlds.

A short walk brought them to Taverna O Thanasis, Day's favourite restaurant since moving to Filoti. The tables in front of the taverna were all full, the tourist season being in full swing. Thanasis, the portly owner, saw them arriving and turned from the bar to greet them. He smiled broadly when he saw Day.

"Martin, my good friend, how are you? And good evening, sir, you are most welcome!"

"Thanasi, this is Edward, my friend from the UK. Edward, this is Thanasis, owner of my favourite restaurant in all Greece!"

Thanasis offered them a good table near the open front window, overlooking the terrace and the street beyond. He brought them a bottle of cold mineral water, glasses, menus and a basket of freshly sliced crusty bread nestling against cutlery tightly wrapped in paper serviettes.

"I'll leave you in the care of my son, Vangelis," said Thanasis, beckoning the younger man, "and I shall just say that this evening I recommend my wife's katsikaki. It's her own recipe."

Thanasis gave a small bow of the head and retreated to welcome more guests.

"Remind me, Martin, my Greek's a bit rusty?"

"He was recommending the baby goat," said Day. "Thanasis's wife, Koula, never fails to do something amazing in the kitchen. I recently had her souvlaki, and although I don't much care for souvlaki as a rule, well, it was astonishing."

"Then our choice is made. I take it we'll order to share? Good. Perhaps you'd do the honours?"

Day asked for some small bits and pieces chosen by Vangelis to start, followed by a portion of the baby goat, a Greek salad and Naxos fried potatoes. Day had a particular fondness for chips. Moreover, on Naxos the locals claimed to grow exceptionally tasty potatoes. Day could not dispute this, and happily put it to the test as often as he could.

"Do you already know, Edward, that you are now in the home of the finest potatoes in Greece?"

"I had heard the rumour," Edward nodded. "One can hardly know Naxos without hearing it. I have to say, they're right. I'm fond of potatoes, as anyone with Irish blood must be, and I've never tasted better."

"You have Irish blood?"

"A little. A love of potatoes, and an ability to tell a good story at great length, is all I have to show for it."

"Ah. In that case, you should tell me a good story! But before you do, shall we order some wine?"

"Please, let's do that. Red wine? Barrel?"

Day regarded his guest with approval, and beckoned the attentive Vangelis. He ordered a litre of the local red wine 'from the barrel', light and young, and good for your head the next day.

"It sounds as if you've been to Naxos before, Edward? Do you know the island well?"

"I've tried to visit as many of the islands in the Cyclades as I can. I have friends on Naxos now. I also remember the Archeological Museum. Wonderful curator there, I recall. Many good pieces too, although the Roman things aren't so close to my heart as the older material…"

"You know the Curator? He's a very good friend of mine. Aristos Iraklidis."

"Ah yes, that's the name. He's still here?"

"He's been here for ever, I think. I'll take you to see him, you can renew the acquaintance."

"That would be excellent, Martin. I must say, …"

Day didn't discover what it was that Edward had to say, as Vangelis arrived with their first dishes. There was a small plate of crispy fried squid in a delicate batter, another of courgette balls, and a bowl of homemade tzatziki dip, flavoured with mint and cucumber. The bright metal jug of red wine and two glasses then appeared, and Vangelis wished them Kali Orexi.

"Oh, this is a real pleasure. Thank you, Martin."

"To your good health, Edward."

Contrary to their plan, they devoted themselves to the food before beginning to talk of the project. Once again, Day approved of Edward Childe for this. It seemed they had certain preferences in common as well as at least one friend. When the food arrived they found that Koula, who brought the dish of roasted baby goat to their table herself, had again cooked something special. The meat was tender, tasty and not too strong, nestling among chunks of the famous Naxian potatoes which were ideal for absorbing the juices. Day was in potato heaven. He helped himself to a second portion of chips when he thought Edward was preoccupied.

When sufficient justice had been done to the dinner, Day divided the last of the jug of wine between their glasses, and sat back in his chair. He suggested that Edward tell him more about his friend, the marble artist.

***

"I met Konstantinos Saris in 2013 in Cambridge. He was visiting the Fitzwilliam Museum for an exhibition called 'Marble Art in the Islands of the Mediterranean'. It was a collaboration between the Fitzwilliam, The Greek Ministry of Culture and various senior curators and academics. Behind the scenes, most of the administration was being done by a very gifted PhD student of mine. Anyway, it was a wonderful exhibition, featuring the work of some really exciting contemporary sculptors at the height of their powers. At the exhibition you could see their new work alongside examples of ancient marble sculpture from the same islands. There were representatives from Cyprus, Sicily, Crete, Sardinia and the Cyclades.

"I went along to the Fitzwilliam one day to congratulate my student, and she introduced me to Konstantinos. He and I went for dinner together that night, and formed a plan for me to visit him on Naxos a couple of months later. Well, I was retired, so there was nothing to stop me. That was six years ago, and I've visited him a couple of times since. His home is in the hills near Kato Potamia, not too far from here, in fact. You have to see it to believe me, it's an artist's paradise.

"Anyway, Konstantinos is almost exactly my age, but his career is going from strength to strength. The Niarchos Foundation have taken an interest in him, and have funded a three year project in which Konstantinos will collaborate with a different marble artist each year at his 'atelier' (as he calls it). The visiting artist will work alongside Konstantinos during the winter months, and each spring there will be an exhibition of work on Naxos. At the end of the three years, the entire output will be shown at the Niarchos Cultural Centre in

Athens, where it will be on display for six months. Not bad work for an old man, eh?"

"You're right, Edward, I shall enjoy meeting your friend Konstantinos. I'm ashamed I haven't heard about him already, and he's practically a neighbour."

"And do you see how he fits in so well with my current project, Martin? I haven't talked about it to him yet, but I'm hoping he will agree to be involved. Maybe he would give an interview, as part of the comparison of modern and ancient marble work on Naxos."

At this moment Vangelis, almost apologetically, interrupted their conversation to give them complimentary glasses of liqueur. It was a clear liquid but looked thicker than tsipouro, the traditional spirit digestif which Thanasis usually gave to his favoured customers.

"Mastika!" said Vangelis by way of explanation, with a smile of pride.

"Mastic liqueur? I haven't tasted this for many years," said Edward. "Cheers, Martin, and here's to our collaboration. That is, I hope you're considering it after what you've heard?"

Day sipped his drink politely, although he always found mastic too sweet for his taste. He replaced his glass gently on the table.

"I think I might need another glass of red," he said quietly. "Then yes, I think we can drink to the collaboration."

***

Day and Edward took their second jug of wine to an outside table under the vine-draped pergola. Most of the tourist families had finished and left, and the table was relatively private. It gave a good view down the village street, where brighter, more popular cafes were busy with people who had gathered to talk and drink away the balmy evening.

Day quite suddenly realised that Edward was tipsy, and felt a pang of guilt. He poured them both fresh glasses of water. Edward talked on, true to his Irish heritage as he would say. Day almost stopped listening. He was thinking about their visit the next day to see Konstantinos Saris at what he called his 'atelier' in the hills. Edward's project appealed to Day in many ways, especially if this marble artist would take part. It would all provide something of a welcome change from the affairs of the late Nikos Elias. He was pondering these things in a pleasant, wine-induced reverie when Edward changed the subject.

Edward had been telling a story about an Italian girl whose doctorate he had supervised many years ago and who had become a renowned yachtswoman, when he stopped and gave a short laugh.

"I'd like to tell you a different story, Martin, if you permit me. It's one which until now I've kept to myself. I'd like to share it with you."

Day rallied himself from his thoughts. "By all means," he smiled.

"Something rather special brings me to Greece this month, in addition to seeing you about the marble project. My plans were already in place to come here when I was invited to a different kind of meeting.

"It has to do with a lady I met many years ago. I suppose she's the reason why I've never married. I've certainly been in love. I was twenty-one when I met her, here in Greece. I had recently finished my undergraduate degree in Classics and had decided to use all my savings to travel round Greece with a knapsack - that's what we called backpacks in 1959. I bought a cheap rail ticket and headed to Athens, intending to visit all the ancient sites round Greece which I'd studied only from books. I wanted to stand there and experience them for real.

"I planned to hitch lifts, take trains, buses. The Greek buses were very good, I remember. Before going anywhere, though, I visited the Acropolis of Athens, of course. After that, all the other sites in the city, cutting my teeth on the Hill of the Pnyx, the Areopagus, the Agora … you know, all the endless delights of Athens. In 1959 it looked very different indeed from today….

"My next stop was Sounion, on a local bus service. The adventure had started. By then - I was an arrogant youth, I'm sure - I thought of nothing but antiquity. I traced my finger over Byron's name where he'd etched it into a blue-white marble column of the Temple of Poseidon, and gazed out to sea imagining the Venetian fleet passing in the distance.

"I remember I got a lift from Sounion to Brauron. It was August like it is now, very hot. We didn't wear shorts back then - it was cream suits or white slacks, and ties, and terribly old-fashioned hats!"

Edward chuckled, and Day could imagine him in the kind of light jacket, dusky trousers and old-fashioned hat he had seen in many an old black and white photograph in worthy archaeological tomes.

"Those were the days when the excavation of the Temple of Artemis at Brauron was in full swing," continued Edward. "It had begun in the 1940s and it went on until sometime in the 1960s, under the supervision of the great man himself, Ioannis Papadimitriou. Exciting times.

"At the village of Brauron I found a room in a local house for a few shillings a night and arranged to stay two nights. The next morning I carefully prepared myself with my Baedeker and notebook, and walked to the excavation site itself. Perhaps it's only the benefit of hindsight, but I think even then I felt that something very important was going to happen to me that day.

"I walked round the remains of the Temple of Artemis in a daze. In those days, of course, you were allowed to touch the columns, even stand on the column bases if you wanted, and I remember striding from corner to corner of the temple to understand it and get a feel for its dimensions. There was only one other person around, an old man in a blue shirt and dark trousers who was sitting in the only bit of shade. He wasn't looking at me, but I couldn't stop looking at him. I thought I recognised him, but it was impossible. I hesitated, I can tell you. Then I went over to him.

"He saw me walking towards him but didn't get up. I worked out afterwards that he was 72. 'Excuse me, sir,' I said, 'Are you Professor Carl Blegen?' The old man smiled, quite a kind smile. He had a grey moustache and bushy grey eyebrows in a suntanned face. His eyes were as blue as his clothes. 'I can't deny it, young man,' he said. He had a strong American accent.

"I muttered something about the honour of meeting him, and he allowed me to shake his hand. He lived another twelve years, you know, but he seemed extremely old to me that day. He asked what I was doing. I told him, and he didn't ask me any questions. He just said, 'I can see you'll be following in my footsteps, Edward Childe. Good luck to you.'

Day had no doubt how pivotal this meeting must have been for young Edward, back in 1959. To meet the great Carl Blegen, the American archaeologist who had excavated Pylos and Troy, at the impressionable age of twenty-one, must have been life-changing.

"Had you already decided on a career in ancient history, Edward?"

"I'd played with the idea, but after meeting the Great Blegen I never considered anything else. I still don't know what he was doing there. Probably just making a visit, like me. I thought it odd that he was sitting on his own, although maybe he was waiting for someone. Occasionally I wonder whether I dreamed it all."

"Surely he would have visited all the sites, and you were just fortunate to be at Brauron on that particular day?"

"I'm sure you're right. Anyway, the story doesn't end there. It was only the beginning.

"That afternoon, after I'd gone off to the village and bought myself something for lunch, I went back to the site again. A girl was sitting on a column drum sketching the great columns and the broken architraves of the temple. She wore a long-sleeved white shirt and a brown skirt that reached down to her stout leather boots. Her only concession to the heat was a broad-brimmed white hat. She didn't notice me, she was intent on her drawing. I watched her from a distance for a few minutes, and then went back to exploring the temple.

"Later in the afternoon I came across her again. We said hello and I admired her sketches. She was very easy to talk to, and remember this was 1959 when girls tended to be rather more reserved than today. A boy had to tread quite carefully. Her name was Artemis, and that got us talking. She thought it huge fun that she shared the name of the ancient goddess of Brauron, and we laughed together. Artemis. She had no airs and graces, and no problem with talking to a young man from England. She was Greek, of course. She had the most beautiful long black hair, I remember admiring it at the time. Well, of course, we soon developed a liking for each other. I extended my stay at the little room in the village, and we spent our days together, I reading and mapping the layout of the site, she drawing and painting everything that she saw.

"When our time at Brauron ended she agreed to go with me on my summer exploration of the other sites of Ancient Greece. She wanted to see Corinth, so we headed there, and then we saw Epidauros and carried on to Nafplio, and walked round Mycenae together. It was a very hot August, which matched our mood perfectly."

Day nodded, not wanting to interrupt the old man's flow. Edward was right, he did tell a good story. Artemis of Brauron, ancient and modern. It was a real 1950s romance on so many levels.

"Unfortunately, the idyll didn't last. My Artemis finally made love to me in Nafplio, and I did nothing to stop her. I was out of my wits in love with her, and she was a truly independent spirit. I was away from home, and so was she. We were so happy. I fell asleep one night, I remember, with Artemis in my arms, and I decided to ask her to marry me before we parted that summer. There seemed to be no urgency. I was wrong. When I woke the next morning she had gone. She left me a sketch she'd done of me while I was sleeping."

"Did you see her again?"

"No. I never heard from her and I couldn't find her. I barely knew anything about her, not even her family name. She would say that she was more interested in hearing about me, and I could never get her to talk much about herself.

"I finished my summer tour on my own, sad but determined. Carl Blegen's words kept me going, even though I was in the depths of misery in my heart. I went back to England and started a doctorate on Bronze Age Greece. That's the end of the story, I'm afraid. At least, it was until a month ago.

"I received a letter from Greece. It was from a lady called Angelika, who said she was Artemis's granddaughter. The letter explained that Artemis died in 2011, and at the time nobody had gone carefully through her personal things. Angelika had recently done so, and found a diary from 1959 in which her grandmother wrote about her relationship with me. Angelika had written to me care of King's

College, Cambridge, and thankfully the College had forwarded it to me.

"To cut to the best bit, Martin, I'm going to meet Angelika next week in Athens. I plan to spend some time in town seeing people at the National Museum and the British School, but the meeting with Angelika, the granddaughter of my lovely Artemis … I can't tell you how much that means to me."

"You don't need to, Edward. What a story. Isn't it incredible how things work out if you wait long enough? You might discover what Artemis wrote about you, and why she moved on. I hope it isn't too painful."

Edward laughed quietly.

"I'm too old for that. I have wonderful memories, and whatever made Artemis leave me I would respect it. These things happen when you're young. She clearly married and had a family, which I'm pleased about. I should have asked her to marry me sooner, that's all."

4

Day woke late the following day, his mind immediately full of the story of Artemis. Edward's proposal for a series of programmes on Greek marble was very interesting, but Day found himself much more excited by the romantic tale he had heard in the warm darkness outside Thanasis's taverna the night before.

He could hear his guest moving about already, probably in need of coffee, so he forced himself out of bed and into the shower. When he emerged from his room, Edward was already sitting on the balcony with a glass of water, smiling into the distance, watching the peaceful movement of the shadows as they slowly slid away in the face of the rising sun.

"Good morning, Martin. Another beautiful day in Paradise!"

"You're too kind, Edward!" said Day quickly, always swift to pun on his name.

Edward laughed, and nodded eagerly as Day waved the empty cafetière at him from the kitchen counter. The smell of fresh coffee soon permeated the house, and when Day carried it out to Edward on the balcony, he thought for the first time that he had nothing to offer his guest for breakfast. Edward seemed unconcerned.

"I should apologise for being excessively talkative last night, Martin. Undoubtedly I enjoyed rather too much wine, but I must say it did me good. Thank you for listening."

"Not at all, it was very moving. It was the stuff of romance. It *is* the stuff of romance, I should say. Look, have you booked somewhere to stay in Athens yet?"

"No, I usually find somewhere at the last moment."

"I know a small hotel that I think you'd like. It's central and convenient for you. It's called the Hotel Lykavittos Comfort. It's in one of the streets right at the foot of Lykavittos Hill, up from the British School. You know the area, I'm sure?"

"Sounds a pricey area, but I don't mind that. I only need a basic single room anyway."

"It's close to my apartment, actually. I thought I'd pop over to Athens next week and we could meet up again before you go home, discuss the project. I could make the hotel booking for you now, if you like?"

"That would be wonderful. From tomorrow night for six nights in total. Is that OK? I'll get my credit card for the deposit…."

Day booked the hotel and they arranged to meet again before Edward returned to England. The arrangement suited Day well. He would spend a couple of nights in his studio apartment in Kolonaki and do some errands in town. He would call his agent in London before committing himself to Edward's scheme. Day was now quite enthusiastic about the marble project, but he was in no doubt that what he really wanted next week was to hear all about the meeting with Angelika.

***

Day and Edward were due to meet Konstantinos Saris at roughly two o'clock, so Day suggested a light lunch first. They closed up the house and drove the short distance to the centre of the village, where they took a table under the ancient plane trees overlooking the little covered market. Day remembered sitting here for aperitifs with Helen not long before she had returned to England. It seemed a long time ago.

"Gentlemen, what can I get you?" asked the lady of the taverna.

"Ah, good afternoon. A portion of moussaka, please," said Edward in his formal Greek.

"Calamari fritti, please, and we'll share a salad, and a large bottle of water."

The lady left, and Edward looked sheepishly at Day.

"All the tourists ask for moussaka, don't they? I feel I should order something different, but I do love it! It's a must for me when I'm in Greece."

"I sympathise. My equivalent is the chips here, they're just so amazing, I can't resist them. It does make me feel like a Brit tourist. We must remember how much the Greeks like both moussaka and fried potatoes. Now, while we wait, I'd love to hear more about Konstantinos."

***

Day's car could almost drive the road to the west coast by itself; it was his usual route to the Nikos Elias house. Not far outside Kato Potamia, one of the hill villages along the way, a sign at the side of the road said SARIS EM, the letters standing for Ergastyria Marmarou or Marble Workshop. It was no wonder that Konstantinos Saris used the word atelier, Day thought He drove down the private track to a pair of closed wooden gates, where another sign politely asked visitors to park on the grass before ringing the bell for admittance. Day obeyed. He and Edward got out, not troubling to lock the Fiat, and looked round.

The marble workshop commanded a panoramic view of rolling countryside and hills. Three low, brick buildings faced with decorative black wooden panels stood round a courtyard, and what looked like a large family home was just visible at the top of a ridge behind the property. Everything was modern and well tended, and spoke of success. To their right, overlooking the road and the valley below, and forming the open fourth side of the courtyard, was an inviting terrace shaded by a pergola. From one of the beams of the pergola hung several large, paper-thin, discs of marble which were cleverly suspended so that they would move in the slightest breeze, catching the light in their translucent white forms. An enormous marble table, its rim carved with the Greek meander design, waited hospitably beneath the pergola, surrounded by red canvas chairs and several pots of red geraniums.

Inside the five-bar gates stood a welcoming dog. This was not the customary Greek guard dog, chained to an outdoor kennel. This was a beautiful creature which looked to Day like an almost white Labrador, and it was behaving as if he and Edward were members of its family. Edward rang the bell, a smile of delight on his face.

"I told you it was wonderful, didn't I, Martin? This is Konstantinos's dog, Dali, after Salvador Dali. He's a gentle creature. I have no proof, but I surmise he sleeps on the end of Konstantinos's bed!"

A young Greek man emerged from the nearest building to open the gate. He wore sturdy boots and a dark overall over his working clothes; his trousers and hands were pale with marble dust.

"Ah, Foti. Good to see you again. I'm Edward, do you remember me? I was here last year. How are you? This is Martin."

The young man called Fotis nodded and smiled shyly, shaking hands first with Edward then Day. He closed the gate after them saying only the word 'Konstantinos', and indicated they should follow him. They walked towards the large building at the furthest end of the courtyard, Dali running ahead with wagging tail.

The building turned out to be the main workshop, and it seemed chaotic at first. They walked carefully through a host of free-standing display units on which were set many ceramic items in various stages of completion. There was a pleasant smell, a mixture of clay, paint, varnish and straw. They reached a broad counter which prevented visitors accessing the room behind it, where Day saw several kilns. An old man with white hair and moustache stood behind the counter, playing with a lump of clay; he seemed not to have heard them enter, which was clearly impossible.

Nothing Edward had told him could have prepared Day for his first meeting with Konstantinos Saris.

The old sculptor suddenly looked up and walked round the counter, arms outstretched towards Edward. So far he had not said a word. His deep-set eyes twinkled mischievously, but Day was equally struck by an inherent sadness in his face. His Mediterranean complexion was liberally freckled with age spots, his bushy brows were frosted with white, even his stubble was white. He was, in his way, immensely attractive, charismatic even. So far, not one word. Day thought he had never met anyone quite like this before.

Edward seemed to be in on the charade and also said nothing. The two old men stood facing each other, and then Konstantinos threw his arms wide open and embraced Edward, chuckling. Neither gave any thought to the wet clay on Konstantinos's ancient apron.

Suddenly Edward and Konstantinos were both talking at once.

"It's been too long, Edward, my friend. And you choose the hottest month of the year to come and see me! How English of you! And this must be Martin?"

Edward made the formal introductions. Konstantinos Saris looked at Day appraisingly, retaining the hand that he had shaken for a second longer than Day found comfortable.

"Martin. I am truly honoured that you have come with Edward to see my atelier. You are most welcome. Please call me Konstantinos. Foti, please, would you make us some coffee? We will have it on the terrace. Now, Martin, Edward knows the place well, but you are here with fresh eyes. What do you think?"

Day avoided voicing the awe he felt in this place and this man, and instead gave an expressive shrug in the most Greek manner he could muster.

"I'm looking forward to seeing everything, Konstantine. For instance, what are you doing here with the white clay?"

"Ah, you are thinking that I am a marble sculptor so what am I doing with clay? Good point, Martin. I do two things with clay. The first is that it can be useful to work out in clay some ideas I have for marble. The second is that I make pretty objects for the public, because not everyone wants a big piece of marble, do they? And anyway, I like clay, it relaxes me. I have my kilns back here, you see? That's how I started, with ceramics. It was my first study, my first love. Nothing is wasted, is it? Every piece of knowledge we acquire feeds our soul and our head and our heart, and we use all of these to make beautiful things."

Konstantinos placed a hand on Martin's arm and gently guided him across the room as he talked. His English was expressive and fluent. So fluent, in fact, that he held the floor completely. They stopped at one of the tall display units, on which stood half a dozen small figures resembling ancient Cycladic figurines in white clay awaiting finishing, and a dusty CD player.

"Come, see. This is very important. You know what this means to me, Martin? The restoration of the soul. When I want to relax, when things aren't going too well, I play my CD of your wonderful English lady, Miss Alison Balsom. She's my favourite. This room rings with the magnificent sound of her trumpet, and I am consoled!"

Day laughed. Clearly Konstantinos had no intention of explaining the Cycladic figures, only the CD player. Trumpet indeed, he thought. That was unexpected.

"So, this building is the heart of my atelier, Martin. The ceramics are made here, and through that door over there is where I work with marble. I'll show you later. For now, please follow me and I will give you a small tour, arriving at the terrace in time for our coffee."

He swept Day away, followed mutely by Edward who appeared completely content. As they left the workshop Day realised that Dali the dog was still sitting patiently outside, getting to his feet only when he saw Konstantinos.

"Good dog, Dali! Dali knows he isn't allowed in the workshop or the shop."

"Shop?"

"Yes, we have a little shop on site where visitors can buy something to take home. Here it is. Let's go inside, and I'll introduce you to Xanthe, if she's in here. Ah yes, here she is."

They entered the single-roomed building, which was full of good light from the large front window. Ceramic bowls, vases, crockery and small sculptures were displayed on tables and shelves, discreetly lit with modern LED lights. Day only had time for a first impression, but it was enough to tell him that these ceramics were very much of the kind that he liked.

Xanthe turned out to be an efficient, middle-aged Greek woman with hair which had probably been lightened a few shades, and modern, dark-framed glasses. She was concentrating on a computer in the corner of the room. She took off her glasses as they entered and stood to greet them. As he made the introductions, Konstantinos explained that Xanthe was basically in charge of the whole place: the shop and its customers, the online enquiries, placing the orders for clay, marble, packing material, glazes, pigments and so on, and in short was indispensable.

"I have the best job on Naxos," smiled Xanthe, shaking hands. "Hello Kyrie Edward, how are you? You look extremely well."

"I'm very well, thank you, Xanthe, and you, as always, look radiant."

"We're about to have coffee on the terrace, Xanthe, can you join us?" asked Konstantinos.

"I'm sorry, not at the moment, Konstantine. I'm in the middle of the monthly account and I'll lose my place."

"I'll ask Fotis to bring your coffee in here, then. Many thanks!"

Outside, Dali was waiting in the sunshine, panting eagerly, watching their movements and pushing a small marble pebble towards them with his nose.

"Dali likes people to kick his stone for him," explained Edward. "Just gently. He likes to play 'fetch' with it. Very appropriate for a marble artist's dog, don't you agree?"

The coffee was waiting for them on the white marble table under the pergola. The terrace faced across the valley to where the distant hills lazed in the heat haze. Day and Edward sat in the red chairs, and Konstantinos joined them after arranging for Xanthe to be given coffee at her computer. Day's attention was transfixed by the discs of fine white marble which hung from thin steel wire at the furthest corner of the pergola, cloudy white in the sunshine.

Konstantinos gestured grandly towards Edward. "Edward and I are like a good marriage, Martin. Our passions coincide but each brings a slightly different set of interests to the relationship. Edward adores ancient marble, and I adore contemporary marble. You see? The perfect match. We always have plenty to talk about - and sometimes to argue about."

"I'm looking forward to it, Konstantine!" laughed Edward. "In fact, I have a new subject for us to debate. It's a new idea of mine to use my collection of travellers' accounts of Greece as part of a series of programmes about Greek marble; it would cover Greece area by area. For each location we would see history through the eyes of an early traveller, and then look at the marble work to be found there."

Konstantinos pursed his mouth and nodded, as if considering the merit of the idea. He took a sip of coffee and replaced the cup on the table. Edward continued.

"Martin presents history programmes and writes intelligent books about Greek history. He and I are thinking about working together on the programmes; my material would be used in the planning of the series, and Martin would be the presenter."

"That sounds excellent, Edward. Many congratulations on such a novel idea. At last your collection can be put to good use. But you should have told me we have a celebrity here. I apologise, Martin, I haven't seen your work. I live in something of a - what's the expression? - something of a bubble up here."

"There's no reason you should have heard of it, Konstantine."

"Edward, how do you propose to explore *modern* marble work in your otherwise excellent plan?" asked Konstantinos, turning back to Edward.

Day concealed a smile. Konstantinos Saris was sharp.

"As usual you're ahead of me, Konstantine. I'm hoping I can persuade you to be involved. Naxos has been a major marble centre since ancient times, and I would like you to be central to the programme talking about modern Naxian marble art. Perhaps I could send you some ideas, and we can discuss it over the phone in a week or two?"

"Naturally I'd be honoured, Edward. I'm going to have a busier winter than usual, as you know, but I always have time for things that interest me. Have you told Martin about the Niarchos Project?"

"Yes, I've certainly mentioned it."

"It's going to keep me busy over the next three years, Martin, especially during the months when the Visiting Sculptor is here and we work alongside each other. This year my collaborator will be the Sicilian, Peppino Berducci. He's going to stay in accommodation in Kato

Potamia at the cost of the Niarchos Foundation. I've asked Xanthe to order some very interesting pieces of marble which will arrive in a week or two, including some very large pieces of exceptional purity. Our smaller work will be shown in an exhibition in the Kastro in Chora at the end of Peppino's stay, then everything made in the three year project will be packed up and taken to Athens to be exhibited in the Niarchos Cultural Centre. Next year and the year after I will be working with different sculptors."

"Congratulations, Konstantine, a collaboration with the Niarchos Foundation is a great honour and opportunity. Do you know who the sculptors will be during the second and third years?"

"Not yet. I'm lucky, the Foundation will give me the final choice. I didn't hesitate to agree to Peppino Berducci. You must come back and see me, Martin, and I'll introduce you to Peppino."

Konstantinos was about to continue when they heard the approach of a car from the main road. An old Land Rover Defender, on which the paintwork had been scorched by exposure to sun and salt, pulled up by the gate and parked next to Day's Fiat 500, making it look particularly small and new. The driver got out and Dali ran to greet him.

"Ah. Here's Markos. I wasn't expecting him today. Martin, this is a good friend and colleague of mine, Markos Ioannakis. We should avoid talking about the Niarchos Project in front of him. I'll explain later."

With that, Konstantinos rose and walked slowly towards the gate. Day noticed he had a slight limp and favoured his right leg. He and Markos greeted each other with a friendly handshake and began to walk back to the terrace. Konstantinos offered coffee and Markos accepted. With a friendly shout, Konstantinos called Fotis and asked him to provide it.

"Marko, I think you've already met my friend Edward Childe, who has been here before? And this is Martin Day, a historian and well-known presenter of history programmes, I understand. Martin, this is Markos Ioannakis. Markos is the owner of Blue & Gold Naxos."

Everyone rose and shook hands. Markos explained to Day that he owned two art boutiques on Naxos called Blue & Gold, one in Chora and the other in Halki, and that Konstantinos's ceramics and smaller marble pieces were his best sellers. He had been Konstantinos's exclusive local outlet for ceramics for the last six years, he went on, making it sound like the highest honour. His smile was genuine. All the same, Day thought he detected a tension arrive with the latest visitor.

Markos sat with his coffee amicably and Dali sat at his feet to have his head scratched. From time to time Markos would nudge the dog's little stone for him to retrieve. He seemed very much at home at the atelier, and talked comfortably about the good tourist numbers and items that had sold well over the past month. He was smartly dressed in the style Day too preferred, cotton trousers and sharply ironed long-sleeved shirt; he had come straight from the Halki shop, he said, leaving it in the care of his wife for the rest of the afternoon.

Day was glad of the shade of the pergola which, in true Greek style, had a considerable amount of climbing plants across its cane roof panels, providing dappled protection from the sun. There was just enough room for all four of them to shelter from the worst of the heat, watching the bright white marble decorations shine against the greens and greys of the fields beyond and the distant blue-grey hills.

Markos finished his coffee and rose to leave. He left a sheaf of papers with Konstantinos, explaining they were requests for more stock to cover an order from the owner of a new boutique holiday rental in Apollonas for a ceramic coffee set with fish motifs and some matching bowls. He shook hands round the table and petted Dali, who accompanied him to the gate.

"I'll come by in a week or so for the order, Kosta. I'll phone Xanthe first," he shouted belatedly. Konstantinos nodded and raised a hand. Markos drove away.

"'Thank you, Martin. I didn't have time to explain why it was better for us not to mention the Niarchos Project in front of poor Markos. It's quite simple. One of the rules attached to the funding is that I may not sell any new work made after the arrival of Peppino Berducci up till the end of the three year agreement. Unfortunately that includes my ceramics. It means that Markos will only have my old stock to sell in his shops for the next three summer seasons. There's no shortage of pieces ready to go, but no flexibility with designs, and once the stock is sold there won't be any more. He's not happy about it, but what can I do?"

"I see. As you say, there's nothing anyone can do. Will it seriously affect his livelihood?"

"I shouldn't think so, he'll just sell other artists' work. His pride is bruised, and some of his customers will be upset if they can't continue buying a set of something. He'll get over it. He's a good man. His wife is more angry than he is and she doesn't give him any rest."

"I'll pop in to one of his shops and buy a few bits for my house in Filoti," said Day.

Edward excused himself politely and went towards the shop where, Day remembered, there was a public bathroom. Fotis came to take the coffee cups and ask where Konstantinos wanted some delivery to be stored. When Fotis had left, Day and Konstantinos sat contentedly in silence. Day realised that his host was as relaxed in companionable silence as he was himself, but on this occasion Day's curiosity got the better of him.

"Fotis and Xanthe are great assets to you," he observed. "Do you have anyone else working here?"

"No, they look after all my needs. Xanthe has been working for me for about ten years, I rely on her completely. Fotis is like a son to me."

Day was surprised. Fotis had seemed rather more like a handyman than a son. He must have somehow communicated his thoughts, because Konstantinos threw him a perceptive glance.

"Fotis lost both his parents in a car accident when he was fifteen. Somehow my late wife came to know about it and talked to me most urgently about helping him. She wanted us to give him a home, and promised me she'd take care of everything and that young Fotis would be a great help to me, especially as I was nearly sixty and there's a lot of heavy lifting involved in what I do. She said a strong young man about the place would be an excellent thing. I gave in to her, as I always did. She was right, of course."

Konstantinos stroked his chin thoughtfully before continuing.

"Fotis had been extremely upset by his parents' death, as you can imagine. Probably a better word is damaged. Little by little he settled down with us, and he adored my wife. Now that she's passed on, he and I have become very close. As you'll have noticed, he's very shy with strangers, but I think he's happy enough."

"Does he live here at the atelier?"

"Fotis? No. He has a nice little place in Kato Potamia. My wife set him up there, she thought he'd be better with a small house of his own. She hoped he'd find someone, a wife perhaps, but that hasn't happened yet. He's only thirty-four, there's still plenty of time. So, I rattle about with Dali in the big house up there behind us, and Fotis drives back to the village each night in the old van."

Edward was walking back from the shop. He seemed a little breathless and his face was flushed. He explained he'd just been throwing the pebble for Dali. Martin was concerned at the difficulty breathing that Edward appeared to be having.

"It's nothing, I'm just a little late taking my tablets," he said. "Curses on old age, eh, Konstantine? My body is a lot less robust than my brain. Could I ask for a glass of water, please?"

Fotis was requested to bring a glass of water and looked on in concern as Edward used it to swallow four or five different pills. Edward tried to reassure the young man that the medicine kept his heart in excellent condition, he had just forgotten to take them at lunchtime. He spoke to Fotis slowly in Greek, and Fotis seemed to understand him.

"Come and sit with us, Foti," suggested Konstantinos. "We're all friends here."

Fotis shook his head and took a step back shyly, but stayed close to the terrace and smiled towards them at intervals as he came and went doing small jobs. Edward, who had recovered from his breathlessness, surveyed the magnificent view with his customary placid smile. Fotis, standing nearby, looked with interest to see what Edward saw.

"I leave tomorrow for Athens, Konstantine," said Edward, his eyes twinkling, "but I hope to be back soon to work with Martin. Let me know how things go with Peppino. Don't give me that nonsense about you not knowing how to email, and anyway you can pick up a phone! We must keep in better touch, we're not so young any more. And I may have some interesting news for you in a few weeks. I'm going to meet with a beautiful young lady while I'm in Athens. She's the granddaughter of a lovely woman I met when I was twenty-one, the love of my life, as they say. How's that for good luck?"

Konstantinos nodded. "You'd better take care of your old heart, Edward my friend. Too much excitement is bad for us at our age."

"Don't worry, old friend, I couldn't feel better. Trust me. Well, Martin and I should take our leave and let you get on with your clay."

"Already? I thought you'd stay for the evening. Have you another engagement?"

"For the evening? No."

"Fotis is going to barbecue some lamb chops from a farmer in Ano Potamia, and Xanthe has brought us a salad. I have some good wine from the Saint Anna Winery over there." Konstantinos waved his hand in the direction of a distant building down the valley. "I was hoping you would both stay."

Day and Edward didn't need convincing. Fotis supplied them with a bottle of ouzo and some ice, and they drank together in the warmth of the terrace. As the sun sank in the west, they watched as the marble discs gradually turned from white to amber. Fotis barbecued the meat in a brick shelter over coals covered with vine clippings, and when they had all eaten they talked quietly as it grew dark.

5

"Good morning, I'm Martin Day and this is Professor Childe. We have an appointment with the Curator."

"Good morning, Mr Day. The Curator is expecting you. Do go up, you know the way, I think?"

Aristos Iraklidis, Day's friend of many years, had been the Curator of the Archaeological Museum of Naxos for more years than anyone could remember. Universally respected on the island, Aristos was often addressed simply as 'Curator'. The museum housed a significant collection of artefacts from several ancient periods, in particular the Cycladic and Mycenaean civilisations. Aristos guarded his domain fiercely. He cleverly maintained connections with the Greek Archaeological Society, many members of which were personal friends, in order to prevent the most important artefacts from being transferred to the National Archaeological Museum of Athens.

Day and Edward began to climb the interior stone staircase of the Naxos Archaeological Museum. The Curator's office was on the top floor and, in deference to Edward, Day took the steps more slowly than he would normally. It gave him time to think of the last occasion he had visited Aristos's office. He had been carrying a bag containing three objects recovered from a Mycenaean tomb. Day had acquired the artefacts through his work on Nikos Elias before bringing them to the museum for safe-keeping. The thought of those three ancient pieces of art still made him shiver with pleasure.

The Curator's office was small but had a stunning view over the old Kastro, the medieval Venetian castle which occupied the top of the hill in Chora. The museum building itself was steeped in history, having originally been a seventeenth-century Jesuit school. Day ushered Edward in before him. Books on shelves, tables and chairs, and in piles on the floor, made the Curator's office a cosy sanctum. Day made the introductions and Aristos waved his visitors to chairs, sweeping an open book off one before Day could sit.

Edward thanked the Curator for making time for them.

"It's my pleasure, Professor Childe. I always make time for my friend Martin, especially when he brings such an important guest to talk to me. What can I do for you?"

"At this stage, it's perhaps rather early to bring our ideas to you, but Martin and I are hoping to put together a rather exciting series of television programmes which you might find interesting. Whether or not you would like to join us in some way is up to you. The idea is …"

Edward outlined the project to the Curator, who listened keenly. As a man with the same overwhelming passion for ancient history, Aristos quickly saw the merits of Edward's vision.

"The marble theme provides a very strong connection with Naxos and the Museum," he mused. "I'd like to think along the lines of some filming taking place here, perhaps? It would be good publicity for us too."

"Splendid. Once Martin and I have done some preparatory work, we can talk about that in greater detail, but it sounds excellent. There will be a major focus on Naxos, not only as a historic centre for Greek marble but also because I have some letters written by Mrs Mabel Bent to a friend in London, in which she describes how she and her more renowned husband Theodore were exploring Naxos in the late nineteenth century. I also have a couple of her photographs. One of them shows the Kouros of Apollo."

"How on earth did you get hold of the Bent material, Edward?" interrupted Day.

"The letters were left to me when I was a student by an Oxford classicist I very much admired. His name was Augustus Bent Middleton. I don't know if there's a family connection with the famous Bents - perhaps you'd like to look into it, Martin? I want to make good use of the letters for Middleton's sake, rather than simply leaving them to the Fitzwilliam Museum."

"Well, you can count on my support," said Aristos. "Do you have time for a little lunch, perhaps? I know a very good place nearby..." Aristos knew some excellent places to eat.

"Unfortunately, my ferry leaves at 12.50, so I won't have time. Maybe when I'm next back on Naxos. I'd like that very much."

"Most certainly. I shall look forward to it."

"You know," said Edward, "I believe we've met before, a few years ago, in Athens at a lecture at the British School. We could try to recall the occasion, perhaps."

"Yes, we must do that. I'm sure we know people in common. Well, goodbye until your return, Professor!"

Aristos gave Edward his business card and the group said their goodbyes. Edward was beaming as he and Day retraced their steps from the Kastro. They retrieved Edward's small bag from the Fiat and Day left him standing in the queue for the passengers boarding the Blue Star Naxos ferry to Piraeus. The port was already humming with people, and Day found himself keen to get away. He wished Edward a safe journey and made sure he had the details of the Hotel Lykavittos Comfort in Athens.

"When are you meeting with the wonderful Angelika?" Day asked as they shook hands.

"Tomorrow. We're having coffee at a rooftop cafe near Thissio, and I've reserved a table at Paximadia, my favourite restaurant in Athens, in case I can persuade her to dine with me."

Day grinned. "Good luck, Edward. Be happy!" he said.

***

Day began to walk back to the car, wondering how to spend the afternoon. In his new home village of Filoti, as in many of the other hill villages in central Naxos, today was the start of a three-day religious festival, so it might be wise to occupy himself elsewhere. He decided on an afternoon at the Nikos Elias house, where the late archaeologist's papers and finds were beginning to give up their secrets to him after several months of work. There was one problem: he was hungry. Day rarely ate a great deal before the evening, but had fallen into bad habits when his friend Helen had been staying with him, as she rather liked regular meals. His appetite would not now be denied. He changed direction, crossed the square, and headed for Katerina's Taverna.

Day had been introduced to Katerina's by Aristos, whom Katerina adored. Her very first question as she showed Day to a quiet table concerned the Curator. Day confirmed that his friend was well, and privately reflected how his friendship with Aristos Iraklidis enabled him to enjoy the best tables at a number of excellent Naxos hostelries.

He always ordered the same thing at Katerina's, and he ate it with relish now. Her red peppers and tomatoes stuffed with special rice were really very good. He would only need a snack for supper, which was good because he had nothing much in the fridge. He brought out his mobile while he waited for his coffee, and began to check for messages. His breath caught involuntarily when he saw one of them was from Deppi. She was the niece of Aristos's wife, and Day was entranced by her. She was announcing that today was her name day and inviting him for drinks on their yacht that evening. He noted with a little disappointment that it was a message to multiple recipients.

Since he had met Deppi and her husband at the Curator's house in May, he had not been able to stop thinking of her. She was married to an energetic Greek-Australian who restored old buildings and was a man he genuinely liked. They had a nine-year old son who was bilingual, Greek and English. Everything about Deppi impressed Day, but more to the point she was manifestly married. Day permitted himself only to admire from afar. Why not? A cat could look at a queen, he told himself for the hundredth time.

He would need a gift. Name days were more important than birthdays in Greece, and the tradition was that the person whose name day it was would invite their friends and family for drinks, cakes or even dinner, while the guests brought a little gift, usually of food or drink. Fortunately for Day, an ideal shop was nearby; in fact, he had a choice of good places. One gift option was chocolates or fancy cakes, and he was close to a Zacharoplastia, or confectioners, which sold wonderful things. On the other hand, chocolate would be messy in this heat and he didn't know a good cake from a bad one, as he didn't eat sweet things himself. So, he would go to a delicatessen instead. There would be something suitable there.

The shop he had in mind stood on a corner near the centre of town, its interior dark and cool, its walls clad from floor to ceiling in dark wood, with products in packets, jars and tins tastefully arranged on shelves amid sprigs of dried herbs, lavender or olive leaves. The big room smelled as good as it looked. He was the only customer. He noticed a girl almost hidden behind the cash desk, who greeted him and offered any help he might need. Day thanked her and began to browse, attracted to the large baskets under the window containing bags of dried oregano tied with striped ribbon, piles of hand-made olive soaps in different colours, an array of natural sponges (undoubtedly imported), and cellophane bags of artisan biscuits.

On the shelves were jars of spoon sweets of all kinds. Day wondered whether Deppi liked these traditional pieces of fruit or nuts in syrup that many Greeks enjoyed with their coffee. His own lack of sweet tooth made the decision more difficult. Further along he found jars of local capers, which he adored, and the inevitable array of Greek honey, some with walnuts, others created by bees who had visited flowers as diverse as white thyme and oak. Finally there was a huge selection of tea and coffee, beautifully packaged and an ideal gift. He was spoilt for choice.

He settled for three items and asked if the girl would kindly wrap them as a single present. She found a small basket and a roll of cellophane, from which she created an attractive gift finished with blue ribbon. The gift consisted of a packet of Greek Mountain Tea, a jar of white thyme honey, and another jar of Siphnian capers. Day paid for them, and at the last minute bought another jar of capers for himself.

Pleased with his purchases, he retrieved the Fiat and drove home. It was too late now to start any work at the Elias house, and anyway he was ready for a siesta. The car was fiery hot, and the air-conditioning took a while to take effect. He had forgotten about the festival, and saw no sign of it anyway. By the time he reached home in Filoti, any chocolate he might have bought would have been totally ruined.

***

Day slept deeply for over an hour, waking as if from a deep underwater adventure. He reached for his mobile and saw it was just after four, and sank back on the bed with relief. Deppi's invitation was for six thirty, so he still had plenty of time. He headed for the shower, switching on the iron as he passed the ironing board which was a permanent feature of his room. He only ever ironed one shirt at a time, when he needed it. No opportunity seemed to present itself to press the entire wash in one session.

Enjoying the feeling of a newly ironed Oxford shirt, Day filled a large glass with cold water from the bottle in the fridge and took it to the balcony. Condensation glistened on the glass, and Day drank the entire contents with relish. He then stared at the peaceful view across the valley, where the afternoon heat caused a slight haze near the hills. His mind was full of Deppi, and he was looking forward to seeing her again with an excitement that surprised him. She was not only beautiful, but she had made an impression on him in the tender way she treated her young son. This was something to which Day was particularly susceptible. He had lost his own mother when he was a boy, and Day had always been sentimental about the rapport between a young mother and a small child. It was a relationship he could barely remember having, but which he treasured.

He resolved to be completely calm and sensible in Deppi's presence that evening, and of course he would behave himself perfectly. It was one thing admiring her, and he thought he could allow himself that, but there was every reason to hide his feelings for Deppi. The most important of these was that she was already married, which ended the matter as far as Day was concerned. She was also the niece of

Rania, Aristos's wife. Rania was a perceptive woman and had once noticed the expression on Day's face as he looked at Deppi. Day had told her about his mother, and how watching Deppi with her son made him nostalgic. She had accepted what he said without making a judgement, and Day had made her a silent promise to leave Deppi alone. He meant to keep his word.

***

The sleek yacht *Zephyro* was tied at the far end of the moorings, furthest from the ferry port. Ribbons had been tied round the ropes of the gangplank, and Nick Kiloziglou, Deppi's husband, stood ready to hand guests on board. Their nine-year-old son Nestoras stood excitedly behind him and waved when he saw Day. Nick grinned.

"Martin, welcome! Good to see you, mate. Come on board. Aristos and Rania have just arrived, and some other friends."

Stepping down into the boat, Day clutched his gift and his sunglasses in one hand while steadying himself with the other and hoping not to lose his hat. He was not a natural sailor and felt precarious. Part of him loved the idea of the yacht: the delight of the water, the shining walnut woodwork, the prospect of freedom and big sky. But for whatever reason, perhaps because he was particularly tall, he never felt completely at ease on a boat. As he released his grip on the superstructure he looked up straight into Deppi's face.

He hoped to goodness he wasn't blushing; it was a hot evening.

"Congratulations on your name day, Despina!" he said, and kissed her on both cheeks while giving her the pretty package tied by the girl in the delicatessen.

"Thank you, Martin. What a lovely present. I can already see it's full of delicious things. Come and sit down - over there maybe?" She indicated a highly varnished bench seat with plenty of headroom.

She made the introductions on the way. There were six other guests already on the boat. He shook hands with Aristos and kissed Rania on both cheeks. He turned to the people he did not know who sat on the cushioned benches along the sides of the yacht. He was introduced to a man called Orestis, Nick's deputy in his restoration business, and his wife Anna, then to Deppi's friends Zenia and Anthoula.

"As we're all here now, what do you say to a little sailing, guys?" suggested Nick. "We thought we might just go out a little way and enjoy the cooler air and watch the sun set?"

There was an enthusiastic response, and as soon as he had made sure that their guests had something to drink, Nick set about preparing the yacht to sail. Orestis clearly knew his way round the boat and took charge of folding away the gangplank and retracting the mooring line. Nestoras, very happy with his role as junior captain, put on his life jacket and went to his mother for her to inspect it. Day registered the action even as he made conversation with Anna and Anthoula.

Nestoras was given the responsibility of sitting at the prow, holding on, and keeping a close eye on other shipping as his father eased the *Zephyro* out of the harbour using the engine. Small boats acting as water taxis and a few yachts carrying tourists were returning to harbour, and, like the *Zephyro,* several boats were setting out to get the best view of the sunset. Deppi, who had been watching the perfectly ordered dance of the boats as they manoeuvred, turned to look at her son in his red life jacket proudly obeying his father's gentle but clear commands. Day noticed her smile to herself before she turned away into the galley.

As the *Zephyro* left the port of Naxos behind, Nick and Orestis hoisted the main sail and cut the engine, leaving only the sound of the wind on the sails and through the rigging, the soft swish of the water parted by the prow, gentle conversation and the clinking of glasses. Soon the yacht was in clear water, joining the few sails on the horizon. It was suddenly an idyllic evening, and Day, finishing his first glass of cold white wine with relish, and settling himself into his place with no intention of moving round the boat, began to really enjoy himself. This was a far cry from London, even from Athens, and another reason to celebrate buying his new house on Naxos. He glanced round for Deppi. She was in the galley preparing food, her back to him. Her black hair was twisted into a fashionably untidy knot behind her head, her T-shirt and shorts revealed her tanned shoulders and legs. She turned suddenly, lifting a tray of food, and met his eyes. She smiled. Perhaps she's indulging me a little, Day thought.

Deppi brought out plate after plate of delicious food. There were little souvlaki sticks, slices of homemade spinach pie, bowls of salad heavy with cubes of Feta cheese, glistening olives, crusty bread, and a bowl of prepared fresh fruit. She chose the moment to thank her family and friends for being with her on her name day and for their gifts, and encouraged them to help themselves. Nick left the sailing to Orestis while he brought tins of chilled Alfa beer and another bottle of white wine from the cool box. He opened a bottle of red wine in front of Day and Aristos, saying he wanted their opinion of his new discovery.

"It's from Folegandros," he told them, showing them the label, "from a relatively new winery there. It's made from Mavrotragano and Mantilaria grapes. What do you think of it?"

Aristos was well known for his love of Cycladic wines, and he applied himself to Nick's task seriously. Day and Nick, who had first met at an evening at the Iraklidis house in honour of Rania's birthday, had been treated to a variety of Aristos's favourite wines, so Nick was returning a favour. The verdict on this particular gem was that it had notes of vanilla and oak that sat well with the warm evening and the clean smell of the sea. Nick couldn't help comparing it with a wine he liked from the Barossa in South Australia.

Deppi and Anthoula cleared the food from the boat's central table and sat down again to enjoy the trip. Nick took a small glass of the red wine to Orestis and replaced him at the wheel. Orestis stayed with him to talk. Anna and Rania were discussing cooking, and the rest of them chatted quietly together. Day alone sat in contented solitude, enjoying his own thoughts. The boat was cruising calmly, the dark water heaving with the small swell caused by the evening breeze. They had left Chora and the port far behind. A ferry could be seen in the distance making its way from the mainland towards Naxos, its white hull slightly pink in the evening light. Deppi told them that sunset would happen in about half an hour, and that before then Nick would lower the sail and drop anchor while they watched it. Day thought it more likely that he would be watching her. The wine had made him deeply content and full of joy, so that for the moment he had everything he wanted.

Nick guided the yacht until he reached the spot he had in mind, lowered the sail and dropped anchor. The sky had darkened and a few stars had become visible. The sun lingered, huge, just above the sea. As they watched, the horizon turned a brilliant orange, with astonishing red and purple streaks in places and a faint line of turquoise light hovering at the place where sky met sea. The Curator pointed to the ferry, which was now heading back out from port, telling the girls to keep their eyes on it. The ferry made a change of direction as it neared open water, and as it turned it caught the light of the setting sun. Its white flanks turned the colour of bronze. The metallic glow was reflected on the calm sea and highlighted the curls of the ship's wake. As it continued its turn, smoke climbing from its stacks, the bronze faded and the ferry became once again an ordinary ship.

With a small pause, the sun slid into the sea. Day waited. He had always wanted to see the green flash that reputedly occurred as the sun set over water, but had never been lucky. There was no flash this time either, but turning back to the group in the boat he saw an expression on Deppi's face which made up for it. She had Nestoras beside her and was stroking his hair, her face still golden from the after-glow of the sunset.

6

The SeaJet 'World Champion', leaving Naxos for Athens, was particularly busy. Day was not surprised. It was Sunday afternoon and the two o'clock sailing was the last of the fast crossings of the day. Not only tourists but Athenians were heading to the mainland. Many of Day's fellow passengers looked reluctant to be returning to the heavy heat of the capital with the prospect of work the next day.

Day, too, felt grim. He suffered from the heat at the best of times, and the wait on the concrete port had been unendurable. On top of that he was not comfortable in a crowd or on board ship. He drank from his bottle of water and closed his mind to the situation as far as he could. He had no clear view out of the SeaJet, as passengers were not allowed outside while at sea and the windows were caked in salt spray. It was easy to feel claustrophobic. At least the SeaJet took less time to make the crossing than the big ferries, so he would reach Athens in just over three hours.

For a while Day managed to sleep upright in his chair. He dozed off while reviewing the last two days, in which he had worked solidly on the biography of Nikos Elias. This morning he had gone for a walk from his house in Filoti to the far end of the village, and extended his exercise by making a loop through the countryside. It had made him realise how unfit he was, and a coffee in a village cafe had been a necessity before he could reach home again. Cafe Ta Xromata, where he had rested, was Helen's favourite coffee venue in Filoti, so he had sent her a text from his brightly-cushioned sofa seat, and promised to call her in a day or so. As soon as he had sent it, he regretted having forgotten to ask about the funeral for which she had returned to London. He resolved to ask her next time.

After showering and packing at a leisurely pace, he had locked the house and taken a taxi down to the port in time to queue with the other foot-passengers for the SeaJet. It was tedious and hot, but he was looking forward to meeting up with Edward the following day and hearing about his meeting with Angelika. Somehow the romance between Edward and Artemis in 1959, and Edward's chance to meet her granddaughter now, filled Day with a personal joy that he was sure had something to do with his current feelings for Despina Kiloziglou. Both Artemis and Deppi had evoked powerful feelings with no possibility of fulfilment, and that was why Day thought they were connected in his mind. Edward now had a chance to experience the joy of talking about his lost love with somebody who had known and had also loved her.

It was odd not to have heard from Edward since his meeting with Angelika. Today was Sunday, and Edward had met the lady on Friday. It was probably just that Edward chose not to put such a thing in an email. Day hoped the meeting had not been a disaster. Perhaps Angelika had failed to turn up. He shook his head; it was pointless to speculate. He would soon find out, as he and Edward were due to meet the next morning.

The SeaJet finally docked at Piraeus port amid the usual scenes of chaos, nothing out of the ordinary. Pedestrians and lorries, motorbikes and cars all mingled on the harbour road amid the cacophony and the stink of fumes. The heat of Athens hit Day as he started down the ramp from the ship's car deck with the other foot-passengers. It even seemed to assail him from beneath his feet as his shoes absorbed it from the tarmac. He knew that the city centre, where he was heading, would be hotter still.

Seeing the waving arm of his usual taxi-driver, Day cut through the madness and reached the relative sanctuary of the yellow Athenian taxi. He always used Nasos, and as a result found that Nasos was always available to pick him up. They had a good arrangement which suited both parties. Day would ring in advance to arrange his lift. The fare was never inflated. The relatively direct road from Piraeus port to the heart of Athens was a route Nasos could drive blindfold and with one hand, which he amply demonstrated on the way to Day's apartment. Day was brought up to date with the latest news about Nasos's gorgeous baby daughter, irritating mother-in-law and possibly criminal cousin. Nothing appeared to have changed very much since Day had left Athens for Naxos six months ago.

The same could be said of his studio apartment in Dinokratous, a wonderful residential street beneath Lykavittos Hill in central Athens. The apartment had belonged to an old couple, friends of his father, who had bought it in their youth when property in Athens was cheap. They had had no children of their own and had left the flat to Day in their will, to his immense surprise. It was perhaps the most generous thing of which Day had ever been the beneficiary. When his father had died last year, Day had decided to spend his inheritance on buying the house in Filoti, and so base himself completely in Greece. As long as he continued to earn enough for the cost of running both houses, he would keep both. He could always rent one out if he needed income.

Dinokratous was a quiet street in an excellent, upmarket area, now greatly sought after. The price of property in Athens was very high these days. Below Lykavittos lay the wealthy embassy area, Parliament Square and the city centre. The Laiki, or farmers' market, took place nearby on a Friday, an event which Day loved when he was in town. He felt a twinge of regret that he had not arranged this visit to coincide with market day.

The apartment seemed more cheerful than he remembered. Even for one person it was oppressively small, and compared to his house in Filoti it was tiny. Nevertheless, it was painted in light colours and the sun flooded in when he opened the shutters. He was aware of the noise of the city, having become accustomed to the peace of Naxos, but this time he found it exciting. He threw his bag on the bed and went to buy some supplies from the local shop. Gin, coffee, milk, lemon, crisps. He bought tonic at the periptero, the useful local kiosk. Back at the apartment he made himself a gin and tonic with a slice of lemon, regretting the lack of ice. He filled the ice-cube tray ready for the next evening, opened the packet of crisps, and pulled a book from the shelf. After a while he wandered out to walk the steamy streets and decide where to have dinner.

***

Day had always needed a lot of sleep, and awoke the next morning refreshed after a good nine hours. The Athens apartment had excellent blackout blinds in addition to the balcony shutters. It had been the road's designated rubbish collection night, which meant the noisy waste lorry grumbling and clattering though the streets in the early hours of the morning, but Day had slept through it. He checked the time on his phone and lay back to reflect. He had time for a leisurely shower and a bit of work on his laptop, before meeting Edward at his hotel for coffee.

Sitting on his sofa, laptop on his knees, Day listed the errands he wanted to achieve while he was in Athens. He should check in on the lady who kept an eye on the apartment for him, and occasionally cleaned it, and give her some money. He would call at his favourite bookshop to pick up the books they were holding for him, and he would like to visit the British School and say hello to friends he had not seen for six months. He answered his emails, checked his social media, and texted Helen, remembering to ask about the funeral.

On leaving the apartment he briefly wondered what had made him feel the need to live anywhere other than Athens. The morning was warm, the sky blue, and the ubiquitous pollution not in evidence from where he stood. No tourists had yet arrived to take the nearby funicular to the top of Lykavittos Hill, and the road was peaceful. He enjoyed the short walk to the Hotel Lykavittos Comfort.

Day took the black marble steps up to the hotel entrance two at a time and passed through the heavy swing doors into the bliss of the air conditioning. The hotel had clearly had a make-over since his last visit, and now boasted a large relief panel showing Greek athletes on one wall, and a modern abstract mosaic on another. The receptionist behind the long counter offered him a welcoming smile.

"Good morning. Welcome to the hotel."

"Good morning. I've come to meet one of your guests, Mr Edward Childe, from the UK. Perhaps you could ring his room for me?"

The receptionist's smile froze and Day suddenly had a very bad feeling. Without thinking, he asked her what the matter was.

"I'm very sorry, Kyrie, but if you'll excuse me I just want to ask the manager to come and speak to you. Would you take a seat, please? I won't be long."

Day did not even consider questioning her instructions and went to stand among the comfortable chairs by the window. He did not sit down. He was alone in the lobby for several minutes. Afterwards he wondered why it had not occurred to him to use his mobile to call Edward. It was as if he already knew he would get no answer. He had not had a reply from Edward since leaving him in the queue for the ferry on Naxos.

"Sir, my name is Matthias Dendrinos, I'm the manager of the Lykavittos Comfort. Would you like to come into my office so we can talk more privately?"

Day obeyed, noting that the lobby was as private as anywhere else given no other people were present. He accepted the chair offered him by Dendrinos, who took another visitor chair to be more informal than facing Day across a desk.

"Is there bad news? I made the reservation for my friend Edward Childe to stay here, and we arranged to meet this morning. What's happened, Kyrie Dendrino?"

"May I ask your name, sir?"

"Martin Day."

"Mr Day, may I offer my deepest sympathy and regret at the bad news I must give you. Your friend Mr Childe is unfortunately dead. He apparently took an overdose of medication while in his hotel room. The police are involved, but that does seem to be what happened. I'm very sorry."

Day found it hard to think. He managed to speak after what seemed longer than it could have been.

"When?"

"He was found by the room service team yesterday morning. The police seem to believe he died on Saturday night, the day before yesterday."

"Saturday 17th?" said Day, pointlessly, aware only that this was the day after Edward's meeting with Angelika had supposedly taken place.

"That's so. Look, I've taken the liberty of asking for some coffee to be sent to us. May I suggest you take a little? You've had a shock."

In England it would have been a cup of tea. Day nodded and thanked the manager. The door opened immediately and a handsome young man placed a tray of coffee on Dendrinos's desk without speaking.

For a minute Day felt choked that he was drinking a coffee with the manager rather than, as intended, with Edward. The strong, hot coffee certainly did help to restore him, however, and before he had finished it, during the whole of which time Dendrinos had respectfully not spoken, Day had put his feelings to one side until such time as he was alone. There would be a private opportunity to grieve for Edward.

"Thank you, you've been kind," he told Dendrinos. "Can you tell me anything more? Anything that the police have said?"

"Well, only what I've managed to pick up, Mr Day. Your friend was found lying on his bed looking quite peaceful, and on his bedside table were empty bottles of tablets which, I think, were his own medication. Heart tablets, were they? And some aspirin, I think."

Day's thoughts went back to Konstantinos's atelier, sitting on the terrace, watching Edward return from the bathroom somewhat breathless having forgotten to take his regular medication. Yes, Edward did take heart tablets, and may also have taken aspirin. What he would not have done, and suddenly Day was quite certain of it, was to kill himself.

There was little else that Matthias Dendrinos could tell Day, although he conveyed the sense that he had nothing more important to do than wait while Day recovered as best he could. At one point he asked whether Edward had family who should be informed, but Day thought not. He assured the manager that he would find out and be responsible for letting them know.

"There's one thing I really need to know, Kyrie Dendrino," he said finally. "The name of the investigating police officer, the person in charge? I want to speak to him as soon as possible."

A quiet voice inside Day muttered: *Here we go again.*

"That is a good idea, Mr Day. I expect the police will appreciate the information you have to offer. The man in charge is Inspector Andreas Nomikos, who is based at Hellenic Police Headquarters in Leoforos Alexandras. That's Alexandras Avenue," he translated. "Would you like me to write that down for you?"

"No, thanks, I'll find it. Again, thank you. I appreciate your kindness. Oh, and what has happened to my friend's belongings?"

"The police have them. His documents too."

"Of course. Goodbye, Kyrie Dendrino."

***

Day left the hotel and walked the short distance back to his apartment. He threw himself on his bed and stared at the ceiling, allowing the shock and sadness to fill him. The only thing that made him get up, eventually, was to use the bathroom. He threw off his clothes and had another shower, putting his face under the water. It helped. He dried himself, dressed and returned to the sofa.

He had to process a few immediate thoughts. One - while he himself had been contentedly working on the biography of Nikos Elias, his friend Edward had been living his last day. That was extraordinarily sad and filled Day with guilt. Two - while he himself was on the SeaJet to Piraeus, in the taxi with Nasos, sipping his G&T, the police were taking away Edward's body and questioning the hotel staff. This filled him with an awareness of how little we know despite thinking we know everything. Three - it was still possible that Edward had met Angelika and spent his last day talking about his beloved Artemis. This thought was bitter-sweet.

His thoughts were overtaken by the powerful conviction that returned with the force of the Meltemi wind. Day could not believe that Edward, who had so many plans for the future and such a zest for life, would ever have committed suicide. Following on the heels of this certainty, however, was a question which came from a sore spot in the pit of his stomach. Was that still true if Angelika had let him down?

He must file that away in his mind for later. The first thing he needed to do was clear to Day. He must speak to Inspector Andreas Nomikos.

Day knew Nomikos. The last time he had spoken to him was in May, or was it early June? There had been a murder on Naxos, the murder of an American archaeologist with whom Day had once worked in New York. Nomikos had been sent from Athens to lead the small local force in the investigation, and the case had grown more complex with the involvement of illegal artefact smugglers and two further deaths. Day had been useful to the police, and Inspector Nomikos had treated him generously in every respect, until finally their combined brain-power had resolved the various crimes. Day's memory of the Athenian policeman was of a large brain in a lion's body. Andreas Nomikos was quite an awe-inspiring man.

Now Day needed to find him and persuade him to allow Day an involvement in a police case once again, and for the same reason as before - Day's personal knowledge of the victim. This time, however, he had known Edward a great deal better than he had known the American scholar. He would not take no for an answer.

7

The headquarters of the Hellenic Police was a striking building. Tall, modern and with an imposing entrance comprising many steps, it was protected by guard posts, decorated with palm trees, and flew the flag of Greece with pride. On that morning the flag hung quietly in the hot, unmoving air.

The officer on the desk had been told to expect Day, so formalities were kept to a minimum. An hour ago, Day had telephoned the police from his Athens apartment and had been surprised to be put through to Nomikos without argument. He had explained his connection with Edward and his concerns about his death, and Nomikos had asked him to come and talk in person. Had Day heard a sigh at the other end of the line, or was it just his imagination? Nevertheless, he was relieved at the Inspector's willingness to listen to him.

Day was shown into an office larger than the entire Naxos Police Station, in which he had sat talking to the same police inspector a few months before. Nomikos walked across the room to greet him, and shook his hand with a smile that contained both genuine charm and a hint of something more steely. Day remembered this from their first meeting. He sensed in Nomikos a certain fierceness of temperament or intelligence.

The Inspector ran his left hand over his mane of fair hair, a striking hair colour in a Greek, and sat down again behind his desk. Day took a chair opposite. Both men hesitated to begin. With a narrowing of his light blue eyes, Nomikos made the move.

"Well, we find ourselves once more involved together in a case of untimely death. How extraordinary. In the best sense, I hope we don't make a habit of this."

"You couldn't be more surprised than I am, Inspector," smiled Day. It gave him a little jolt to realise he was smiling for the first time since finding out about Edward, and it felt stiff and unnatural.

"Andrea, please, Martin, when we're alone."

"Thank you, Andrea," said Day, startled by the policeman's easy use of his first name. "As you know, I'm here to talk about Edward Childe, my friend from the UK who died at the Lykavittos Comfort Hotel. As I said on the phone, I knew Edward Childe, knew him quite well, and I'm absolutely sure he was not in the frame of mind to commit suicide when we parted on Thursday. I don't believe two days is enough to send a man of his fortitude and joy to the brink of desperation."

"Mmm. In my experience, we can never truly know the mental state of others. However, I respect your judgement, especially after our association on Naxos in May. I'm happy to hear what you can tell me. I'm in charge of the investigation into Mr Childe's death, and I attended the hotel myself when your friend's body was found yesterday morning. I haven't yet said how sorry I am for your loss, Martin. It must be a shock. The evidence does appear quite clear as to what happened, but I'm prepared to keep an open mind. I'd like you to tell me more about the man himself, how you knew him, what he was like. And what happened in the last week or so before his death."

Day nodded, relieved. Inconsequentially he noticed that Nomikos's hair was rather too long for a senior policeman, but of course it wasn't the only thing that was unconventional about him.

Nomikos leaned back in his chair and drew towards himself a large notepad and pen. "First of all, tell me about Edward, and why you're so sure he didn't kill himself?"

"Edward said he still had a great deal he wanted to achieve. He told me he was eighty-one, but that he didn't feel old and even now lived a good life in Cambridge. He described lectures, dinners and other events with former colleagues of his Cambridge College - King's, I believe. He said he spent most of his time working in the College Library, devising projects and writing about the history he had loved all his life. He used a memorable phrase, I remember: he said he bounced from one project to the next."

"Did he have any family?"

"No, I don't think so. He never married. I never heard him speak of any relatives. He said he had Irish blood, that's all I remember."

"How was his health?"

"He had heart problems but told me they were kept under control with medication."

"Did you sense he was really well, or might he have been concealing something more serious? People have been known to commit suicide when faced with a desperate illness."

"I appreciate that, Andrea, but in Edward's case I got the opposite impression. I felt he lived well and enjoyed life."

"OK. What was he doing in Greece?"

"He wanted to persuade me to collaborate on a project. It was to be a series of programmes for television to do with marble art in Greece. Edward was inspired to do this because he had a collection of rare documents from nineteenth-century travellers to Greece, letters, that kind of thing. He mentioned paintings too. He was going to base the programmes on this collection, using them to dictate the town or island which was the subject of each episode."

"Would these rare documents be very valuable?"

"Yes. From the point of view of their contribution to our understanding of history, some would be beyond financial value. I don't know what's in the collection of writings apart from some significant letters. There are some works of art from the same period. An Edward Lear painting, which Edward owned, would be worth serious money."

The inspector had been making notes. He looked up thoughtfully at Day.

"Is there anything else you can tell me about the project? Was anyone involved apart from you and Edward?"

"Apart from our UK agents, we mentioned it to two people in order to draw them into the project. One was Aristos Iraklidis, the Curator of the Naxos Museum, whom I think you've met."

"Ah, yes, the Curator. I don't believe I had the pleasure of meeting him, but I certainly heard of him by reputation."

"Aristos agreed to allow some filming at the museum and to lend his support to the project. Then we visited a renowned marble artist and ceramicist on Naxos, a friend of Edward's called Konstantinos Saris."

Nomikos wrote down the name, and raised his leonine head to invite more detail.

"He has a workshop near Kato Potamia on Naxos. He liked Edward's idea and they were going to talk about how a comparison of ancient and modern marble art could be an angle for the programmes. He's truly among the world's best marble artists, apparently. He's won funding from the Niarchos Foundation to work with a different marble artist each year for three years, culminating in an exhibition in the Niarchos Cultural Centre here in Athens."

"I see. Did you say Saris and Edward Childe were old friends?"

"They met in Cambridge just a few years ago, I believe, and have seen each other a few times since. They seemed very amicable."

"Can we take a step back, Martin, and talk about the days leading up to the last time you spoke to Edward? Firstly, when did he arrive on Naxos to see you?"

"Last Tuesday, the thirteenth."

"And he stayed at your home?"

"Correct."

"Where did he go during his stay? Please try to include everything you can remember."

"We ate at the taverna in Filoti run by Thanasis... actually, I'm not sure I know his surname. Taverna O Thanasis on the main road. And we had a lunch together at a place in the centre of Filoti. We met the Curator at the museum, and Konstantinos Saris and his team at the marble workshop."

"Edward took the boat to Athens when exactly?"

"Last Thursday, the fifteenth. I booked his hotel room for him, because it's close to my apartment in Dinokratous. I came over from the island yesterday and slept at my place. We had arranged to meet for coffee this morning."

"Did you hear from Edward at all after he left Naxos?"

"No. And that was odd, because he was going to meet someone important on Friday, he was really looking forward to it. I expected to hear about it. Perhaps he wanted to tell me about it in person."

"Who was he meeting?"

Day hardly paused before coming out with the lie. "I don't know. I'll try to find out and let you know."

Andreas Nomikos looked across the desk at Day with his intelligent light blue eyes and put his pen on the pad of paper he had been using. For a second Day thought his lie had been obvious to the policeman, before a second thought occurred to him. Even if Nomikos sensed a change in his tone, there was no way he would guess the truth: a romance from sixty years ago, and the chance for an old man to finally find out why it had not lasted.

"I've thought of something else," he said. "Edward planned to meet people at the British School and the National Museum this week. I don't know any names, but you could check. His flight home was booked for the twenty-first, I think."

Nomikos crossed his arms and thanked Day for the information. He had been an attentive listener, and used charm in a way which made you feel that a spider was inviting you into its web. Yet he was never dismissive of Day's opinion. He was certainly an unusual detective, and not only with regard to his luxurious mane of hair.

"I'll let you know the result of the autopsy, Martin. The scene at the hotel suggested suicide, but we must wait for the post-mortem examination before we can be certain. Rest assured, I'll be informing the British police, and if the autopsy casts any doubt over suicide I will be initiating a major investigation both here and in the UK. In that case I will come to Naxos myself to interview his contacts there."

Day nodded, wondering what else he should ask Nomikos while the policeman was in such a communicative mood.

"Did you find a suicide note, Andrea?"

"No, we did not."

"Was anything missing from his room?"

"The room was tidy. We have his passport and so on. There was no computer or mobile phone."

"Edward didn't have a portable computer, not that I saw anyway. But he did have a mobile phone."

"Perhaps he mislaid it. Or it could have been stolen. We suffer from pickpockets in the popular tourist sites, you know."

"Perhaps. He replied to none of my messages since leaving Naxos. Did he have any injuries, even small things?"

"No. He was lying peacefully on his bed, a glass of water on the bedside shelf and the empty tablet bottles next to the glass."

"Rather classic, isn't it? Andrea, believe me, there's something very wrong here."

***

As he left the building, Day reflected on his own final statement. One of the things that was 'very wrong' was his impulsive lie to Andreas Nomikos, whom he respected. One of Day's professional skills was the shaping of a narrative, making it convincing, knowing what to include and what to leave out. Perhaps he had felt that the story of Edward and Artemis was a hindrance to his determination to make the police consider murder. It suggested a susceptible old man with fanciful ideas, which was not the Edward he had known. On the other hand, Edward had been due to meet Angelika and had died the day after the proposed meeting. If Edward had been murdered, what business had Day, an amateur, to hide from the police his knowledge of possibly the last person to see Edward alive?

As he could not now turn the clock back on his lie, and had no desire to return to Nomikos and apologise, he resolved to find Angelika himself.

8

Day walked away from the police headquarters in the heat of the late morning, wondering what to do. Should he remain in Athens or return to Naxos? He wanted to find Angelika, but he should waste no time to see Konstantinos Saris. He owed it to Edward to give Konstantinos the news before he heard from somebody else.

He would look for Angelika online to begin with, and could come back to Athens when he found her address. The only thing he really had to do in Athens was give some money to Irini, who took care of his apartment, but he could leave it in the flat for her. He decided to book a return ticket to Naxos as soon as possible.

He took the Metro to escape the throbbing heat of the street. The Metro was busy but cool, clean and well-organised, and Day always liked to use it. He travelled for two stops and emerged into the glare of the sun by Evangelismos Hospital, skirting it by walking through a small park and uphill through the streets till he reached his road. By the time he unlocked the apartment building he was uncomfortably hot but felt better for the walk.

In the apartment he put on the air conditioning, made himself a coffee, sat down with his mobile and called the SeaJets ticket office. Then he called Nasos and booked a taxi ride to Piraeus. Nasos would arrive in an hour and a half. He wrote a note enclosing some money for Irini, threw away the milk and switched off the fridge. What else should he do? He would call his friend Helen in London.

"Helen? It's Martin. Is it a bad time to call?"

"It's a good time, actually. I was just getting up from the computer, where I've been for too long today. What's the matter?"

"I'm fine. How are you?"

"I'm fine too. Missing Filoti and the view from the balcony. Also Koula's cooking, the little Fiat, swimming at Agia Anna… missing Greece, basically."

"We're missing you too. Did the funeral go OK, as far as any funeral can?"

"Yes. It wasn't a very solemn affair. My godfather was in his late eighties, so it was more of a celebration of his life. It seems a long time ago now, but it's only been a fortnight. What's your news?"

"You'll find it hard to believe who I've just seen."

"OK, I give up, Martin."

"Andreas Nomikos."

"The beautiful blue-eyed police inspector from Athens? What's he doing there, and why are you talking to him again?"

"I'm not at home, I'm in Athens. I'm going back to Naxos in an hour or so. I went to see Andreas at the Police HQ here. A friend of mine has been killed."

"Killed?" There was a pause. "Do you mean killed *by* somebody?"

"I think so. It looked like he took an overdose, but I don't believe that. There aren't too many other options."

He had been standing restlessly at the window looking down onto the quiet street below. Now he went to the sofa and sat down. He told Helen about Edward, the project, the planned meeting with Angelika and his conversation with Inspector Nomikos.

"Poor Edward. How very sad for him, just when he was looking forward to so much happiness. If somebody did kill him and try to make it look like suicide, I'd trust Inspector Nomikos, wouldn't you?"

"He's a good man. He said he might come out to Naxos himself, to interview the people Edward met there."

"Well, keep me informed. I might even have to come back and make sure you don't get into trouble again, like last time!"

Helen was referring to the small matter of when Day had misled the Naxos police and confronted a possible murderer alone, a course of action Helen had not condoned. Perhaps it was this implication that stopped Day from telling her that he had deliberately lied to Andreas Nomikos about Edward's meeting with Angelika.

***

The SeaJet arrived at the port of Naxos just as the sun was setting over the sea. It was just after seven in the evening, and Day felt exhausted as he struggled through the crowds. He headed towards his favourite bar, Diogenes, further along the harbour road. He wished Helen was here now. For three months she had stayed on the island to work on her next novel, and as she would call it, tried to keep him out of trouble. He smiled at the memory.

Arriving at Diogenes bar, Day threw his bag on a bench and settled down. His favourite barman, Alexandros, was working that evening and came over to greet him.

"Gin and tonic, Martin?" he asked, without giving Day the cocktail menu he held in his hand.

"Yes, please, Alexandre. Thanks."

The drink went down far too quickly, and despite the little bowl of nuts and crisps which had come with it, Day realised that he was hungry. He had eaten nothing all day. He didn't feel like anything fancy. Within a quarter of an hour, he had a burger and fries in front of him on his table at Diogenes. He decided against a second drink, left a generous amount of money in the small glass in which Alexandros had folded his bill, and went looking for a taxi. Home would feel good. He fancied an early night after an hour or two with a book.

***

The letter was waiting for him inside the front door. Day threw down his overnight bag and took the letter to his bedroom. Switching on the light and the aircon, he lodged on the end of the bed and tore open the envelope.

Saturday 17th August, 9.30am
Plaka, Athens

Dear Martin,

You will think this letter strange, because I shall see you in person in Athens in two days. However, when we meet on Monday we should be discussing our exciting plans for the marble series, and I shouldn't take up your valuable time with my private adventures. All the same, I would like to tell you about my wonderful experience of meeting with Angelika yesterday. You were very kind when I told you my story about Artemis, after some delightful Greek wine in the taverna. I believe you will forgive me this self-indulgence.

I'm sitting in a cafe across from the New Acropolis Museum, having coffee alone. Twelve hours ago I was still talking with Angelika in Paximadia restaurant. We met for coffee in the morning, then took a pleasant stroll round the Hill of the Nymphs before we parted to rest until it was time for dinner. Angelika went to her fiancé's apartment where she stays when she's in Athens. We then had a delightful evening meal sitting at a table on the restaurant's balcony overlooking the quiet street, with the full moon as a backdrop. It was a wonderful day.

So, what of the young lady? Her name is Angelika Spetzou. She seemed to me to be the very image of her grandmother. It was like seeing Artemis again. As you know, Angelika's name means 'messenger of the gods' or 'angel' if you prefer, and it suited her. She is of medium height, trim and pleasant-looking, with a nice easy poise. She has light hair where Artemis's was dark, but it is long and wavy like hers was. She has the most enormous dark eyes, and her smile made my heart lift. She laughed a great deal. We both did. It was such a happy day.

Artemis passed away some seven or eight years ago, having had only one child, Angelika's mother. Sadly, Angelika's mother suffers from some kind of mental complaint, and Angelika cares for her. This takes up much of Angelika's time, and although she had a box of her grandmother's belongings, it went unopened and forgotten for years. A few weeks ago she found some time to herself and she opened the box.

It contained a diary from the year 1959 in which Artemis had written about her relationship with me. As Angelika put it, "the wonder of that brief summer shone from the pages". She said it read like a love story. There were accounts of the places Artemis and I had explored together after leaving Brauron, descriptions of me that were full of tenderness, and private thoughts that showed that her grandmother had held me in very high regard as a person, not just as a boyfriend.

Angelika noticed a reference in her grandmother's diary to King's College, and therefore wrote to me there, with a covering letter to the Provost asking if the letter could be forwarded to me. As you know, this was successful as I still have many friends at the College.

Artemis, I understand, had become quite a well-respected artist. I suppose that if I had ever looked for her on the internet I might have found her work in some gallery or other, but as I told you, Martin, I didn't remember her surname. Apparently it was Pantrakis. I wonder if I could perhaps buy one of her paintings even now?

Angelika understood that I had hoped to discover not only what happened to Artemis during her life, but also the reason she left me and didn't contact me again, but she said she was unable to help me. I respect that. Perhaps the diary didn't explain why Artemis left me. Perhaps Angelika thought it would be unnecessarily painful to hear, but either way I'm sure she did the right thing.

I don't know, of course, if I will see Angelika again, but if she is willing I will try to see her next year. She said she would write to me from time to time. I think we got on rather well. Anyway, I wanted to finish the story I started to tell you in Filoti, Martin, and I think you will agree it's a happy ending.

So, when I see you on Monday I shall simply say that the details are all in the post! I'm looking forward to talking about marble, marble, MARBLE!

Kind regards,

Edward C.

9

Seven in the morning was a time Martin Day rarely appreciated. Indeed, rarely saw. He staggered to the balcony in his dressing gown, where the morning shade made his skin prickle and he retreated indoors to put on some coffee. After a glass of water he felt better, and took his coffee back to the balcony. This time he was prepared for the cool air and revelled in it. He stared out. The valley was glistening in the low morning sunshine, the opposite hills no longer a bland foil for the nearer view but a complex art work of shades and textures. The threat of heat lay dormant within the silence. Day admired the colours, wondering what kind of pictures Artemis had painted and whether she had ever painted anything like this view.

He opened his mobile but there were no messages. It was time to start on his long list of tasks. First, an email to Maurice Atkinson, his agent in London, requesting a call around nine o'clock UK time, which would be eleven o'clock Greek time. Then he sent a text to Konstantinos, asking if he could call at the atelier at half past twelve to speak to him.

There was so much he wanted to do today. He would start with a shower to clear his head. He switched on the iron that stood ready in his bedroom, and on emerging from the shower he ironed his one remaining clean shirt. Unable to avoid it any longer, he threw some clothes into the washing machine, congratulated himself for thinking of such necessary domesticity, and left the house. It was still too early to attempt Elias research. He needed a walk.

As he walked his mind was full of Edward. Edward's letter was absolutely not the work of a man about to kill himself. It was full of joy, of excitement about the future, of plans for the following year. Day knew he must tell Nomikos. He could send him a scan of the letter, perhaps? No, he couldn't do that, because Edward spoke of Angelika, and he didn't want to bring the police down on her head. He would just tell Nomikos how positive the letter sounded, and hope the police would not demand it as evidence until he had spoken with Angelika.

He returned from his walk with a take-away frappé just in time to receive the call from London. Maurice Atkinson had become friend, and Day enjoyed their banter. Maurice was an independent agent with more contacts in the world of historical books and films than anyone Day knew. Thanks to him, Day had not been without a reasonable income for fifteen years. Maurice was about Day's age, nearing the dreaded forty, but still looked wet behind the ears. He was, however, an astute businessman and rarely brokered a bad deal.

"Martin! Where in God's name are you, you devil? Do you ever do any real work?"

"I'm fine, thanks for asking, Maurice! I take it you're as busy as ever?"

"As ever," agreed Maurice Atkinson. "So, what can I do for you?"

"I need to speak to you about Edward Childe."

"Oh yes, the project about Greek marble. Browne and Moore sent me the gist of it and asked me to try to involve you. Jonathan Wells is the agent, a very experienced chap. He thought that you'd be the ideal person to collaborate on it and eventually present the series. The project seems to be in the very early stages, with lots of ideas buzzing about, but I was impressed that Edward Childe had some valuable original material to base the programme around. I suggested he contact you directly."

"Any reason why you didn't tell me about this yourself?"

"Oh, should I have? Are you pissed off with me, Martin?"

"Not at all. It's just not like you to leave things to chance when there's a good deal to be made."

"Sorry. Has it not turned out well?"

"Very badly, in fact, but not in the way you mean. Edward visited me last week and we talked about the project, and it was all set to go to the next stage. I should have been calling you today to get you involved with money and contracts, all those things you do for me."

Day paused. His throat felt unexpectedly dry. He sipped his frappé. Maurice waited, experience having taught him not to interrupt his clients.

"I'm afraid Edward's dead, Maurice. He came and stayed with me here for several days, then went to Athens to catch up with colleagues and friends. I was due to meet him yesterday to discuss the marble project again. I went to his hotel and was told he'd committed suicide on Saturday."

"My God. That's terrible. Do you know why he might have wanted …?"

"I'm sure it wasn't suicide, Maurice. Edward wasn't in that frame of mind, in fact just the opposite. It's in the hands of the police now. Look, would you do me a favour? Would you put together for me everything you have and anything that comes to you from now on that's connected to Edward or the project, please?"

"Sure. Anything else I can do?"

"Yes. Could you send me Jonathan Wells's contact details?"

"Will do. So, are you thinking about making the marble series yourself?"

"It's not the right time to talk about that."

"OK, sorry. I just wondered whether you were thinking of fulfilling Edward Childe's wishes, something like that."

"Something like that. OK, Maurice, I'll give you a call in a few days."

"Goodbye, Martin. I'm sorry about Edward."

Within minutes Day received Jonathan Wells's contact details from Maurice by text. He saved them to his contacts list but there was no time to call now. He did a quick search on Wells. He was the senior agent of Browne and Moore, a literary agency founded in London in 1967. Wells's specialism appeared to be accessible history books. His photograph showed an energetic and unpretentious man in his fifties. The agency, as Day was already aware, had a good pedigree and an impressive list of authors, including some senior academics and one or two popular historians who had become household names.

Day closed his computer with a sigh. It was time to get ready to leave to give Konstantinos Saris the unwelcome news.

***

Konstantinos himself opened the gate for Day with a big smile. Dali the dog was with him, taking every opportunity to press up against his master's legs. Konstantinos wore dark dungarees over his shirt and trousers, and all of him bore signs of white dust.

"Martin! How nice to see you again so soon. Come in! Let's have a cold drink on the terrace."

Konstantinos walked ahead, his limp more pronounced than before. The sun at its zenith shone through the pergola and created a dappled pattern onto the terrace and the marble table. Konstantinos took a bottle of mineral water from a small fridge built into the shaded wall of the workshop next to the terrace, and grunted slightly as he sat down. He noticed Day's look of concern.

"My leg? Just an old accident that I'm paying for now," he volunteered cheerfully. "Before Fotis came to live with us, I was up ladders and heaving blocks of stone around, and one day the inevitable happened. Enjoy your youth, Martin! So, why did you want to see me?"

Konstantinos poured a drink for them both. Day had been hoping for a little time to talk of other things before having to break the news, and accepted his glass of water with a sad nod of the head.

"I'm sorry, Konstantine, but it's not a social call, much as I would prefer it to be. Something very bad has happened. It's about Edward."

"Edward?"

"I'm afraid died on Saturday, Konstantine. He went to Athens, as you know, and we planned to meet there yesterday morning. When I arrived at his hotel, I was given the bad news."

The old sculptor looked leaden. "How did he die? Was it his heart?"

"It looked like he had deliberately taken an overdose of his medication. He was in bed with the empty pill bottles on the bedside table. But I don't believe it."

"You don't? Anyone can suffer from depression or be overcome with fear or sorrow. Although I do agree that I wouldn't have thought that of Edward …."

"I agree. There's a police investigation and I happen to know the man in charge. I've told him what kind of man Edward was, and how full of optimism. I'm sure he'll take it seriously."

They fell silent, and Konstantinos's face seemed to line and age even as Day watched. The old man's eyes, unfocussed but resting on the view across his courtyard, became so saddened that Day was afraid the sadness might spill over. He had no idea what to say, so he said nothing.

"I've only known Edward for six years or so, Martin, but in another way I've known him for ever. We met in Cambridge, did he tell you? I was there for a superb exhibition of marble work at the Fitzwilliam Museum. I met some extraordinary people on that occasion, none more impressive than Edward. He was a very special man."

"Indeed he was. And yes, he did tell me how you met, and that you went for dinner together and have been friends ever since. You must have had a great deal in common."

"A very great deal. In fact, …"

Konstantinos was interrupted by a big man in his forties with masses of hair and a curly, black beard who had emerged from the workshop and was walking towards them. Day wondered if this was the owner of the only other car that had been parked at the gate. When he saw Day and noticed their expressions, the big man hesitated.

"Peppino, please, come and join us. This is Martin Day, a new friend of mine. Martin, meet Peppino Berducci. He arrived yesterday from Sicily. We're going to work together for the next few months. You remember, I explained to you about the Niarchos project?"

"Yes, of course. I'm very pleased to meet you, Mr Berducci."

Peppino Berducci shook hands with a firm grip and insisted on first names. He accepted a glass of cold water from Konstantinos, who looked at him slightly longer than normal and then placed both hands flat on the marble table with an air of decision.

"Peppino, you're part of this family now, and I welcome you warmly. Unfortunately, you seem to have arrived at a time when things are not as I would want them to be as we begin our friendship and collaboration. Martin has come with bad news this morning. Our mutual friend Edward, to whom I was hoping to introduce you, died this weekend. He was here with us at this very table only four or five days ago. He was well and happy, I'm pleased to say, and I'm very saddened by his loss. He had so much still to enjoy. Who knows what his later years would have brought him in the way of further success and happiness? He was not finished with life."

"Please accept my sincere condolences," said the Sicilian, expertly summoning his rather accomplished English. He rubbed the side of his nose with a finger, a gesture perhaps of embarrassment. "I'm very sorry to intrude."

"No, no, Peppino, You're not intruding. Your company, and Martin's, are a great support. Especially today, when something unpleasant has happened here at the atelier, something that has unnerved me a little."

The old artist leaned down to stroke his dog on the head.

"What's the trouble, Konstantine?" said Martin. "Has something happened to Xanthe or Fotis?"

"Nothing like that, thank goodness. It seems we had a break-in last night, that's all."

Pressed for more details, Konstantinos stressed that nothing had been stolen and only one small item had been broken. His right hand flicked occasionally to minimise the importance of the event.

"There was no sign of a forced entry, but the workshop door was open this morning. Some items had been moved around, taken from their usual places and put on different shelves. For instance, some unfinished items were in the packing area, while some completed items that were ready for sending to Markos for the shop were lined up ready to go in the kiln. A row of identical vases were interspersed with different articles from elsewhere in the workshop, and some bigger items were upside down. It was very odd. In the shop across the yard there was more disruption: the items for sale had been moved about so they were against different descriptions and price tickets."

"How bizarre," said Peppino. "Who could have done that? And why would anyone want to?"

"Did you say something was broken?" asked Day.

"Just a small figurine, one of my modern Cycladic designs. It's head was broken off, and it was lying on the table next to it. I'm grateful the damage was no worse. Xanthe and Fotis are putting things back where they should be now. It will all be sorted out soon, apparently."

"Have you told the police?" asked Day. The sculptor shook his head. "Someone has shown they can get in here, and the police ought to be told. Anyway, there's something sinister about it. It seems purposeless, but nobody would do that without a reason. And how did they get in without breaking the door?"

"Perhaps the door was left unlocked last night. Only Xanthe, Fotis and myself have keys, so that has to be the answer. It's not a matter for the police, Martin. Nothing was stolen and nobody was hurt. I don't want any rumours starting in the town, and it doesn't seem necessary."

"I don't agree, Konstantine, I think you should let the local police know so they can advise you on security…."

"No, Martin. It's fine, it's over. Thank you, but no."

Day had to concede. "OK. Look, I have a lot to do today, so I'll leave you and Peppino to your afternoon, but if I can help at all please give me a call. I'm only over the other side of that hill. We're neighbours."

***

"Aristo? It's Martin. Am I in time to invite you to lunch?"

"Ah, well, yes, that would be good. I was going to skip lunch and work through to the siesta, but I'd rather meet up with you. Where do you want to eat?" asked the Curator.

"Katerina's? I'll set off now. It will take me about half an hour because I'm in the villages."

It took Day less time than he thought to drive down from Kato Potamia to Chora, find a parking place and walk to the taverna everyone knew as Katerina's. The taverna may have had a different name, but the locals knew who was in charge: the hospitable Katerina with the smiling husband and exceptional chef. It was traditional Greek cuisine, always cooked to perfection, and the ambiance made it a very popular taverna.

Day arrived less than five minutes before Aristos. As soon as he mentioned that he was expecting the Curator, Katerina's already beaming smile extended further and she waved him to the quietest table in the restaurant. Day sat in what was now his usual place and accepted a menu. Katerina returned with a basket of fresh sliced bread, cutlery rolled tightly in paper napkins, two small glasses and a bottle of ice-cold water. A look on her face told Day that his friend had just arrived, and Aristos opened the taverna door.

"Martin. Thank you for this timely rescue from my duties. Good afternoon, Katerina. What do you have today?"

The taverna owner listed the fresh dishes available that lunchtime before leaving them to make their decision.

"Thanks for coming, Aristo," said Martin, genuinely grateful. "Let's order, then I'm afraid I need to pick your brains."

"Don't tell me you're on the trail of another undiscovered tomb?"

"Nothing like that! I just want to unload a few things and see what you think."

Aristos hid his surprise with pursed lips and a sudden interest in the menu. They chose what to eat and looked cheerfully towards Katerina, who came to take their order.

"We would like a Lamb with Potatoes and a briam, please, Katerina." said Aristos.

"Will you be sharing?"

"Yes, please."

When Katerina had disappeared behind the screen into the kitchen, Day began.

"You remember I brought my friend Edward to see you last Thursday? He took the ferry to Athens straight afterwards, and I heard nothing from him after that. When I got to his hotel yesterday, to meet him for coffee as we planned, I was told he had died, apparently of a self-administered overdose. The trouble is, I absolutely don't believe it."

Day looked across at his friend, expecting some kind of disagreement, and was silenced by the grim expression on Aristos's face.

"Then I would support you, Martin. Your judgement is good enough for me. Edward seemed brimful of enthusiasm, energy and plans for the future. I can't imagine what could have happened to change him so greatly that he should kill himself. He could have picked up the phone and talked to you, for one thing. He was only here a few days ago. Tell me, what were the tablets that he supposedly consumed?"

"His prescribed heart tablets and aspirin. The empty bottles were on his bedside table."

"Hard to believe. Of course, it's just my opinion, but my impression of Edward was of a positive, courageous individual. I saw no signs of a depression severe enough to result in suicide."

"Thank you, I appreciate your opinion. Anyway, I've already started to cause trouble. The hotel where he was staying were very helpful, and gave me the name of the police inspector in charge. It's Andreas Nomikos. I'm sure you remember him, the fair-haired man from Athens who came in May to investigate the murder in the Hotel Philippos? I went to talk to him and I believe he'll look into it properly. If it turns out that Edward didn't kill himself, of course, it's even worse."

"Worse?"

"If it wasn't suicide, it must have been murder."

Day now faced the usual dilemma: was he going to tell Aristos about Angelika, and the letter Edward had sent him from Athens? His decision was postponed by the arrival of their lunch. It was excellent comfort food, no doubt about it. The lamb and potato stew which was rich and warming, and the dish of freshly roasted vegetables, restored him like little else would have done. They continued to talk as they ate. Day told his friend in more detail about the marble project, the collection of unpublished writing and art, and Edward's life in Cambridge. He told him about Konstantinos and his friendship with Edward. He could not, however, bring himself to betray Edward's confidence regarding Artemis and her granddaughter, although he promised himself that he would tell Aristos when the right time came.

"Your friend Edward seemed a particularly agreeable and inoffensive person," concluded the Curator when he had heard all that Day was prepared to share. "I'll think about what you've told me, but I must say he seems a very unlikely victim of murder. What would be the motive?"

The question remained unanswered. Day was reminded of his earlier conversation with Konstantinos and Peppino about the break-in at the atelier, which also seemed to be without motive. He considered mentioning the matter to Aristos, but his friend was showing signs of preparing to return to the museum, or possibly head for his siesta.

"Well," said Day, leaving money for their lunch on the table, "I'm sure when Andreas has the results of the autopsy, he'll let me know. It should confirm whether Edward's death was suicide or murder. Then I think I may have work to do."

10

Day felt that he too would benefit from a siesta after lunch, and slept with the heaviness that the August heat instilled despite the air-conditioning in his room. When he woke, an image lingered in his mind, the remnants of a dream. It was the figure of a headless man, tall, slender and unrecognisable, honed down to the essentials of the human form. Its head was on the floor beside it, regarding its former body sadly.

It was no fantasy. It was an echo of Konstantinos's account of his broken figurine, the single piece of damage to occur during the break-in. Once Day's imagination had shown it to him so vividly he realised that the decapitated model at the Saris atelier had not been broken by accident. On the contrary, it seemed very much like a threat. It was either a threat to Konstantinos himself, or to the atelier as a whole.

Day tried to remember everything that Konstantinos had told him about the incident. There had been no sign of forced entry, the door may have been left unlocked, and only Konstantinos, Xanthe and Fotis had keys. Day found it hard to believe that either Xanthe or Fotis had a grudge against Konstantinos, but even if they did, what had they hoped to achieve by the random relocation of objects round the workshop? What had anybody hoped to achieve by it? Nobody would risk breaking into the workshop during the night just to relocate items at random. No, something sinister lay behind the break-in, and the broken figurine seemed significant.

He took a quick shower, made himself a coffee and sat down with his laptop and phone to begin on his list of calls. It was five o'clock in the afternoon, a good time to call the UK. England was two hours behind Greek time, so currently it would be three o'clock in London. He decided to begin with Jonathan Wells, Edward's contact at Browne and Moore. A young man's voice greeted him courteously and put him through to the senior agent in the firm.

"Hello, this is Martin Day. I'm calling about Edward Childe." He couldn't think what else to say. He wondered whether news may already have reached Jonathan Wells, perhaps from the British police, whom Nomikos should already have informed.

Jonathan Wells had a voice that reflected his online profile. It suggested intelligence, confidence and warmth, a charming combination. It was clear that he recalled Day's connection with Edward but had not heard the news about his long-term client. When Day finished telling him there was no immediate comment from the other end. When he did react, Jonathan Wells sounded shocked, in the unashamedly emotional way of a family member.

"Oh dear. That's extremely bad news. Edward and I have known each other for over thirty years. Thank you for taking the trouble to call me in person, Mr Day. May I call you Martin? Edward spoke highly of you when he called me from Athens."

"Of course. I'm sorry for the shock. I wonder, could I talk to you for a moment? I have something I'd like to discuss with you concerning Edward."

"Naturally."

Day had no intention of discussing his opinion about Edward's death, but he wanted to find out as much as he could about Edward's valuable collection, in particular anyone who might benefit by his death.

"For Edward's sake I'm considering whether I could take forward his ideas for the marble project," he said, not entirely untruthfully. "Can you tell me who else is already involved in it?"

"That's simple. Only Edward, you, myself, and your agent Maurice Atkinson even know about it," answered Jonathan. "Nobody else here at Browne and Moore will have heard of it. So, you might be considering a future for Edward's idea?"

"Possibly. I'd like to look into it, anyway. Do you have any objection?"

"I think it's something Edward would have liked. I'm sure Maurice and I can come to an agreement. I don't know if there's any next of kin, or to whom Edward has bequeathed the collection. Perhaps you know more?"

"I don't, but I'll try to find out. Would you have any objection to speaking to Maurice, and ideally get some details sent to me here, in Greece, where I live?"

"I don't have anything of value, but I do have a great deal of paper which Edward left in my care, his plans for the series. There are several ring binders, I'm afraid. That's typical of Edward." He paused, his professional mind working out the best interests of the firm. "I'll send them over to Maurice as soon as we've agreed how to proceed. Have you considered Edward's collection of travellers' writings? I hope they're secure. They must be of considerable value."

Day reflected on this. It would be useful to know more about the collection. Unlikely though it seemed, it might have been a motive for murder.

"Do you have a list of the travel writing?"

"I believe so. I'll include it in the material I send to Maurice for you."

"I'll tell Maurice to expect to hear from you, then. I'll find out where Edward's most valuable items are, and ensure that they're safe. Thank you, you've been really helpful, Jonathan."

"Let me know if I can do anything else, Martin, and would you let me know about the arrangements, please? The funeral, I mean."

"Of course. Thanks again."

Day rang off. He realised he had no idea who would make Edward's funeral arrangements, or even how a body was returned to the UK when someone died abroad. He hoped, selfishly, that the task wouldn't fall to him. He opened the app on his phone and tried to make a video call to Helen, assuming she was at home in Hampstead.

"Hey, Martin, this is a surprise. We only chatted yesterday. Has something else happened?"

"Not really. You OK?"

"Fine thanks. The novel's going quite well. I just broke off to make a cup of tea."

"Sounds good. So, how do you fancy coming back to Naxos?"

"What?"

"I'll tell you the story. I'm going to try and find out the truth about Edward's death, maybe even continue with his project. If you can come to Naxos I'll tell you everything, but basically I need to see all the material which Edward left with his agent in London. I've asked for it to be sent to Maurice, then I want it over here in Filoti. I thought, if you wanted a trip, you might pick it up from Maurice and bring it in person. Edward left a couple of ring binders, I'm told. How about it?"

"Ah, I see. It would be quicker and cheaper if I brought the stuff out to you than using the postal system or a courier. OK, I'll do it. I can work as well there as I can here, and September in the Cyclades is the best month, so I'll stay on with you for a while. I'll have to work all the hours God sends, though. When do you want me to come out?"

"As soon as possible. O Thanasis's delicious food awaits you."

"So personal, Martin. I miss you too! Koula's cooking is a lot better than yours, though, so I'll try to get there in the next few days. Will you send me Maurice's details, and tell him I'll call him?"

"Brilliant. You're wonderful, Helen!"

***

"Maurice?"

"Martin. I know why you're calling. I just finished talking to Jonathan Wells. You're thinking of continuing with Edward Childe's project."

"Indeed. I thought you could look through the material and give me your thoughts, and then I'll take a detailed look myself. Apparently a lot of Edward's plans were written on parchment with a quill pen, so I've persuaded an old friend to hand-carry the paperwork over to Greece. It will be safer and quicker, and I get intelligent company too. Her name's Helen Aitchison. I'll put you both in touch, and perhaps you could liaise?"

"Will do. I wish I had friends who would put their lives on hold and run errands for me."

"Really Maurice, I only invited her for a holiday in Greece …."

***

It was time for call number three, this time to King's College, Cambridge. Day could not remember Edward mentioning any names of college friends or former colleagues, so he asked to be put through to the Provost's secretary.

"James Dillon, Provost's Office, may I help you?"

"Ah, hello. My name's Martin Day, I'm a friend of Professor Edward Childe. Do you know whom I should speak to on a personal matter relating to Edward?"

"Can you tell me what it's about, please, Mr Day?"

Day realised there was an issue of confidentiality, but he had no choice but to be open with the Provost's assistant. He explained, and received the man's condolences.

"Professor Childe was particularly close to a member of staff in the Department of Ancient History," said James Dillon. "He should be informed of the sad news anyway, and he would be the best person to help you, I think. His name is Dr Cameron Maxwell. I should probably ask him to call you, as it's the summer vacation and he's likely to be at home, on a private number."

"If you would. I'm in Greece, of course, so do advise him of that too."

***

Dr Maxwell telephoned within half an hour. Of all the people to whom Day had so far had to break the news of Edward's death, this proved the most difficult. He spent fifteen minutes answering questions about the how and even the why. Cameron Maxwell was incredulous at the idea of suicide. His disbelief resonated with Day, who found himself opening up to the historian, explaining about Edward's project and plans for the future. He stopped short of complete disclosure; it had become a habit to keep Artemis and Angelika from everyone.

"There are a few practical matters about which I want to speak to you, Dr Maxwell. Firstly, did Edward have relatives who need to be informed, do you know?"

"I believe not. He was, as he would say, short on relatives but strong on friends. A deliberately mixed idiom."

"I see. Which brings me to my next question. What happens to his property now? I believe he had a collection of valuable items."

"Yes, I can help with that. I was in his confidence and am executor of his will. He has left some items to the Fitzwilliam Museum, and the bulk of his estate to the College in the form of scholarships for deserving students and his most valuable artefacts. The will is lodged with Bland and Wilmott in Parkside Place. I'm his executor."

"That's very clear. Another pressing matter is the return of Edward's body and arranging the funeral...."

"I think my wife and I can do that, Mr Day, with the help of the university authorities. I'll see what I can sort out."

"Thank you. That's a great relief. Perhaps you would let me know the details of the funeral, when the time comes?"

"Of course."

"Do you happen to know whether Edward's collection of travel writing is in his home, or securely under lock and key somewhere? I'm concerned about how vulnerable it is." Day kept to himself the possibility that Edward's valuable collection could be connected to his death.

"No need to worry on that score, Mr Day. Edward placed it with the University for safe-keeping. When the will is read, no doubt it will be safely transferred to whomever Edward decided should have it."

Day thanked Cameron Maxwell, they exchanged email addresses, and they ended the call sure they would be in touch again before long.

***

Day's calls to the UK were now completed. It seemed there was no way Edward's valuable collection could have been a motive for his murder. No relatives or any other individuals stood to gain. He had drawn a blank, but it was a useful one.

He emailed Andreas Nomikos with what he had learned, giving the contact details of everyone involved. Edward's will would interest Nomikos, Day thought. If a verdict of suicide was recorded, it would be said that Edward had put his affairs in order first. If murder, the motive must lie elsewhere.

Day suddenly wanted to leave the house and get some air. Before heading off for a walk, he called Konstantinos and asked for Peppino Berducci's mobile number. He then invited the Sicilian to meet him at Taverna O Thanasis the following evening for dinner. It would be an opportunity to get to know the newcomer, and learn more about the strange break-in at Saris EM.

11

Day's first thought on waking was that it was exactly a week since Edward had taken him to Konstantinos's marble workshop. Only one week. In that short period Day's entire focus had changed. Before Edward's arrival he had been immersed in his research, putting together the biography of Nikos Elias which had been his intended labour for the summer. The first draft was supposed to be in Maurice's hands by the end of October. Day hadn't given it a serious thought since Edward's death.

He heaved himself from the bed, flicked on the iron, and went for a shower. The warmth of the water felt good after the cool of the air-conditioned bedroom. He ironed a shirt from his pile of clean washing and dressed carefully, hoping to improve his mood. He made his morning coffee with attention to detail, using a cafetière which had been a gift from Helen at the end of her last visit, and relocated to the balcony. The morning sun had not moved round to the table, but he was warm enough. He drank his coffee staring at the view, his gaze unfocussed. Like many people who live alone, Day enjoyed the company of his own thoughts.

He thought about the mysterious break-in. The broken figurine conveyed some kind of threat against its creator, he was sure of it. Generous, witty, warm-hearted Konstantinos, an exceptional man in his early eighties, seemed an incredible target for malice, and surely neither Xanthe nor Fotis would wish to harm him.

A dislike of the world, an alienation from his fellow human beings, suddenly washed over Day. It was a tendency to which he was prone when forced to acknowledge the dark side of human nature. First Edward's death, now threats against Konstantinos. Those two elderly gentlemen, two friends with scholarly or artistic lives, were undeserving targets of other people's hatred.

Day told himself to apply the power of his reasoning. The break-in at the atelier seemed the most straightforward of the two problems, but he quickly realised he could do nothing as long as Konstantinos refused to inform the police. Then he thought about poor Edward. He was powerless there too, until the news of the coroner's report.

He must find Angelika. She should be told that Edward had died, told by a friend, and it was the one useful thing he could do for Edward right away. Day's real reason for searching for her, of course, was more selfish. He was currently the only guardian of Edward's story, and he wanted to know more.

A pale dove landed noisily on the cane canopy above the balcony table, jolting Day from his thoughts. He got up and fetched his laptop and mobile from the bedroom, returned and poured another cup from the cafetière.

He typed 'Angelika Spetzou Athens' into the search engine, but felt no surprise when nothing useful came up. It was a very common name in Greece, and in other parts of the globe too. Of the many Angelika Spetzou entries, all were for women of the wrong age. He removed the word Athens, only to find countless entries on Facebook and no way to choose between them. Alternative spellings brought no better success. Fair enough, he thought, it was never going to be easy. He would try looking for her grandmother, Artemis. As a professional painter she must have had an internet presence.

He had immediate success this time. Artemis Pantrakis (1939 - 2011). Greek painter. Gallery 'Greece Re-Explored', Kolonaki, Athens.

In amazement he realised that the gallery was only a few streets from his apartment. The Kolonaki district, full of high-end shops and the kind of restaurant to be seen in, was an obvious place to open an art gallery. For a moment Day considered getting the next ferry to Athens and going there in person, but decided to telephone first.

"Oriste?" said a man's voice.

"Hello. Is that the 'Greece Re-Explored' Art Gallery?"

"Yes, good morning. Alekos Georgiades, how may I help you?"

"My name is Martin Day. I'm doing some research into the painter Artemis Pantrakis. I believe she exhibited at your gallery?"

"That's correct, she worked with us exclusively for many years, up until her death of course. I know her by reputation, but was never lucky enough to meet her. I bought the gallery in 2013, so the association with Kyria Pantrakis was before my time."

"Ah," said Day, disappointed. "Can you tell me anything about her?"

"What kind of thing would you like to know?"

"Do you have any of her work at the gallery, or know where it can be found? Is she exhibited elsewhere in Athens perhaps?"

"I can't help with any of those things, I'm sorry. I believe, if I remember rightly, her work was returned to the family at their request when she died. I'm not aware of any venue in Athens which still displays a piece of hers."

"Would you be able to find her address on your files?"

"I could check, Mr Day, but as I said, she died several years before I bought the business. The former owner has retired and I wouldn't know where to find him…"

"I see. No matter. If you do find anything, would you kindly let me know? May I leave you my email address?"

"Certainly. Oh, something has come back to me now. You could try Brauron. I seem to remember hearing that she was associated with the museum there in some way."

Day thanked the gallery owner and ended the call. What bad luck, he reflected. Artemis Pantrakis had died less than a decade ago, but the change in ownership of the gallery had broken the path back towards her. The Brauron connection was interesting, though. He knew that the museum at Brauron was not a large one, although with five or six rooms it was larger than some. Day was sure, all the same, that no modern work would find a place in its hallowed halls. He could not think of another building in Brauron which could accommodate modern works of art, either at the site or in the nearby community. All the same, Edward's story of Artemis had begun in Brauron, where she had been sketching and painting at the moment he saw her. Day wanted to follow it up.

He looked up and dialled the number for the museum at Brauron, though with no expectation of success. The member of staff who answered confessed to ignorance, but suggested that Day call a different number, for a lady called Ioanna Othonos, who, before her retirement, had overseen the refurbishment of the museum.

Day reached the lady, and once again explained that he was researching Artemis Pantrakis, who had painted at Brauron in the 1950s or 1960s. Ioanna Othonos responded without hesitation.

"Ah yes, Mr Day. I never met her, but the museum owns two works by Kyria Pantrakis. They were donated a very long time ago, before I took up my former post at Brauron. Unfortunately, the museum never had the space to display them, but they are considered to be exceptional modern interpretations of the site, and are kept very safe."

"That's fascinating. Can you tell me more about them?"

"With pleasure, I remember them well. One is a beautiful interpretation of a votive statue owned by the museum. It's a young girl holding a hare. As you may know, the goddess Artemis was seen as a defender of children, and young girls were associated with the worship of her. Kyria Pantrakis's painting brings out a feeling of tenderness that is inherent in the statue, the tilt of the little girl's head, the youthful hand that calms the little hare that the child holds in a fold of her garment.

"The other picture is even more impressive. It depicts the head of the goddess Artemis, again painted from an important original sculpture on display in the museum. The artist shows a real feeling for marble and the way it was carved, the way the light reflects from it, the way its texture weathers over the centuries. I could arrange for you to see the paintings, if you wish?"

"Thank you, I'll accept your kind offer one day, although sadly it's not possible for me just at the moment. What you've said is very helpful, Kyria Othonos. Do you have any information about where the artist lived? That would be very useful to me at this stage of my research."

"I'm afraid not, at least I don't think so. I'll ask my former colleagues and if they can help I'll gladly let you know. I believe she used to exhibit in Athens, but I don't know which gallery."

Day said goodbye and closed his mobile thoughtfully. Artemis's feeling for marble, which Ioanna Othonos had talked about so warmly, struck him as a direct connection with Edward. The girl Edward had fallen in love with had been sitting in the sun sketching the temple of Artemis at Brauron, with its marble columns and what was left of the carved metopes above them. Day wondered whether Edward's profound love of marble, on which he had based his entire career, might have begun when he met Artemis. Alternatively, perhaps Artemis had been influenced by her love for the young Edward Childe. Had it been the memory of Edward which had made Artemis return in her more mature years, paint the ancient marble sculptures of Brauron, and later donate them to the museum?

The most frustrating outcome of his morning's enquiries was his failure to find Angelika. He spent another hour on the internet, but came up with nothing. Another annoying thing was that his searches under Artemis's name had not brought up a single image of her, or of her work, especially unusual in an age when so much is posted on social media and image-sharing forums. Nor was their any personal information on the artist. He pondered on this as he left the house and took a walk into Filoti.

Although it was noon and the lunch period had just begun, Day found his favourite table free at Cafe Ta Xromata. He ordered a frappé and a sandwich, and set up his laptop, opening his Nikos Elias folders. It was time to get back to the biography. For an hour or so he managed to do some work, or at least remind himself of what he had been doing last.

When he looked up, the village had begun to fill up with tourists, attracted by the many good tavernas and the other great attraction of

Filoti, its traditional hardware shop. This emporium of delight sold everything from wine jugs to goat bells. In addition, it was a magnet for photographers, who struggled to capture the floor-to-ceiling displays of terracotta bowls, kitchen utensils, baskets, sling shots and colourful wine jugs. Day packed his laptop away, left money for his lunch on the table, and walked home away from the bustle.

***

He did not manage to sleep despite lying down for his customary siesta in the cool of his air-conditioned room. He lay with his eyes shut, thinking about Edward, about Artemis, about Konstantinos. In the middle of his attempted rest he heard a text arrive on his mobile, but decided it could wait. He tried to empty his mind by thinking of Greek words and their English counterparts, and dozed fitfully. He stirred when his lace curtain began to move gently with a new breeze from down the valley. He had forgotten to close his window. So quiet was the back of his house that unless the neighbour called out, there was virtually nothing to disturb the peace.

He reached for his mobile. The text had been from Helen, telling him when she was due to arrive on Naxos. Immensely cheered, despite his life-long enjoyment of living on his own, Day fetched himself a glass of water, returned to his bed, and picked up his book. The rest of the time before the hour of the aperitif would be profitably spent reading about one man's walk down the valley of the Meander river. Never likely to take such exercise himself, Day loved reading about those who did.

***

There was nothing more cheering, Day thought as he showered, than the prospect of a quiet and well-earned gin and tonic prior to a meal with an interesting companion. He found himself now in just such an enviable position. He chose a pink Oxford shirt, ironed it with more than his usual care, and went to the fridge to begin preparing his signature aperitif. When the glass's rim had been brushed with a slice of lemon, the ice cubes were cracking beneath the gin and the tonic, and a fresh lemon slice lay among the rising bubbles, he took the drink to the balcony and prepared to enjoy the evening light of the Filoti valley.

He had about forty minutes before he was due to meet Peppino Berducci at the Taverna O Thanasis. He had time to look forward to the evening. Walking to the taverna was an excellent form of exercise, in Day's opinion. Thanasis's wife Koula, matriarch of the family and head chef, never failed to instil in Day something very like awe when he tasted her food. Peppino Berducci, moreover, promised to be an interesting guest.

He suddenly realised quite how beautiful the view in front of him actually was. This balcony overlooked no other house, if you discounted a distant building which somebody was slowly refurbishing as a holiday home. In the early evening light a pink glow seemed to infuse the valley. The sun, sinking towards the west, would shortly disappear behind the hill. Mildness spread across the landscape. Whether due to the warm air or the gin and tonic, Day felt more relaxed than he had felt for a week.

He checked the time on his mobile and prepared to leave the house. The walk to the taverna was easy going. Local people were sitting outside their houses to enjoy the balmy temperature of evening, calling greetings to each other and to passers-by, nursing a coffee cup, or playing with their komboloi, the smooth beads used to pass the time in Greece. Suddenly someone called out to Day, wishing him a good evening, and he replied at once, filled with pleasure that he was beginning to be recognised as a resident.

He arrived at the taverna five minutes early and Peppino had not yet arrived. It was a good opportunity to greet Thanasis and let his host know that he was expecting a new colleague to dine with him.

"Ah, you have so many friends, Martin! And how is the Belle Helene? When will she come to visit us again?"

Day laughed. Thanasis teased Helen flirtatiously as if she were Helen of Troy. Day thoroughly enjoyed Helen's exasperation. "She'll be back in a few days, Thanasi, I'm pleased to say. You'll see a lot of us, you can be sure."

"Excellent! Ah, is this your guest arriving?"

Peppino Berducci, looking very Italian and impressive in a red floral shirt, waved as he entered.

"Peppino, nice to see you! Meet Thanasis, owner of my favourite taverna."

Day and Peppino took a table on the terrace in front of the taverna. It occurred to Day that they made an interesting contrast to each other. He guessed the Sicilian was only slightly older than himself, perhaps in his mid-forties. There the similarities ended. Peppino was a large-shouldered man with a natural bulk, yet it was clear that he kept fit. He looked as if he could move at speed. Day, an Englishman in a pink Oxford shirt, was conscious of his own fitness level, or lack of it, although he was thin by comparison to the Sicilian. Peppino Berducci dressed casually but with flair, the floral shirt bright and positive, the jeans clean but not new. He had thick, wavy, dark hair that he pushed back from his forehead frequently, revealing the silver that was beginning to take over at his temples. His beard and moustache showed signs of careful grooming without which they would be wild. He was a good-looking man, Day thought, and one given to smiles and laughter.

"This is fantastic, Martin," said Peppino, echoing Day's current mood. "I've not really stopped running around since I first arrived. I've moved into my little house in Kato Potamia, bought a car, been to the supermarket, got myself a Greek SIM, all those practical things… I haven't really eaten much at all, and certainly not in good company."

"Well, I can promise you won't be disappointed with the food here, Peppino. That is, if you like Greek cuisine."

"Of course I do! You know, there are many connections between Sicilian food and Greek food. Simple, honest ingredients are central to both. Sicilian food was greatly influenced by the Greeks who settled in Italy, and a famous Sicilian cook called Mithaecus actually brought Sicilian cookery back here to Greece."

"I didn't know that. So tell me a few Sicilian specialities… Oh, hang on, shall we order some wine first? Do you prefer red or white?"

Day looked back into the taverna and saw Thanasis's son, Vangelis, watching with a professional eye. He came over to the table.

"My father would like to offer you a small glass of cold white wine from his family vines, on the house. Yes?"

"Yes, of course, please thank him for us."

Vangelis returned with two small glasses of cold white wine, which was zesty and lively, fresh from the barrel. It made Day smile as he sipped, and he wondered whether his guest would smile or grimace. The wine was coarse and young, there was nothing refined about it. Day liked it very much as an aperitif. He watched Berducci, who gave a similar smile as he drank.

"That wakes up the taste buds!" he said, and gave his first loud laugh of the evening. Day remembered it now from when he had first met Peppino at Konstantinos's atelier.

"So, let me see, Sicilian specialities," said Peppino. "Pasta, of course. Pasta with seafood especially. Have you tried pasta *ai Ricci*? That's pasta with sea urchin. My family came originally from the Catania region, so pasta *alla Norma*, which comes from there, is another favourite, it's a regional speciality made with sardines. And there's a delicious pasta sauce made from dried tomatoes, called *Capuliato*, which is very rich and wonderful."

"I see a theme, Peppino," Day grinned. "It sounds fantastic, I could eat it now. So, have you spent much time in Greece and tried all the Greek favourites?"

"I've certainly been in Greece several times, but not for a few years. I'm looking forward to many months of Greek food. I won't be at all homesick in such a cuisine."

"How long are you going to be on Naxos?"

"At least until the end of February. The Niarchos Foundation have put a great deal of thought into this project, with Konstantinos at the heart of it. My part is just for the first season of three. I'm very excited about it. There are specific requirements associated with the funding we've been given, and I believe we will need at least six months to complete the work, maybe longer. My accommodation is completely paid for by the Foundation, and my allowance is extremely generous. All our costs are taken care of by the Foundation too - the purchase of some good marble, in particular. I'll probably stay on Naxos after February, to be here for the exhibition in the Kastro."

"And the work is to be shown later in Athens, is that right?"

"That's right. All the work made during the project goes to Athens for the big exhibition at the Niarchos Centre in three years' time."

"I'd like to hear more about your work, both in general and what's planned for the project."

"And you must tell me about what you do, Martin, and how you come to be living here on Naxos."

They were interrupted by the arrival of Thanasis.

"Gentlemen. Would you like to keep this table for the evening, or would you prefer a table indoors for when you have your meal? No rush, of course, but I'll reserve your favourite table, Martin, if you would prefer to eat inside."

The terrace was beginning to fill up with summer visitors in families and larger groups, which may have prompted Thanasis's suggestion. They accepted his offer, and said they would move inside in a while.

"Before we talk of other things, Peppino, is there any more news about the break-in? How is Konstantinos?"

Peppino ran his finger down the side of his nose, a habit Day had already noticed in him, apparently a sign of unease. "Nothing new on the break-in, and Konstantinos is refusing to think or speak about it. He wants to put it behind him. It happened on the night I arrived, you know. I feel somehow guilty, like the bringer of bad luck. I sat with Konstantinos after you left yesterday morning and listened to him, and I think he's afraid that somebody he knows may have done it. I think that's why he wants to forget the whole thing."

"Mmm. The only people who have keys and could have got in without damaging the door seem to be the two people he most relies on and likes. It's hard to believe it of either Xanthe or Fotis. Has Konstantinos found anything missing, or anything else damaged?"

"I believe not."

"There's no obvious motive, then. I would have expected some kind of message or demand."

"Why's that, Martin?"

"I've been thinking about the broken statuette, the small Cycladic figure with the head broken off. Don't you feel that it's some kind of threat?"

"I hadn't thought of that, but it does seem bizarre. Sinister, even."

"I wish Konstantinos would speak to the police. He's not going to, though, is he?"

"Not that I can see." Peppino finished his white wine in a single swallow.

Day sighed, seeing his own anxiety reflected in the Sicilian. He suggested they move to their table inside. He was ready for food.

***

Vangelis showed them to their table in a quiet corner inside the taverna. The dark blue tablecloths overlaid with fresh white paper covers made the restaurant look fresh and clean. Sepia photos in simple wooden frames completed the atmosphere of a traditional Greek taverna, and Day was pleased to imagine the good impression it must be making on Peppino. Vangelis returned with a bottle of cold water and two glasses, a basket containing cutlery wrapped in paper serviettes and freshly sliced bread. Handing them each a menu, he smiled at Day.

"Can I bring you something to drink while you choose your food?"

"Red?" suggested Day to Peppino, already feeling that they shared the same taste. "A kilo of your red wine, please, Vangeli. Thanks." Day turned back to Peppino when they were alone. "You order wine using the kilo not the litre in Greece," he explained, as Peppino was looking faintly puzzled. "I've ordered the barrel wine, as they call it, the house wine. It's quite good, and it's good for you the next morning too!"

"Fine by me. So, what do you usually eat here? And do we order to share?"

Day warmed even more to the Sicilian; sharing dishes of food was his favourite way to eat in Greece.

"Yes, sharing is best. First I should consult the family on what they recommend today. Koula, that's Thanasis's wife, cooks special dishes according to what she finds fresh on the market."

"Home from home. I said so!" said Peppino. He unwrapped a knife and fork from their paper serviette and laid the cutlery in anticipation in front of him, reaching back to the basket for a piece of bread which he bit into with relish.

Vangelis returned with a large jug of red wine and two wine glasses of the kind that probably bounced if you dropped them on the floor. Day loved all this. He had no need of elegant crystal, he far preferred the tooth glasses and stubby wineglasses of traditional Greek tavernas.

"So, Vangeli, what do you recommend this evening? I think some seafood might be what we're looking for tonight."

The young waiter grinned. "We have octopus and shrimp, fresh today, I highly recommend them. We also have mussels cooked in my mother's own sauce. For meat, we have lamb chops grilled, and rooster in red sauce. The special salad today is 'politiki' salad."

Peppino's smile reached the complete width of his face as he asked how the octopus and shrimp were cooked.

"The shrimps we can grill, fry or cook 'saganaki', Kyrie. That's with Feta cheese. The octopus grilled, or with lemon sauce, or my favourite way, which is with macaroni in a tomato sauce. It's a dish we usually eat in Lent, but it's very popular so we offer it at other times of the year too."

"Peppino, I think you should order," said Day.

"We can decide together," Peppino conceded, "but for me the fried shrimp and the octopus speciality both sound excellent."

"Shall we have, then, those two, and a few of Koula's mussels? I'd like a portion of chips to share, and perhaps we ought to have something green?"

Peppino laughed and agreed, and Day asked for a portion of horta, a generic name for the local green leaf vegetable found everywhere in Greece.

Vangelis smiled and disappeared to the kitchen.

"What is horta?" asked the Sicilian.

"It's just very simple steamed green leaves, grown locally, probably picked today. There are a number of different leaves they use, but they're all delicious. The octopus should be excellent, good choice. We don't really need a filler, but the potatoes on Naxos are renowned for their flavour, the locals are extremely proud of them. You have to have them at your first meal here."

Thus Day concealed his love of Naxian chips beneath a veneer of hospitality.

***

As the food was placed on their table, in the order in which it became ready in the kitchen, they put modest amounts on their plates and gave themselves over completely to the pleasure of eating. The Sicilian declared the shrimps excellent, and that dish was soon empty. The octopus with pasta in a rich tomato sauce was topped with the local Mizithra cheese, which was Peppino's first taste of the island's pride and joy. He declared himself 'at home', then corrected it to 'in heaven' as he tucked into the seafood.

Day usually felt he over-ordered in Greece, but on this occasion there was clearly no cause for concern. Peppino Berducci was a big man, and a hungry one. He seemed to relish the last bite as much as the first, and when there was nothing left on the table he sat back with a smile. Day lifted the empty wine jug in a silent suggestion, and Peppino nodded. Vangelis, seeing this and knowing his customer, indicated that he would bring another.

When the table was cleared of empty plates and they sat with replenished glasses, Peppino began to describe the work that he and Konstantinos planned to do together.

"Do you know much about Konstantinos's sculptures, Martin?" he asked. When Day shook his head, he launched enthusiastically into his lecture.

"He's famous for his full-length, life-sized human figures, sometimes a single person, sometimes a couple. I shouldn't really say 'person', and probably not 'human' either. Konstantinos makes sculptures that are subtle, emblematic shapes, reminding you of Cycladic simplicity, often androgynous. His single figures are contemporary and simple, almost always sad. The couples express the importance of love, but all his work suggests disillusionment with the modern world, the heads usually turned away slightly. He's also made some figures that are meant to be laid horizontally, showing the death of the spirit."

"My God, that's very bleak."

"In concept, yes, but the work is also uplifting, I promise you."

"And how would you describe your own sculptures?"

"I make some full-length figures also, but mostly heads. With the heads I like using extraordinary pieces of marble with colour and pattern in the stone, creating the facial expression using the grain and shading of the marble. My work is more 'busy' than Konstantinos's - mad, unruly hair, that kind of thing. I'm afraid I too produce more sad faces than contented ones! I find the lines within marble can work well to suggest a 'long face', as I think you say in English, or even a tearful one. Certain marble, of course, can suggest a dead face. History shows us that sculptors have always known this about marble."

Day was familiar with this already. "Yes, the grave stele from the Classical period come to mind, the grave markers."

"Indeed. My full-length figures are very much influenced by the sculptures of that period, and in these I can express all my Sicilian passion! My figures are in motion, they are dynamic. Do you know about ancient Greek sculpture?"

"Not as much as I'd like to. Treat me like a blank page!" Day said with uncharacteristic modesty, in the face of someone with far greater expertise.

"I'll send you a few links tomorrow, you can look them up online. They will show you the kind of thing I do. There's an acroterion, a statue designed for the very top of a roof, from the ancient Temple of Asclepius at Epidauros, which is twisted and dramatic. It's in the National Archaeological Museum in Athens. There's another great piece called the Raging Maenad that we only know because the Romans made a copy of it, the original is lost. Both are clearly in the middle of dramatic movement. My figures, like those, are twisted or tortured souls, or triumphant ones, always in movement. Unlike the ancient sculptures, on which time has changed the patina, I emphasise the gleaming surface of the marble, with minimal suggestion of human traits. My figures express emotion through violent movement. Konstantinos expresses himself through the very smallest positional hints in an otherwise static, monumental statue. We complement each other."

"I'm now going to have to learn a lot more about contemporary marble sculpture, Peppino. You're a great ambassador for the subject. Do you have any ideas for the pieces you're going to make while you're here? If it wouldn't be giving anything away …"

"I'm happy to tell you. The project stipulates that between us we make three large pieces for public spaces. Working in that way will be new to us both. We have some ideas. The most interesting to me is a work that the viewer can see through in places, so that the view beyond becomes part of the meaning. These three pieces will be abstract. Then Konstantinos and I separately will create works based on the theme of climate change, conserving the planet. For my part, I'm thinking along the lines of some heads emblematic of clean air, water, the sea, ice… Konstantinos is interested in exploring nature myths, like the Greek goddess of nature, Artemis. He plans a full-length sculpture of her."

Thoroughly enjoying the images that Peppino was conjuring up, Day was drifting pleasantly in a miasma of red wine. He registered the name of the goddess and it made him remember Edward. Edward, who had eaten at this same table with him only a few days ago and was now dead. Day reached for the wine jug.

"We've ordered some fantastic pieces of marble," Peppino was saying. "Naxian, Parian and Pentelic from Greece, and some special, coloured pieces from Sicily. It's really exciting. I just hope we have time enough for everything we'd like to achieve. And I'm a bit concerned that Konstantinos doesn't wear himself out. He doesn't seem very robust."

"Are you thinking of the break-in? Or his limp?"

"No, more of his emotional state. He likes to be witty and hospitable, and play the energetic old man. But apparently his wife died some years ago and he's still grieving deeply. He can't seem to even say her name aloud. It's hard to recover from such a loss at his age. He clearly adored his wife. They were clearly soulmates."

Into Day's mind sprang a vivid picture of Deppi. He considered telling Peppino about her, and opened his mouth to do so. The introverted side of him came to the rescue, much as it had when he had decided not to share the story of Edward's early love with anybody. Deppi would remain hidden inside him, at least for as long as he could keep her there. Peppino was a natural listener, he showed signs of empathy as he talked of Konstantinos, and yet Day could not open up to him about Deppi. He must not. He forced his thoughts back to marble sculpture, and they talked for a while longer about the qualities of marble, its colours, its challenges.

"You know, Martin, I think one of the most exciting things about working with marble is simply that you become part of an enormous history of exceptional artists. Yes, we have a modern approach, and yes, we want to express different things. But … Have you heard the completely unsubstantiated quote about Picasso? He is meant to have said it when he saw the Neolithic cave paintings at Lascaux."

"No, what?" Day managed to say.

"Basically, that thousands of years have passed since those pictures were painted on the cave walls, and yet we know nothing more about art now than what those first artists knew. Something like that. I feel the truth of that when I'm working with marble. I'm working in a tradition that is one long continuity from ancient times, Greek and Roman particularly. We take ideas from here, influences from there. We make our own work. Maybe we even imagine that we are creating something really new."

12

The first visitors were beginning to queue for tickets at the reception desk of the Naxos Archaeological Museum. Day edged round them, climbed the stone stairs to the top floor of the museum, and pushed open the door to his friend's office. Aristos looked up from his computer.

"Ah, Martin, good to see you. Are you well?"

Day certainly was. He felt this visit was rather momentous, and had been looking forward to it since Aristos's invitation. The Curator wasted no time, and they walked down to a gallery in which discoveries from the Mycenaean tombs at Aplomata, in central Naxos, were displayed. Day was familiar with most of the artefacts in the Naxos Museum, having spent a great deal of time examining them closely, but one new object had recently been added to this display case. He stopped in front of it, surprised how moved he felt.

It was a small rounded jar with a narrow top, a curious false spout, and two handles high on its neck, and came from a tomb on Naxos. It was called a stirrup jar because of its shape, and had been in two pieces when Day himself had recovered it. After being restored as a priority at the special request of the Curator, it was now on permanent display. This was one of the things Aristos had brought him to see. Day stood smiling at the Mycenaean artefact, and experienced a strange pang of ownership.

Having given Day a moment for reflection, the Curator could not resist giving his account of the jar's restoration.

"Beautifully done, isn't it? I enlisted the help of my old friend Aliki Xylouri at the Archaeological Society. You remember her? Of course you do. She prioritised the restoration, and it's now one of my favourite exhibits in the collection. In many ways it's clearly akin to the stirrup jars that were found at Aplomata, but it isn't decorated with the marine motifs so prevalent in these islands around this period. Instead it has these lovely botanic designs. Actually, I believe we'll be able to confirm that they represent plants that would have been growing along the shoreline at the time. It's very fine, don't you think?"

"I do. The restorer has done a good job. What date have they given it?"

"Early 12th century BCE. That's still to be confirmed, though, so it will be a while longer before we make the display label. When we do, it may have your name on it."

"Why on earth would you do that, Aristo? No, let it stand for itself. What about the other objects I gave you, are they on display too?"

"Come with me."

They went to another gallery, politely circumventing groups of visitors. Metal artefacts and decorative personal items were displayed in these cases, mostly from the Mycenaean tomb at Kamini on Naxos. There were various items of jewellery, sealstones, semi-precious stone beads and objects made of gold. Day was less familiar with this gallery, as his real interest was in pottery, but Aristos drew his attention to a case near the window which held gold jewellery. In the middle of the highest shelf was a gold bracelet, the second of the three items which Day had recovered. There was a display label against the bracelet which said, simply, 'Gold bracelet found near Melanes. Late Mycenaean. 1200 - 1100 BCE.'

"This is an extraordinary piece," said Aristos in a low voice so the visitors would not overhear.

"It's stunning, isn't it? And the third object? Is the figurine out on display too?"

"No, not yet. It's proving of interest to a scholar in Athens, but it will come back to us at some point. I have her letter in my office, you might be interested to read what she says."

They returned to the Curator's office and Aristos went to his filing cabinet to get the letter for Day. Day felt his phone vibrate in his trouser pocket and brought it out. The screen said Peppino Berducci. He apologised to Aristos and took the call, already uneasy.

"Martin? Peppino. I'm at the atelier. There's been another break-in. Serious damage to a kiln full of Konstantinos's ceramics. And this time there's a message. Whoever did this wants the Niarchos project to be stopped before it's even begun."

Day said he would be there in twenty minutes, corrected himself to thirty, and asked Peppino not to do anything else till he got there.

***

Forty minutes later, he drew up at the gate of Saris EM.

As on Day's first visit, it was Fotis who emerged from the store building to open the gate for Day. He wore a different expression this time, a face clouded with concern and incomprehension. There was no sign of Konstantinos's friendly dog, nor was anybody else in sight. Without a word, Fotis led the way across the courtyard to the workshop, where Konstantinos, Peppino and Xanthe were seated on wooden chairs, empty coffee cups on the floor beside them, and Dali pressed up against his master's feet.

Peppino rose to shake Day's hand and indicated the chair next to Konstantinos which he had just vacated. The older man shook his head gently as Day sat down beside him.

"I didn't want to listen to you, Martin. I know you thought that the first break-in was more than just a stupid prank… Nothing like this has ever happened to me before. I must have really upset somebody…"

Konstantinos looked mournfully round his workshop, avoiding the eyes of everyone in the room. He reached down and stroked his dog's head. Dali got to his feet and laid a large paw on the old man's knee, his tail moved slightly in a faint wag.

"Whatever the truth of the matter, Konstantine, this is not your fault. I take it the police have been called?"

"No, not yet," Peppino answered. "Konstantinos wanted to wait for you."

"Will somebody tell me exactly what happened? Peppino?"

"As soon as I arrived this morning, we came in here to start work," said the Sicilian, "just Konstantinos and I. Xanthe was over in the shop, and Fotis was still on his way from Kato Potamia. Everything was as normal. There was no sign that anybody had been in the atelier during the night. Konstantinos went to the kiln room, where a batch of ceramics were fired overnight. That's when he saw that the back wall of the kiln room was covered with red writing. You could only see it once you were inside the room. He called out to me. We couldn't understand it at first. Someone had scrawled in red paint the words NIARCHOS OXI. 'No to Niarchos'. We called Xanthe, and Fotis arrived just then, but they didn't understand it either. There's been no trouble about Konstantinos winning the Niarchos funding, only positive reactions. Then Konstantinos noticed the firing temperature display on the kiln. The setting was far too hot. We both knew what we would find when we opened the kiln."

Konstantinos stood up with some difficulty and asked Day to follow him. They went behind the counter and into the kiln room.

"I have four kilns, Martin. This big one here is my best old one, a serious beast with thick walls, it holds my large items. Outside I have an old, traditional kiln which I don't use much, but I love it. For practical reasons I bought these two modern kilns here. They're easy to transport to the island and very useful for small batches of firing. I can load one while the other is in use. You see?"

Day nodded. They were inside the kiln room, and although he was listening to Konstantinos he was transfixed by the vulgarity and violence of the red letters on the wall. They reminded him of old films where the threat is scrawled in the victim's blood. This was a deliberate attempt to frighten Konstantinos. It was certainly making Day's heart pound. He dragged his attention back to the sculptor.

"Modern kilns are electronically controlled, of course. This is the control programmer, and this thermocouple leads from it to the kiln. See the temperature setting? That's how we found it, at 1300 degrees centigrade. Earthenware needs to be fired about 1000 to 1040 degrees centigrade. If the temperature is set incorrectly, for example at above 1250 degrees, the pots will be spoilt, and not only that but the interior of the kiln will be ruined, there's a lot of damage. I knew what I would find before we opened the lid. The figurines in pieces, the heating elements destroyed...."

"It's hard to say what is the worse loss, Martin, Konstantinos's work or the kiln itself. But that's not the point, is it?"

"I agree, Peppino. The damage is serious, but it's the writing that worries me the most."

Day walked to the kiln, the lid of which was open, and looked inside. A mess of ruined clay shapes were melded onto the body of the kiln. He looked at the control that was attached to the wall next to it. The temperature setting was very high.

"Do you think we could all go and discuss this somewhere else, Konstantine?" he suggested.

"Of course, Martin. Shall we go up to the house? I think I might need to take a rest after we've finished talking. This way. Come on, Dali."

Konstantinos's large and beautiful house stood on a ridge behind the workshop and commanded a view over the rolling uplands of the island's heart. The nearest slopes were a busy pattern of abandoned terracing. Several small white-painted homes nestled in the valley, surrounded by their few olive trees and small fields. Beyond, the larger hills rose in an escarpment. The idyllic landscape was in sharp contrast to their mood.

The main door opened into the living room. Konstantinos let himself down into an armchair, his movements heavy. The others took chairs near him except Xanthe, who went to the kitchen to find refreshments.

"So, the temperature setting on the kiln's controller was changed to 1300 degrees," began Day.

Konstantinos was again defensive. "That's the maximum setting on that kiln, quite unsuitable for the job. I would never make that mistake. Believe me, Martin, I did not leave it on that setting."

"Of course not, Konstantine." Peppino assured him. "But who would have had the know-how to change it on the controller? And when could they have done it?"

"I filled the kiln yesterday afternoon and set the temperature control on the timer. I had no need to go back in there until this morning."

"Is there any sign of a forced entry this time?"

"No, Martin."

"And Dali didn't bark in the night? He didn't hear the intruder?"

"No. Dali and I wouldn't hear anything in the house. It has thick walls and it's quite a way from the workshop. We were here from about six-thirty or seven o'clock last night."

"Right, so the kiln could have been sabotaged at any time between seven last night and this morning?"

" I suppose so. Fotis and Xanthe went home soon after five. Peppino, when did you leave yesterday?"

"Yesterday was Sunday ... I was home by four o'clock. You remember, we talked about the marble deliveries and then I went home for a siesta."

"So, between seven o'clock last night and the time people arrived this morning, nobody was in the workshop and that's when the kiln was tampered with."

"Yes," said Konstantinos. "The kiln computer might tell you when it happened, Martin, but I don't know how to find out."

"Don't worry. I don't think it would help us much anyway, I'm afraid. Nobody will have seen the intruder, this area is too remote. Could you tell me, though, how difficult it would be for someone to change the temperature setting?"

"It's an automatic electric kiln. You fill it, programme it, and once you're used to how it works, it's very easy. I set it to warm and then bisque fire at the rate and for the amount of time I want. I suppose it must be possible simply to over-ride this and enter new instructions. I wouldn't know."

The old man's head bowed, and Day resisted the temptation to reassure him again; Konstantinos was far too intelligent to want empty platitudes. One thing was clear, at least. The intruder had needed a basic knowledge of the kiln, and an outsider would not have known that Konstantinos was planning a firing for Sunday night. Whoever was responsible had to have had some inside knowledge.

At this point Xanthe came in with a jug of coffee and some cake. She had made an individual cup of Greek coffee especially for Konstantinos, and the traditional drink seemed to cheer him. When the room had settled and with everyone now present, Day addressed them all.

"Before we bring in the police, I'd like to understand where everyone was yesterday, and whether anyone noticed anything unusual."

"Do you think one of us did this?" asked Xanthe.

"Not at all, I just need an idea of where people were," Day said as reassuringly as he could.

"I'll start," said Peppino. "I was here from about half past ten until four o'clock, when I went home. It being Sunday, I didn't return in the evening. I saw nothing unusual while I was here. I was with Konstantinos until about noon, then he did his own potting and I did some design work. I sat on the terrace. Xanthe spent her lunch break with me there before some visitors arrived and she took care of the shop after that. As I was getting into my car to leave, I saw Markos Ioannakis's landrover pulling off the road, but I didn't speak to him."

"He had come to see me," said Xanthe, "He wanted to change a few items on a recent order. Some hotel customers had changed their requirements. Not a problem, and the order had grown larger. We chatted and Markos left after about twenty minutes. That was probably about half past four. It was otherwise a very normal day. We had several groups of visitors throughout the afternoon, which is usual for a Sunday, but they only went into the shop. I went home at five."

"Foti, did you see anything unusual yesterday?" asked Day gently; the young man had not said a word so far.

Fotis shook his head. "Nothing," he said, and to Day's surprise he continued. "I finished at about five, a few minutes after Xanthe."

"OK. I have one last question. The red paint that was used on the wall - could the intruder have found it in the workshop?"

"It's not from here, Martin," Konstantinos said. "You might think it could be red glaze, but glazes are strange colours before they're fired. That's paint on the wall, and it's not ours."

"Right. I think it's time you called the police. This is a lot more serious than before. There's actual damage and a very real threat. Inspector Cristopoulos is in charge of Naxos police, and I can tell you he's very approachable. I got to know him quite well earlier this year. Why don't you call him now?"

Konstantinos looked at Peppino and nodded, and at that moment Day's mobile rang. Coincidentally it was the police, but not Inspector Cristopoulos. Day took the call in the kitchen and mostly listened, asking the occasional question and finally asking for a meeting with the caller.

"That was Andreas Nomikos," he told them when he returned to the living room, "the police inspector in Athens who's investigating our friend Edward's death. He has the results of the autopsy on Edward. The cause of death wasn't suicide after all. It wasn't even an overdose. It was suffocation. According to the toxicology report, none of the medications Edward had with him for his heart condition were present in his body to any abnormal level, only what was consistent with his prescribed daily dose. I'm afraid Edward was murdered. His pillow was used …"

Day stopped. Konstantinos was white with shock and his mouth was slightly open. Xanthe, who looked nearly as pale, leaned across and put a hand on his arm. Konstantinos covered her hand with his own.

"Go on, Martin," he said, his voice tight.

"The forensic team are revisiting their findings, but the hotel room was covered in finger marks. It will take a long time to eliminate staff, for instance, and then some of the marks could be from former guests. There was no CCTV at the hotel or in the adjacent streets. It's a quiet area of Kolonaki, and the only CCTV is on rich people's houses, none of which are positioned where it might help the police. So Andreas is coming to Naxos soon, and he will want to speak to us all because he's tracing Edward's movements before his death. I'm sorry, Konstantine."

Konstantinos was still looking pale and Peppino urged him to go for a rest, promising that he would take care of phoning the local police. Konstantinos seemed drained. He took his leave politely and went to his bedroom. Xanthe began to clear the cups, and Fotis left the house to return to the workshop. Peppino looked thoughtful.

"Would you like to meet this evening to talk about all this, Martin? I think it's time we pooled our resources."

"Your English really is extremely good! Yes, of course, I had the same idea. When and where would suit you?"

"Shall we get away from round here?" suggested Peppino. "Maybe somewhere in Chora about 8? By then I'll have spoken to the police and can update you on that. Some bar with a bit of food, perhaps?"

They agreed to meet at Day's home from home, Diogenes Bar, at eight.

13

Day arrived at his favourite bar before Peppino. He particularly liked this place because you could sit as long as you wanted and watch people walking past. Tonight, however, the pavement was less busy than usual. The volta, or evening stroll, was over and local families had gone home for their evening meal. It was too dark to see the ancient Portara, the massive marble doorway on the little islet of Palatia not far from the bar. In the darkness around the Portara, the dark sea would be lapping on the rocks and the small fringe of sand, unseen by anyone.

Day walked past his favourite table by the pavement and chose one at the back of the bar where he and Peppino could talk privately. He shook hands with Alexandros, the waiter he had come to know, and ordered a gin and tonic. Alexandros, a cheerful man who came to Naxos to work during the summer, brought him the drink and a generous bowl of salty nibbles.

Peppino joined him and ordered a large Alfa beer. He moved his chair so that he could talk easily to Day and still watch the goings-on on the pavement. He lodged his feet on the rungs of another chair,

Greek-style. The cold beer seemed to revive his spirits, and he ate a great many of the nuts which Alexandros had put before him.

"Happy Hour? At eight o'clock?" Peppino said, reading the sign on the wall.

"I think at Diogenes it's probably Happy Hour all day in the summer season. How did you get on with the police?"

"Inspector Cristopoulos and one of his men came out to the atelier and spoke to everyone individually, but apart from recommending vigilance, the police can't do much."

"Mmm, I suppose not. I wish I thought this was the end of it, but I don't. What do you think?"

"I agree, Martin. The demand has been made and when we don't comply there could well be another incident."

"It's also worrying that the second break-in was much more serious than the first. It's escalating. Whatever happens next may be worse still."

Peppino Berducci took a drink from his glass thoughtfully. "So, who could be behind this? There was no sign of forced entry on either occasion. Whoever broke in last night must have known that a firing was planned, and how to sabotage a kiln. I don't believe it was a stroke of luck for the intruder."

"OK, in that case we have a very limited set of suspects. If we discount Xanthe, Fotis and the two of us, who else has that special inside knowledge, somebody we haven't yet thought of?"

Peppino sighed. "Unfortunately, we can't take Fotis and Xanthe off our list just yet, Martin. Impossible though it seems that either of them would hurt Konstantinos, they both have keys and inside knowledge.

There's Markos Ioannakis too. I saw him at the atelier yesterday. He stands to lose business through the Niarchos project because of the rule that we can't sell work through him."

"We add Markos, then. Anyone else? Do you know if Konstantinos has any family, anyone who might have keys but whom Konstantinos didn't think to mention? They might have known about his plans for the day …"

"Konstantinos hasn't mentioned any other family, and anyway a member of his family would be even less likely to want to harm him."

"Neighbours? Rivals?"

"I don't know any other marble artists on the island, not of Konstantinos's stature. I'm afraid I just don't understand it."

"Nor do I. Cristopoulos has a difficult job."

"Beyond Naxos, there might be people jealous of Konstantinos's success," said Peppino thoughtfully. "Disappointed rivals, that kind of person. But they wouldn't have the access, would they?"

"No. This feels close. People outside Greece wouldn't come all this way just to …" He let his words hang unfinished, and sipped his drink.

"Martin, just how dangerous do you think this situation is?"

"I thought there was a degree of malice in the first break-in, particularly when I saw the decapitated figurine. It made me concerned for Konstantinos, I thought it seemed a personal threat against him. From the writing on the wall, though, it now seems the target is the Niarchos project. Konstantinos could still be in danger. What do you think he'll do? I imagine he won't concede to the demand?"

"No chance. And I support him completely. I can provide some protection to Konstantinos. I'm a Sicilian, I was brought up in a place where young men know something about self-defence! The trouble is, Konstantinos is there alone at night. I'll try to persuade him to let me stay at the house till this is over."

Day nodded. "Good, although I don't know how we'll know if it's over. We probably have to wait and see what happens next."

They ordered two of the largest burgers on the menu and generous fries. The trouble with Diogenes, Day reflected, was that it was very easy to eat comfort food and drink too much. He felt considerably better after eating, though. Chips really were the answer.

As they ate, Peppino began to tell a story about a romance in his home town of Erice in Trapani. The province of Trapani, he told Day, produces some of Sicily's best wine and is close to a historic marble-producing area called Custonaci, so Peppino had chosen to live there as soon as he had the means to buy a place. He had also heard that the number of marriages for the size of the population was higher in Erice than anywhere else in Italy. Day nodded. He allowed himself to drift off to Peppino's tale, a romance as good as something taken from a history play. He too propped his feet on another chair and stared dreamily at the nearby nightlife of Chora.

"That's quite a story," he said when Peppino had finished. "Romeo and Juliet with a happy ending, and the Mafia thrown in for good measure. No, no, I believe you that it's all true! Some stories must have happy endings. I have a story to tell you, actually. This one didn't end all that well, but it's certainly true."

Peppino grinned and signalled to Alexandros for another drink. Day drew the line at this point, thinking of the drive back to Filoti and the steep bends in the road. He already felt very relaxed. Thanks to the effect of the drink, he believed that the moment had come to share Edward's story of Artemis with somebody, namely this warm-hearted, romantic Sicilian.

***

"Our friend Edward, the retired history professor from England, was the hero of this story when he was a student. He went off alone round Greece to visit classical sites, and one of his first visits was to Ancient Brauron - it's about thirty kilometres east of Athens, and is the home of a temple dedicated to the goddess Artemis.

"While he was there he met a beautiful young Greek girl whose name also happened to be Artemis. She was an artist, and Edward fell deeply in love with her. They began a relationship, and together they continued Edward's planned tour of the archaeological sites of Greece. One morning when he woke he found she was gone. She had left behind her a drawing of Edward asleep. No explanation. He never managed to find her, and went back to England, became a professor at Cambridge, and never married.

"Then one day, very recently, he received a letter. It was from a lady called Angelika who had found some diaries belonging to her late grandmother, whose name was Artemis, in which she found the story of her grandmother's romantic summer with Edward. She wrote to him at his former Cambridge college and asked if he would like to meet her. Edward arranged the meeting, full of joy and excitement. At last he would hear more about his lost love."

"My God, Martin, what a romantic story. What happened?"

"The meeting took place, a few days after Edward left Naxos. They met in Athens the day before he was murdered."

Peppino could find nothing to say. He just stared at Day.

"You told the police?" The assumption of Day's confirmation was clear in Peppino's tone.

"No, I didn't. You're the only person I've told. I'm going to find Angelika myself."

"What if there's a connection with his murder? You should tell the police, Martin. Really."

"When I find her I can make that judgement."

"I still think you should tell the police, but if you're not going to, it's important you find this woman immediately. Do you know if Edward told other people about Artemis and Angelika? Colleagues, friends?"

"I'm sure he didn't. He only told me when he'd had quite a lot to drink. I felt entrusted with a secret."

"Well, I hope you're doing the right thing, Martin, in keeping this to yourself."

14

The next morning, Day decided to get out of the house early and take his laptop to Cafe Ta Xromata to work there. The owner, a widowed lady with an adult daughter, had become very friendly and welcoming recently, realising that Day was fast becoming one of her regulars. Little slices of homemade cake would sometimes appear next to Day's frappé, which was awkward because he disliked all forms of sweet food. If only Helen were here, he thought when this happened again; she could be relied on to help him out with cake.

The solution occurred to him. He wrapped the slice in a paper serviette and explained he would enjoy it later, as he had only recently finished breakfast. The cafe owner beamed. Day felt even worse, as he rarely ate breakfast and certainly had not done so that morning.

He worked on his laptop for over an hour, completing a chapter of his biography of Nikos Elias. His mobile rang as the clock tower of the village's historic orthodox church sounded the hour. It was Dr Cameron Maxwell from Cambridge. It must be exactly nine o'clock in England, as it was eleven o'clock in Greece, so Dr Maxwell was calling as soon as he reached his office.

"Hello, Mr Day, this is Cameron Maxwell. We spoke before, about Edward Childe. I thought I should update you. Do you have a little time now?"

"Certainly, thank you very much. Is there some news?"

"The will was read yesterday, and I was present as Edward's executor. I learned what is to happen to Edward's body, which I know you were concerned about. The Greek police informed the British Embassy of Edward's death, and they arranged for him to be cremated in Greece and the ashes returned to Cambridge. It was Edward's wish to be cremated. The ashes will be sent to me, and I will organise a commemorative event. The University have agreed to a small memorial on university grounds. My wife and I are arranging for a private ceremony and reception at the College, to which friends and colleagues are most welcome, yourself included if you should be able to come over."

"That's all a great relief to me. I only came to know Edward recently, but I feel we became friends."

"That's the kind of man he was. Now, there's something else I should tell you. You asked me about Edward's collection of early travel writing, and whether it was safely under lock and key. I answered that the university was taking care of it, which was true, as far as the letters and so on are concerned. However, I didn't realise that Edward's collection also included some paintings, in particular a valuable one by Edward Lear. I'd seen it, of course, in his house, but I didn't make the connection when we spoke before. Edward strongly believed that works of art should be looked at and enjoyed, so all his paintings are hung round his house. I've arranged with the solicitors, as Edward's executor, to pay for extra security at the house with money from the estate. I can reassure you that this is now done. After probate the collection will be given to the beneficiaries whom Edward stipulated. The Fitzwilliam Museum is to receive some items, and the rest will go to King's College. I believe that the Lear watercolour of the Athenian Acropolis is to hang in the Senior Common Room."

"I see. Would you be able to let me see a complete list of Edward's art collection?" Day's curiosity was aroused now; he would soon see the list of travel writing, but he wanted to know about the art too.

"I don't have such a list personally, but both the solicitor and the art curator at King's have a copy. I'm not sure whether they will be happy to share it."

"I'd be very interested to see it, if that would be possible, Dr Maxwell. If the future owners of the works were to agree, I might possibly like to do some work on Edward and his collection … a tribute to Edward and a fulfilment of his wishes …"

"I understand. I'll see if I can get permission to send you a copy."

"Thank you. If it's a lot of trouble I can apply to the solicitor myself."

"I'm sure it will be quicker if I ask them, as executor. So, I'll keep you informed of the arrangements for the memorial gathering and send you the list of art works if possible. Do you have any news for me? Have the police come up with anything new?"

Day sighed. There was no good way to say what he had to say.

"I heard from the police only yesterday. I'm afraid Edward was murdered. It wasn't suicide."

"Oh dear. I didn't see how it could have been suicide, of course, but for a friend to have been murdered … How dreadful. Appalling. Do the police have any idea …?"

"Nothing yet. They'll be coming here soon to question anybody whom Edward met in the week before his death. I'll let you know you if there's significant news."

"Right. Thank you. Goodbye for the time being, then."

***

Day stood at the port of Naxos waiting to meet the Blue Star Delos, the ferry on which Helen was arriving from the mainland. The little port area was even more busy than it had been when he had travelled to Athens. August had certainly been an excellent month for tourism.

With a cloud of offensive black smoke, the ferry reversed into its dock, lowered its vehicle ramp and released its passengers. Cars and vans drove down the centre of the ramp, and passengers dragging luggage struggled down the sides. Vehicles and pedestrians intermingled alarmingly, horns were hooted, police whistles blown, but no sign of ill-temper appeared anywhere.

Day looked for Helen among the foot-passengers. Ah, there she was, her fair hair visible slightly above the heads of the people around her, trousers and shirt creased from the journey. She held a small wheeled suitcase firmly behind her, and a larger one was virtually pulling her down the ramp. Descent from a ferry around here required skill. Helen cleared the ramp, escaped the crowds and looked round for Day. He was not hard to pick out.

"Oh my God, how do this many people find anywhere to stay on the island?" she gasped and gave him a hug.

"Good trip?"

"Yes, not bad at all, thank you. All I crave is a shower and I'll be human again. You OK?"

"I'm fine. Shall we go straight home?"

"Perfect. Let's get away from here and make a dash for Filoti."

Helen was relieved to be back. As soon as they left Chora and began the drive into the hills of central Naxos, she visibly relaxed.

Day unlocked the front door, waved Helen inside, and returned to the car for her luggage. Helen walked into the front room, sparsely furnished but welcoming with its familiar smell of old wood and slightly creaking floorboards. She continued into the larger room at the back of the house, opened the shutters to the balcony, and pushed them wide. The view, the sunshine, the fresh smell of grass and wild herbs, filled her with joy. Day dumped her bags in the middle of the room and grinned.

"It's really good to be back, Martin. Can I have my old room?"

"It's yours," he said, recalling how strange he had felt showing Edward into the bedroom that seemed to belong to Helen. "Want a cup of tea, or the shower first?"

"The shower, please. But you can put the kettle on, I won't be long."

Day never drank tea unless it was with Helen, but the colour seemed right when he added the water. She soon returned in a cool blue dress and sandals, damp hair and sunglasses, looking younger than her forty-three years. She took her favourite old chair on the balcony. The sun was now falling directly where they sat, fingering its way through the old cane awning above the table. Helen sat in full sun to dry her hair, while Day brought the tea to the table.

"Oh, thank goodness!" Helen said, ruffling her wet hair. "I feel as if I've just escaped a world of madness! The peacefulness here is superb!"

"Did Hampstead not suit you?"

"It has been a funny sort of summer in the UK," she said. "I missed the slow pace here and the heat of the sun." Nevertheless she moved into the shade, away from the burning rays of midday.

They spoke of London, mutual friends in England, and the funeral of Helen's godfather. Helen asked after Naxos friends such as Aristos and Rania, and how Day was getting on with his biography of Nikos Elias. Day gave her a report that covered most things except Deppi's name day celebration, which he kept for another time. He also held back telling her the Artemis story. He would do so soon. He felt there should be a better moment than this.

"Maurice asked me to tell you," said Helen, "that he would appreciate the first draft of the Elias book, or as much as you can send him, by the end of September. He knows that's a lot to ask, and a synopsis of the final chapters would do at a push. He has a publisher interested."

"Good for Maurice, although this is probably just a tactic to make me work harder. Thanks for going to see him. I take it you were able to bring Edward's papers? Was there very much?"

"I've put everything on the dining table for you to go through at your leisure. There's quite a bit, and a letter from Jonathan Wells which Maurice included. I had a good talk with Maurice. He's a clever man, isn't he? He asked me to say to you that once Edward's will has passed probate we'll know whose permission needs to be sought if you wanted to fulfil Edward's plans for the material, and, if you want him to, Maurice will follow this up with the solicitors. It looks like King's College Cambridge will own the material, he thinks."

"Yes, I gathered as much from speaking to an old friend of Edward's who is the executor of the will. I was only talking to him this morning. Cameron Maxwell, his name is, and he's a Professor of History at King's. He told me that the travel writing element of Edward's collection, the original documents, which must be priceless in historical terms, are already in the university's safe-keeping. Edward arranged that some years ago. However, his art collection is apparently hanging in his house, and when Dr Maxwell realised this he had the house secured, pending probate and the paintings being given to their proper recipients. Some will go to the Fitzwilliam, most to King's."

Helen turned her gaze to the valley, unconsciously seeking the mule which she had got used to seeing grazing in the shade of a solitary tree.

"So, are you really interested in taking on this project, Martin? Presumably after completing the Elias biography you could move on to it?"

"I don't know, to be honest. It would be very hard without Edward. I'm certainly interested in the collection, it sounds fascinating, and possibly contains extremely rare material. Edward said he had original letters from the wife of Theodore Bent. Do you know about him?"

"No, who was he?"

"He was a young Englishman from Yorkshire who lived at the same time as the giants of archaeology, like Arthur Evans and Heinrich Schliemann. Bent was completely self-taught as an archaeologist, very young and inexperienced. Undeterred, Bent committed his short life to travel and archaeology, and his equally young wife Mabel went with him. Among other places, they travelled through the Cyclades, writing about what they saw, not only about the ancient remains they found but also the lives of the local people. I'll lend you the book, it makes good reading. It's called something like *Life among the insular Greeks*, I have a copy here in the house." Day gestured with a loose sweep of one arm towards his huge bookcase. "The Bents were travelling in Greece at the end of the nineteenth century. Theodore was an Oxford graduate with no experience of practical archaeology, but when he had an opportunity to excavate the remains on the islet of Antiparos, off Paros, it made his reputation. He died tragically young, in his mid-forties, but not before travelling a lot further afield than Greece.

"Theodore's writings are hugely respected, but his wife also wrote travel notebooks, which are in library collections in London. Edward told me that he had some letters she wrote to a friend describing their time on Naxos. Although she wrote about her experiences in her notebooks, I'd love to see her personal accounts in the letters. They might shed light on her marriage too."

"I'd like to read that. But you don't sound certain about working on the project. What's against it?"

"Nothing, I suppose. You're right, though, I'm undecided. I wanted to find out about Edward's collection because it might have been connected to his death. It must be valuable, and love and greed, they say, are the most common motives for murder. I was wrong, though. Killing Edward was never going to obtain the collection for the murderer."

Helen regarded Day steadily. "I see you're more deeply involved than I thought. What do the police say?"

"There's been no news since the coroner's report. Inspector Nomikos is coming out in a few days. It sounds as if they've drawn a blank in Athens. I call him 'Andrea' now, by the way."

"Mmm, I'm not sure it's a good sign being on first name terms with the police, Martin."

"I like Andreas Nomikos. Anyway, gin and tonic? It must be an appropriate hour."

"Of course it is!"

***

They ate a relaxed dinner of salad, cheese, ham and prawns, washed down with a very light red wine, all purchased locally by an unusually well-organised Day. The evening was warm enough to be outside, but the insects were biting so they ate at the large wooden table in the main room which served as kitchen, dining room, living room and library.

Then Day decided to tell Helen about Edward's youthful romance with Artemis and recent meeting with Angelika. As he expected, Helen was moved by the story but alarmed that he had kept it from the police. Day assured her that he intended to tell Andreas Nomikos when the inspector came to Naxos.

"By then I hope to have found Angelika and told her in person what happened to Edward. If I don't succeed in that, Nomikos or one of his men will find her and tell her while questioning her like a suspect."

"Has it occurred to you that she might actually be a suspect?"

"Rubbish. Who would go to such elaborate lengths to find an old man only to kill him? Why?"

"I don't know why, Martin, but that could have been why she sought him out in the first place."

Day chose to ignore her.

"Well, I haven't had any luck finding her so far, and I don't know what else to try. I also searched for Artemis the artist, but the gallery where she sold her work in Athens has been taken over by a new owner, one who couldn't help me at all. At Brauron, where she donated a couple of paintings, there are no leads either."

Helen nodded, apparently thinking of something else.

"Poor Edward," she said quietly.

"Yes. But you know, he wasn't sad when he told me his story. He said he'd had a good life and never blamed Artemis for leaving him, only himself for not telling her how he felt. I believed him, at the time."

"He was clearly a very emotionally intelligent man. All the same, it's a sad end."

"He met Angelika, at least we can be sure of that. He wrote about it in his letter from Athens. Anyway, I'm not finished yet. When I find Angelika I'll tell her that she meant a great deal to Edward."

"I'd like to go to Brauron, Martin," mused Helen. "We could see Artemis's paintings and also the museum and temple. When Inspector Nomikos has gone back to Athens, why don't we make the trip?"

"Fine, as soon as everything's sorted. A friend of mine is having problems at the moment, there have been a couple of break-ins at his place, and I have to stay here until that's resolved. I'll tell you all about it tomorrow. You look like you've had enough for today."

"I was up at five this morning. You're right, I'll probably go to bed soon. Thanks, Martin, it's wonderful to be back!"

"Thank you, for coming back."

15

Helen was already at work on her laptop when Day emerged from his room the following morning. Early rising did not suit him, and he had indulged himself in not setting an alarm. He drank a large glass of cold water from the bottle in the fridge, refilled his glass, and poured one for Helen. He made coffee and took everything to the balcony table, where Helen joined him.

"Good morning, Martin. Are you sufficiently awake for communication?"

"Am I that bad?" he grinned. "Did you sleep well?"

"Wonderfully. I was woken by the sound of a mule. I don't remember hearing one so close before. I immediately knew I was back here."

"Are you working well? Want to keep going? I thought I'd have a look through Edward's papers after my shower."

"Yes, I'd like to get on with work today. What do you want to do for food tonight?"

"We could go to Thanasis's, or to Chora?"

"Let's go to Thanasis's."

"He'll be pleased. His 'Belle Helene' is back! He's been asking after you."

"Belle Helene indeed! Silly man!"

They finished their coffee and Day went for his shower, switching on the iron as he passed it. He suddenly had a good feeling, as if the morning would bring a break-through, either in his work or in the mystery of Artemis of Brauron. Perhaps today he would find Angelika, or hear news from Nomikos, or find something important in Edward's papers. He ironed a blue shirt, chose his lightest trousers because of the heat - Day abhorred shorts - and took his laptop to the balcony, where he checked his emails.

There was a message from Jonathan Wells saying that he had sent the documents to Maurice and had checked with other members of his firm, but nobody else had known about Edward's project. Day typed a quick reply to him and checked for other messages.

Andreas Nomikos's email told Day when he would be arriving on Naxos, and that Inspector Cristopoulos would be fixing a schedule of interviews for him, although in the case of Day himself they would make an informal arrangement. He asked Day to give Cristopoulos the details of everyone who had been in contact with Edward Childe during his visit, including contact information. Day did so at once; he had already kept too much from the police.

It was time to examine the folders from London. He took them to his room, where he opened the window and carried the small table onto his bedroom balcony. The air outside was already warm, and the view of his neighbour's small-holding was peaceful. The only things moving were a group of small brown birds in the pomegranate trees.

He sorted through the papers. There were letters from people all over Greece responding to Edward's enquiries about involvement in his series. Day found replies from various marble sculptors, from the marble museum on Tinos, from the ephors, or curators, of ancient sites, and from a number of people who appeared to be the owners of private collections. Edward clearly had a deep knowledge of his field. Without exception the replies were positive, usually enthusiastic.

In addition to the letters, Day found a pile of papers which turned out to be Edward's detailed plan for the series, episode by episode, location by location. There was a post-it note on it from Jonathan, which explained that he believed this to be Edward's latest proposal for the project. Ten episodes were outlined, and although there was no suggestion where the money was to have come from, fundraising was the *raison d'être* of people such as Maurice and Jonathan, and Day had no doubt it would have been forthcoming.

Finally Day turned to the document in which he was most interested. It summarised the collection of travel writing from the nineteenth century which Edward had intended to use as the structural basis of the series. No reference was made to the paintings and drawings. The list of written material, however, contained some astonishing names. Without doubt this small private collection was of huge value. In addition to the letters from Mabel Bent, Day saw several famous names, from Edward Dodwell in 1802 to E. M. Forster in 1901. This was the collection of a lifetime, accrued through luck, skill and expertise.

Day asked himself what, if anything, this list told him that might have a bearing on Edward's death. The collection of writing was of great value, but killing Edward in Athens would not have led to the murderer acquiring it. It was a dead end as far as understanding the murder was concerned. Nomikos could follow his own lines of enquiry, but Day was sure they would both reach the same conclusion: Edward had not been killed for his collection.

He went to find Helen, who was taking a break from work to prepare something to eat. They took their usual light lunch to the balcony table; it consisted of cheese, rocket, olives and grilled flatbread moistened with thick local olive oil. It was another hot August day, and they drank most of a bottle of cold mineral water.

"We'll need to visit the supermarket in Chora soon," observed Day. "I've run out of lemons."

"That will never do. What will you put in your gin and tonic? Let's go later this afternoon, when it's a bit cooler."

Although lemons were absolutely essential for Day's signature gin and tonic, which he had turned into an art form, Helen had noticed that the stock of food in Day's kitchen was very low. Day was less than enthusiastic about most fruit, and only knew vegetables when they were brought to him in a restaurant.

"Has work gone well today on the magnum opus?" Day felt pleased with himself for remembering to ask.

"Quite well, thanks. Did you read through the papers I brought from Maurice?"

"Yes. Edward had some astonishing things. Many are written by relatively unknown members of well-to-do families, but there are some really big names too, even my personal idol, E. M. Forster. There's something by Edward Dodwell, the writer and artist, and a memoire by George Cochrane, who published a book about Greece in the 1830s. I don't think it matters that some of the names would be unknown to the television audience; Edward would have made it interesting, and used the material cleverly to introduce each marble location."

"Still not tempted to do the project without Edward?"

"I'm not really thinking about it. I just needed to know that the collection can't have any bearing on his death."

"When is Inspector Nomikos arriving?"

"Thursday. He's asking our friend Cristopoulos to make arrangements for him to interview the suspects. He's going to see me separately. I want to talk to Andreas anyway. I need to tell him about Angelika."

"About time! He needs to find her."

Day's mobile emitted a ringtone that jarred in the quietness of the balcony. It was a call from Peppino, which Day took in his room.

"Martin? Look, I've just spent an hour with Konstantinos, who seemed to want to talk. No, he's reasonably well, just unsettled. There is something else worrying him, I think, but I don't know what it is. I sense that he's not telling me something. I'm wondering if he's considering giving in to the demand to call off the Niarchos project, although it's my understanding that he's now contractually obliged to fulfil the whole three-year agreement. Anyway, I've talked to him about how I see it, and put the point that one lunatic shouldn't be allowed to ruin an outstanding artistic enterprise. I told him I'd be happy to move into the house rather than stay in my rented place in Kato Potamia. He turned me down, but I'll try to change his mind…"

"I think you're right that he shouldn't submit to the threats, but Konstantinos isn't a young man any more…"

"No. Actually, that's not my main reason for calling you, Martin. Once we finish this call I'm going to send you a picture I took on my phone. I took it in Konstantino's study, where we were talking. There are bookcases, a desk and an amazing oil painting. That's what I'm going to send you. I took a photo of it when Konstantinos went out of the room. It's a portrait of a woman."

Day saw no significance yet, and said nothing. Peppino continued.

"The portrait is signed 'Artemis'. There's no date. But there is a small title. The picture is of a woman called Angelika."

The adrenalin that shot across his chest actually made Day squirm in his chair. His mind raced, but in circles.

"Martin, I don't think this can be a coincidence," Peppino continued. "I think that Edward's Artemis and her granddaughter Angelika are the same women as Konstantinos's late wife and *his* granddaughter Angelika."

"My God!" Day could say nothing else. Konstantinos had never mentioned the name of his late wife or mentioned a granddaughter. Presumably, Edward had never seen the portrait in the study, nor heard the names of either woman. That in itself raised questions in Day's mind.

"Are you still there?" asked Peppino.

"Sorry, yes I'm here. I just can't get over the chances against this. It can't be a coincidence, can it? *Can* it? What else could it be? Sorry, I need some time to work this out. Did Konstantinos say anything about the picture?"

"I did try to get him to drop some clues by admiring the picture. He was very reticent, but he said it was a picture of his granddaughter.

We agreed she's beautiful. I asked whether he sees much of her, and apparently she lives here on Naxos."

"My God!" said Day again, this time more loudly.

"I'm not surprised you're finding this hard to take in. I was the same. I'm sure Konstantinos doesn't suspect I know anything about his granddaughter. He sounded very proud of her and quite protective, but didn't say anything more. I feel awkward about telling you what he told me during a private conversation, but it might have a bearing on Edward's death, no?"

"That's what I need to work out."

"I had a call from Inspector Cristopoulos an hour ago, saying that his colleague, the policeman from Athens, will want to speak to me. Look Martin, should I say anything about this to the police? It might be relevant to their investigation into who killed Edward…"

"Yes, of course, tell them everything. I will too. If you're interviewed before me, you can tell him I'll explain. Andreas Nomikos is a good man but I realise he can't work without the facts."

"I thought you wanted to protect Angelika?"

"I do. I'm going to have to find her very quickly."

***

Peppino's photo of the portrait of Angelika arrived on his phone some minutes after they ended the call. The woman in the picture was mesmerisingly lovely, but it was the effect of the painter's lavish brush strokes that gripped Day's attention first. It was easy to see that he paint was put on thickly, lovingly and with generosity. The background was given depth by layers of marks in all shades of yellow and ochre, in front of which were the head and shoulders of a Greek woman with large, almond-shaped eyes, full lips and a perfect Greek nose. Her hair, its roots carrying a suggestion of Grecian black, was fair and wavy, falling around her shoulders with the same generosity that the painter had given to the background. The woman, Angelika, looked directly out from the picture and held the viewer's gaze.

It was now an easy matter to find Angelika, knowing she lived on Naxos, but Day hesitated. He believed that Angelika Spetzou should hear from a friend about the death of Edward, the old man she had found from her grandmother's diary, the old man she had clearly bonded with, who was a living link with her grandmother. It would be a shock to discover that he had been murdered only a day after they had met. If he did nothing, Angelika would find out from the police. Nomikos would certainly find her and question her about it. Yet he felt he was betraying Konstantinos by speaking to his granddaughter behind his back.

Konstantinos and Edward: how strange their friendship had been. Edward must only have learned from Angelika that his youthful lover, Artemis, had become the wife of his friend, Konstantinos. What an enormous shock that must have been. And Konstantinos had met his academic English friend years after his wife's death and not been aware of the connection she made between them. Two elderly men who had loved the same woman but had never realised had become friends.

Day found Angelika's address on Naxos within minutes. His head had started to ache, and he decided to take his siesta, even though he did not expect to sleep. He would contact her, but first he had some thinking to do.

16

Day drove out of Filoti with excitement and anticipation in the pit of his stomach. He followed the familiar road from the villages towards Chora, going due west initially along the Naxos-Halki road, past Konstantinos's atelier, and onwards to the quiet bay where he regularly went to do his research at the Nikos Elias house. A lovely taverna stood at the opposite end of the bay from the Elias house. The locals called the bay Paralia Votsala, meaning beach of shingle or pebbles, and the taverna was called Taverna Ta Votsala, Pebbles Taverna. The owners, with whom Day and Helen had become friends, placed tables on the beach where their guests could sit within a metre of the water.

Day was on his way to meet Angelika Spetzou at Taverna Ta Votsala. He had called her the previous evening and introduced himself, explaining his friendship with Edward. When she had overcome her surprise, Angelika had confirmed that she was the person Day sought. Day was elated. He had found her, the Edward's Angelika, the granddaughter of Artemis. It had then been necessary to tell her the reason for his call. Having given it some thought, Day had told her gently that Edward had died, but not that he had been murdered.

As he had feared, this was upsetting enough. Angelika had thanked him for telling her in person, and then to his delight had diffidently asked if Day would agree to meet her, to tell her more about Edward.

Day was on his way to that meeting now. He had suggested Taverna Ta Votsala as the meeting place because it was quiet and only a short drive from Chora, where Angelika lived. The peaceful taverna with its position right against the sea appealed to Day's sense of the special importance of this meeting. It also suited Angelika, who could only leave the house for a couple of hours at most, for the sake of her mother. There was a friend who would stay with her mother for a while, but it was better if Angelika was not gone for too long.

He was greeted outside Taverna Ta Votsala by the owner, Vasilios Papathoma, who gave him a full man hug, something which had never happened before. Day felt guilty for not having called into the taverna sooner, despite frequently working at the Elias house at the other end of the road, where his car would have been visible.

Vasilios stretched out his arm to indicate that Day's guest was already seated at one of the tables near the water. She sat facing the sea, her fair hair falling over the back of her shirt, which was the light blue-green colour of shallow water.

Angelika heard Day's footsteps as he walked over the shingle, and stood up to greet him. Day realised he was smiling broadly, with a mixture of pleasure, relief and smugness. He gave an embarrassed laugh and shook her hand, thanked her for coming, and suggested coffee. They gave their order to Vasilios, both grateful of the chance to take stock of each other. before starting to talk.

Without seeming to do so, and while talking to Vasilios, Day admired Angelika's face. It was the face from the portrait which Peppino had sent him. Despite the untidy golden hair which seemed to have a life of its own, this woman had strong Greek features, in particular a splendid straight nose and astute dark eyes. It was the face of someone with a shrewd intelligence who knew her own mind, but who would do everything possible to give you the benefit of the doubt. That is how Day saw her. Even as he assessed his companion, he knew that those same intelligent eyes were assessing him in return.

"You look like your voice, Martin," she said. "I imagined what you looked like very closely."

Day liked her directness and smiled. Edward must have found that rather endearing too.

"I'm very happy to meet you, Angelika. Even though I needed to give you bad news, I really wanted to find you after what Edward told me."

"I'm happy too. It's good to be able to talk with you about Edward."

Their coffee arrived, and with it another short opportunity to assess each other.

"Have you always lived on Naxos, Angelika?"

"Yes. I was born in the house in Chora where I live now with my mother. It was my grandparents's house first, but when my mother married they left the house to her and found a new house for themselves. It's an old Greek custom."

"And your father?"

"He went many years ago. I look after my mother, who needs constant care. Thankfully my grandfather can support us financially. Please, tell me about Edward. First, what happened to him?"

Her big dark eyes were fixed on Day with a strength and determination which surprised him. He realised that he could tell this woman the truth, and she would not thank him for prevarication. She already knew much of the story, but now he must let her know that Edward's death had been neither natural nor accidental.

"Edward came to stay with me in my house in Filoti for a few days, because we had plans to work together. On Thursday of that week Edward took the ferry to Athens, and was looking forward to meeting you the next day. We arranged to meet at his hotel before he went back to England. It was the hotel manager who told me that Edward had died. He died on the Saturday night, the day after you met him. I think I told you most of this on the telephone. However, there is something I decided not to tell you, perhaps through cowardice. There were empty pill bottles by the side of Edward's bed, and it was assumed that he had taken his own life."

"Edward, kill himself? I don't believe it. I would have felt his sadness, or some kind of desperation."

"I'm sure you would. I didn't believe it either. I went to the police and told them as much as I could about Edward, and how much he was looking forward to the future. They have ifound out that Edward did not die from an overdose of pills, but that he was deliberately suffocated with the pillow. I'm sorry, Angelika, it's horrible to hear…"

She said nothing at first, but her eyes had become even larger.

"No, Martin, you're right to tell me the truth. Seriously, the police believe somebody did that to Edward?"

"Yes. The police inspector from Athens is coming to Naxos to speak to everyone who knew Edward. That's why I wanted to find you myself first, and tell you in person."

"Thank you. That's very kind."

Day felt guilty. What he had said was true, but it glossed over his curiosity to find Angelika and follow the trail to Edward's lost love, her late grandmother Artemis. There was no time now to examine his motivation.

"I'm afraid I wasn't completely honest with the police in Athens, Angelika. I didn't tell them about you, that you had met Edward the day before he died. I thought, well, I felt that Edward had confided in me, entrusted me with something very important to him… I wanted to be the one to tell you."

Angelika gave the first truly large smile he had yet seen. He sensed she was tempted to rebuke him for his sentimentality. He saw no sign of relief, no indication of guilt, just an innocent pleasure in another person's kindness.

"I see why Edward liked you," she said, and finished the last of her coffee.

"I'm not sure what I can tell you about Edward that he didn't tell you himself. Is there anything you want to ask me?"

"I think you will tell me what else I need to know as we get to know each other better. You already know my grandfather, you told me on the phone, and I hope you will come to my house for dinner and meet my mother. You live on Naxos, we shall be friends and neighbours."

"I'd like that. Would you tell me the story of how you found Edward?"

"Of course. I read about Edward when I looked through a box that had belonged to my grandmother. It contained personal things. I hadn't wanted to open the box when she died. I'd forgotten about it, actually, but then I found it again. I no longer felt upset by her passing by then, and I was curious to know more about her. She was quite well known as a painter, did you know that? My mother and I both love to paint, but my grandmother's work was special.

"In the box I found two old diaries, and I read everything. One diary contained the story of her first love, when my grandmother was twenty, and the man she loved was an English student called Edward Childe. They met at the ancient site of Brauron in a very hot August, like this one. My grandmother wrote that she and Edward spent several weeks going round ancient sites together. There were sketches of this handsome young man in her diary. I think she had fallen very much in love."

Day smiled. "Did the diary tell how the relationship ended? Edward told me that he never knew why Artemis left him, although he didn't blame her at all."

"Edward asked me the same question, of course. No, the last entry is a happy one, and the rest of the pages are empty."

"How did you find Edward?" asked Day. "Was there an address?"

"No, I don't think grandmother knew where he was. The diary mentioned Edward's university, and I found an old reference online that told me that he had taught there before he retired. I sent a letter to the college, asking them to forward my letter to Edward if they could, and they did.

"I felt a bit unsure about writing to him, so I didn't give my address. I used a post office box near my fiancé Loukas's apartment in the Pangrati district of Athens. Loukas brought me Edward's reply when he came over - he often spends the weekend on Naxos with us. Edward wrote that he planned to visit Greece this month to see a friend, which presumably was you, Martin. He asked if I would like to meet, and suggested a date and time, and the name of a nice café in Thissio. I wrote back and said I would be there. I never gave my address or phone number to him, I didn't know then how trustworthy he was."

"He was overjoyed that you'd found him, and doubly overjoyed that he'd be able to meet you. I believe I was the only person he told that he was meeting you, and I think he'd never spoken of your grandmother to anyone before he shared it with me. I felt honoured; I still do."

"I arranged for my mother to be cared for in a retirement care home on the island for a few days," Angelika continued. "I feel bad about this, because my grandfather paid for it so that I could spend a few days in Athens with Loukas. I still haven't told him about my meeting with Edward. I haven't even told him that I read my grandmother's diary. Do you understand, Martin?"

"Yes, I see that it's difficult. But you did visit your fiancé, and I don't think you should feel guilty. Was your mother all right in the home?"

"Oh yes, I think so. It was a holiday for her too, and I was only away for two nights, I returned early the day after I saw Edward. Martin, can I ask you please not to speak of this to my grandfather?"

"I promise. We'll talk about it later. Go on …"

"I stayed with Loukas on the Thursday night and met Edward the next day. Loukas went to work, and I was pleased because I wanted to see Edward alone. Loukas knows all about it, he thinks I'm being sentimental, but he's promised not to tell my mother or grandfather.

"Edward didn't know what had happened to my grandmother after they parted from each other, until he heard from me," Angelika continued. "He had tried to find her but not succeeded. He was keen to hear everything about the family. I was happy to talk to him about my grandmother, and I could see the pleasure he felt when I talked of her. When I talked about my grandfather, Konstantinos, and the life he had led as a marble sculptor, Edward became very quiet, as if he was trying to decide what to say to me, and I could see it was important. Then he told me that he was actually a friend of my grandfather, and about how they had met, and his recent visit to the marble atelier with you. It was like a dream. Edward called my grandmother Artemis, and my grandfather always called her Temi, which is one way we shorten the name in Greece. I sometimes felt we were talking of two different people. Edward talked of my grandfather with great fondness, with love almost. He clearly liked and admired him deeply."

Day nodded abstractedly. He focussed on the quiet edge of the sea, which brushed the shingle with a delicate touch not far from their feet. When Peppino had told him about the portrait of Angelika in Konstantinos's house, he had struggled to understand this strange connection between the two old men; he could barely imagine Edward's shock on learning it from Angelika.

Angelika had fallen silent, and Day allowed himself some private reflections of his own. In his letter, Edward had not mentioned the connection with Konstantinos. Day wondered why, but had to shelve that question for the time being. Possibly Edward had wanted some time to think, unaware, sadly, that there would not be another opportunity to explain it to Day.

People are so fond of keeping secrets, Day reflected. Himself included.

Angelika reached for her coffee cup, realised it was empty, and left it on the table. She folded her hands across her waist as if she felt cold, despite the warm morning.

"Martin, there's something I'd like to ask you. Perhaps Edward said something to you which might help me. It's quite personal."

"Really, everything you say to me will remain just between us. I can keep a secret, as you already know."

"Thank you. It's not really important - well, yes it is - but it's only important to me. I've been thinking that Edward might have been my mother's real father. He might have been my grandfather by blood, don't you think?" Day was alarmed to see the hint of tears in Angelika's eyes. "Did my grandmother find out she was pregnant, and that's why she left Edward? It's a possibility, I think."

Day was astonished. He tried to remember what Edward had said about when he and Artemis had become lovers. His mind refused to produce any details.

"Don't you know the date of your grandparents' marriage and your mother's birth?"

"Of course. But if there was a pregnancy before marriage, it would have been arranged that dates on documents were suitably adjusted, or the documents hidden or lost. I have seen no certificates. Whatever the truth, my grandmother must have met Konstantinos immediately after her summer with Edward, and married him almost at once."

Day smiled at her as reassuringly as he could, trying to think. Artemis and Edward had seemed very much in love; Edward certainly had been, and her diary suggested that Artemis had felt the same. Could she have left him because she knew she was pregnant, perhaps for Edward's sake? Could she have fallen into the kind arms of Konstantinos, who had married her to save her from the shame of being an unmarried mother in 1960s Greece?

"I don't think, in that case, that it will be possible to find out the answer to your question," Day replied. "The only person who knows the truth is Konstantinos. Unless you think your mother ...?"

"No, my mother's memory has been affected by her illness. Anyway, my family have always been very unwilling to discuss matters involving sex, and never talk about the past. It has never mattered to me before, but now that I've met Edward, I would like to know the truth, Martin. Konstantinos he has been there for me all my life, and for that reason he will always be the man I think of as my grandfather. I think I have to accept that I'll never know the truth."

"I'm sure you've thought of this, Angelika, but does your mother look anything like Edward? Forgive me, but you have the look of a lady who is a hundred per cent Greek."

Angelika gave a genuine laugh.

"So does my mother, Martin, that's true. I had just hoped somehow to be certain."

Day pondered on the secrets in the Saris family that had been closely guarded to protect the ones they loved. This made him think of more recent problems in that same family. He wondered how much Konstantinos had told his granddaughter of the break-ins.

"Has your grandfather told you about the recent incidents at the workshop, Angelika?"

"No. What do you mean by incidents?"

"There have been two break-ins at your grandfather's atelier recently. The first seemed just petty, moving objects around so as to worry Konstantinos, and only one thing was broken. The second was more serious, and the police have been told. The kiln was turned to maximum temperature in the night, and everything inside exploded. The kiln was damaged too. Your grandfather is anxious now, because a threat was written on the wall of the kiln room in red paint, telling him to call off the Niarchos project."

"My God, I didn't know. Poor Pappou. This is much more important than any of my worries. He definitely must not be allowed to hear anything about my meeting with Edward, Martin. It would be too stressful, on top of all this. You agree?"

"Of course. Konstantinos won't hear anything from me."

"Thank you. I'll call on grandfather and get him to tell me about these troubles. Martin, I'm sorry, but I must go now. Will you come to dinner with mother and me, at home? She likes seeing new people, it will do her good and you will hardly notice her problems. You can see for yourself how Greek she looks! Saturday night?"

They made an arrangement and Angelika explained where best to park for her house in the Kastro. They got up to leave.

"I'd like to bring a gift for your mother on Saturday," said Day. "I understand she isn't well. Would you please tell me what she would like?"

"I should have said, I'm sorry. She has bouts of severe clinical depression. Between these she is quite well, but they always come back. Really, when you meet her on Saturday I'm sure she will be at her happy best. She loves chocolate, and dark chocolate is meant to be very good for her state of mind."

"Then I shall bring her some. I look forward to meeting your mother, and perhaps we can talk more too on Saturday."

Day walked Angelika to her car, and she gave him a Greek double kiss as they parted.

17

Helen, looking and feeling wonderful after a long siesta and shower, joined Day on the balcony. He had already poured a small glass of red wine for each of them. It was seven o'clock, and the sunset was under an hour away. The light in the valley was already rich with the promise of the deep orange that would soon fill the horizon.

Day turned to greet her. "My God, it's an imposter!" he said, unable to contain his admiration.

Helen laughed. "I thought I'd put in a bit of effort tonight. And not just for our friend Thanasis! I did seven hours of good work and had a terrific nap, the first since I went back to London. Anyway, it's only a bit of make-up. You wouldn't know about these things, Martin."

"Indeed not, dear friend. So, I propose a toast. Not only to your successful day of creativity, but also to Angelika Spetzou and her grandmother, Artemis. We have found them at last."

"That's worthy of a toast. To Artemis and Angelika. Mmm, I like this wine."

"It's not a posh bottle, it's an island wine that Aristos recommended to me. I'm glad you like it because I bought a case. Friends of Aristos's make it."

"It's lovely. I think we should have a glass or two here, admiring the sunset before we go to the taverna. Fancy that?"

"Good idea. I'll tell you all about my meeting with Angelika. Vasilios says hello, by the way. I felt very bad about not having called to see him before. He greeted me like a long lost brother."

"It was a good idea to meet Angelika at Vasilios's, where it's quiet. What's she like?"

"In looks, she's the woman from the portrait I showed you that Peppino sent me. The picture in Konstantinos's house, painted by Artemis."

"So there's no doubt that Edward and Konstantinos loved the same woman?"

"I don't think there can be any doubt at all. And I think neither man knew the truth until Angelika told Edward. Konstantinos still doesn't know."

"Did you like Angelika?"

"Yes, very much. She's quite strong-minded but also seems very kind. She's pleasantly direct - she invited me to dinner with her mother and herself on Saturday. She's engaged to a chap called Loukas who lives in Athens. She doesn't seem to have a job, she cares full time for her mother, who suffers from depression. She adores Konstantinos, her grandfather. He supports them both financially."

"That's hard on her, caring for her mother full time. How old do you think she is?"

"Late twenties? I'm not good at that sort of thing."

"And did she tell you what happened between her and Edward?"

"From what she said and what Edward told me in his letter, I have a good idea. They seem to have liked each other from the start. Angelika was genuinely upset to hear that Edward had died, and even more so when I told her today that he was murdered. Of course you would expect that, but I was looking out for even the smallest sign that she already knew anything or had any involvement. I'm sure she doesn't."

"Mmm. You really are going to tell Inspector Nomikos about her now, aren't you, Martin?"

"Yes, yes. Talking of Andreas, he'll be on Naxos tomorrow to question everyone. I wondered whether to invite him to have dinner with us. He would probably eat alone otherwise. What do you think?"

"Well, up to you. You're the one on first name terms with a police inspector!"

"Right, hang on, and I'll give him a call now."

Helen went into the house to fetch the bottle of wine and some nibbles, while Day dialled Nomikos's mobile. When she returned, he was smiling.

"It's sorted. He was quick to accept. I said we'd cook and eat here, unless he preferred a restaurant, and he was very pleased at the thought of a home-cooked meal. He'll be arriving just after six tomorrow evening."

"Right, supermarket for us tomorrow morning, then. I'll do the food, you sort out the drink."

They sat for another half hour with their wine before reluctantly making a move to walk to Taverna O Thanasis while there was still light. Along their route they walked past neighbours who were chatting, or just sitting on chairs at their front doors, and once again Day was wished a friendly good evening, this time by more than one person. He looked so happy. Helen smiled, and asked herself aloud whether Day was now infamous.

"I think you mean famous?" he suggested.

"I'm a writer. I chose the word deliberately. It think they've heard about the scandal at the Elias house and your part in bringing the truth to light."

Day grinned, surprised by gratification, and returned the small wave of an elderly grandmother who was sitting in front of her house gently rocking an ancient pram.

On arrival at Taverna O Thanasis they were greeted by the owner himself, looking rather smart in black trousers and a dark blue shirt. They were ushered to the best available table under the awning on the terrace, where Helen would have a good view of the comings and goings along the road as night fell. Thanasis brought two glasses of aperitif wine, placed them ceremoniously on the table, and bent to kiss Helen's hand in welcome.

"You've made a hit there, Helen," said Day, once Thanasis had gone. "Remember his wife Koula is preparing our dinner."

"I shall take care not to be too flirtatious until after dinner, then. What do you fancy to eat?"

"I'm in the mood for meat tonight," said Day. "Perhaps some lamb, or some chops of some kind. Let's see what Koula is cooking."

Thanasis brought them menus, bottled water and glasses, and the traditional bread basket and cutlery.

"Tonight my wife has some fresh octopus with lemon sauce, some small fish cooked in the grill, cockerel in red sauce with orzo, and lamb chops grilled. To start there is baby squid, fava, Cretan salad. Also Koula's own pantzaria salad."

"Wonderful. What would you like, Helen? I really fancy the lamb chops, and shall we share some pantzaria, and some fried potatoes?"

"Yes, and I'd like to try your wife's fava, please, Thanasi."

"Excellent, Kyria Helen, Martin. Shall I bring you some wine?"

"Yes, please, your excellent local red. Thanks."

Thanasis left with their order and returned almost immediately with a jug of red wine.

"Have you eaten here a lot in my absence, Martin?"

"A few times, mostly on my own. I also brought Edward here, and more recently Peppino Berducci."

"The Italian sculptor? I'd like to meet him some time."

"He's a big, warm-hearted man and very interesting, you'll like him. He's the only other person I told about Angelika. By the way, when we see Andreas Nomikos tomorrow, he'll already have spoken to Peppino, so he'll know that I've kept the details of Angelika from him. It could be embarrassing."

"And you deserve it! I plan to hide in my room until you've cleared it up with him."

Day waved his hand dismissively, and was saved from comment by the arrival of Thanasis with the fava and the pantzaria, a fresh beetroot dish. Day took the cutlery from the bread basket and placed one set by Helen's plate before taking another for himself. He passed her the bread, and they began with the warm fava dip, made from yellow split peas and topped with a little green olive oil and some delicate slivers of raw onion.

"So, tell me more about your talk with Angelika," Helen asked, when their first flush of hunger had been assuaged.

Day told her everything he could remember from what he and Angelika had said. As always, he wanted Helen to know all the facts and the direction of his thinking. Her perspicacity and imagination had in the past given him insights or raised useful questions in his mind. Two minds were better than one, as the old saying went, especially when they thought in complementary ways.

Helen began as soon as Day had finished his account.

"How is it possible that Angelika is unable to find out the true dates of her grandparents' marriage and the birth of her own mother? It doesn't seem such a difficult thing to do in these days of internet searches and ancestry websites."

"I asked Angelika the same thing. She tried to tell me that a pregnancy outside marriage would have been shameful even in the 1960s, and would have been concealed. She's a modern woman, though, and if she wanted to find out, I think she could."

"Perhaps she doesn't really want to know?"

"I suspect she's now quite keen, having discovered Edward and his story. More likely, she doesn't want to start such a search out of respect for Konstantinos."

"Did she say much about her fiancé, this Loukas?"

"Only the basic details that I told you. He works in Athens and has an apartment in Pangrati, where she visits him sometimes. She stayed there when she met Edward. The fiancé also visits the island to see her at weekends, when he isn't working. I didn't ask what work he does."

"Does this man know about Edward, and Angelika's meeting with him?"

"Yes, Angelika has been open with him, just asked him to keep the secret between them. So I started to be suspicious of Loukas, who had knowledge of Edward, lives in Athens, and could have used his connection with Angelika to get Edward to open the door to him. He *could* have killed him. I just don't see much of a motive. He might be protective of Angelika, but Edward didn't pose a threat, did he? Would an extra grandfather, even if that were true, cause Loukas to resort to murder?"

"It seems unlikely. Do you know where he was the night Edward was killed? It was a Saturday night, maybe he came to Naxos with Angelika. Or perhaps he was in Athens still?"

"I don't know the answer to that. I didn't think to ask - but I could hardly ask Angelika without her realising why I was asking."

"True. I wonder whether the fiancé will be at the house when you go to dinner on Saturday?"

At this point their meal arrived at the table, brought by Thanasis's son Vangelis, who shook hands with Helen and welcomed her formally back to their taverna.

"You're Mrs Popular here, Helen!" Day said when the young man returned to the kitchen.

Helen smiled and moved the chips closer to Day before helping herself to a succulent lamb chop and another piece of bread.

"Why do you think Edward said nothing to you in his letter about Konstantinos being Angelika's grandfather and Artemis's husband? Don't you think, having told you everything else, he might have told you that?"

"I have two theories about that. He might have felt that it would be better for me not to know, as I would be seeing Konstantinos both socially and professionally in future. Or perhaps he wanted to tell me in person, not knowing, of course, that he wouldn't have the chance."

"How sad," said Helen, laying down her fork and sitting back. She took a deep drink of water and looked round at the other tables, lit now by bulbs in the awning and around the posts that held up the structure. "I wonder if he would ever have told Konstantinos."

Day divided the last of the wine equally between their glasses. He had no answer for her, and was rather tired of his inability to see clearly through the puzzle of Edward and Konstantinos.

"Don't you think it's particularly hot and stuffy tonight, Martin?" Helen asked.

"Yes. The weather's turning, and there'll be a storm tonight, they say."

"That explains it. Good, I like storms in the Cyclades, you can sometimes see them coming for miles across the sea."

"Not in Filoti, you can't!" Day laughed. Considerable hills stood between Filoti and the Aegean.

"Well, maybe a storm will clear the air. I feel very muddled by a lot of this story. I had an odd thought just now. I was wondering how it is that the box of Artemis's diaries and private writing was at Angelika's house, rather than with Konstantinos? Wouldn't you expect the widower to keep this late wife's most personal possessions? So, how did Angelika come to have them at all?"

18

The wind rose in the night, and just before dawn the rain began. It was heavy, its big drops driven slantingly by the wind, dramatically noisy round the house and thudding against the shutters. At some point the wind became more gentle and allowed the rain to fall directly to the ground. In the relative quietness that followed the deluge, the storm wasted to an end. As the sky lightened, the fresh-scented valley beyond the balcony began to steam in the morning sun, and Day and Helen dried the chairs and the table on the balcony, brought out the cushions and made their first pot of coffee.

Finally they could put off the supermarket trip no longer, and finding some carrier bags in a drawer threw them in the back of the car and drove to Chora. The supermarket was on the outskirts, just off the road from Filoti to the centre, and it was popular, its large gravel carpark already busy. Most people preferred to shop before the day became hot, so the atmosphere in the store when they arrived was buzzing and convivial, with neighbours greeting neighbours and much banter over the fresh produce.

Day, who was in charge of drinks, had little to do because the house was already well stocked. He picked up two six-packs of mineral water, three large bottles of tonic and a bag of lemons. He noticed some packets of roasted pistachio nuts from Santorini and added two to his trolley. Meanwhile, at the fish counter, Helen was laughing and stumbling over her order for fish with the young lady behind the counter. Once she had what she wanted she moved across to buy some olives from the vast quantity of loose fruit in brine at the next counter.

"How are you doing?" asked Day, who had already finished his shopping.

"So far, so good!" she replied. "Still need to get salad, cheese, bread, milk and coffee."

"I'll get milk and coffee, shall I? What cheese do we want?"

"Some good local Feta and a little Mizithra."

"OK, I'll do those too, and you get salad and bread, and meet me at the tills."

When Helen joined Day at the till he was astonished how much food she seemed to have acquired, and there were grapes and peaches in her trolley too. Day would not think of buying fruit unless Helen told him to. He looked again and saw a pack of Greek rocket in the trolley, and also a large juicy-looking garlic, tomatoes of all shapes and sizes, and a cucumber. That was much better.

As they were loading their purchases into the boot of the Fiat, Day remembered something he had to do.

"I need to buy chocolate to take for Angelika's mother tomorrow night. We could get it now, if you wouldn't mind."

Helen had no objection to buying chocolate. They drove further into town and parked just outside the centre, a short walk from the zacharoplastia, or confectionary shop, which sold some of the best cakes and chocolates in Chora. The last time Helen had been in the shop, in May, they had bought a gift for Rania before going to her birthday celebration. Once again she was dazzled by the quality of the fancy confectionary and gleaming chocolate on display.

"Angelika suggested dark chocolate would be the right thing to take for her mother," Day explained. "What do you think would be good?"

Helen scanned the glass shelves. It would be her decision, as Day knew nothing about sweet food. Suddenly finding the words in Greek, she chatted to the girl behind the counter, who filled the bottom of a small box with a mixture of dark chocolate-covered almonds, dark chocolate truffles studded with niblets of pistachio, and some crystallised orange segments dipped in dark chocolate. The girl made the box look attractive and then wrapped it deftly in several silver ribbons and a final flourish of red ribbon bearing the name of the zacharoplastia. She surveyed her work with pride and placed it on the glass shelf before Helen. Day looked on mutely, reached for his wallet and prepared to pay.

"Just a minute, Martin. Let's get a few nice things for the meal this evening too."

They added another box of delicacies and Day paid. He hoped the chocolate would make it back to Filoti in solid form. Helen had similar concerns about her fish.

***

They worked separately for the rest of the morning and into the afternoon, pausing only for a light snack at lunchtime. Day then took his laptop to his room as if to work again, but he was clearly heading for a siesta. The afternoon was hot but not clammy, the island seemingly cleansed by the storm. Helen closed her computer and set to work on the food. She cleaned the fish and the prawns, rinsed the salad, prepared plates and dishes, and surveyed her work. That was enough. She had planned a tasty but easy meal, and the rest of the preparation would be better done nearer the time. She took a book to the balcony, made herself comfy on the old sunbed in the small area of shade, and read contentedly until she fell asleep.

When she woke her phone said five o'clock. Perfect, she could go for a shower and then take her time in order not to emerge from her room until Inspector Nomikos had berated Martin for not telling him about Edward and Angelika. Wasn't that some kind of criminal offence? She hoped that Martin was on as good terms with 'Andreas' as he appeared to think.

***

Inspector Andreas Nomikos was late, but only by a polite amount. A little after six in the evening he stood in front of Day's house, waving away the police car that had brought him. They shook hands and Day invited the inspector in, closing the door behind him. He turned to find the tall policeman facing him, arms crossed and feet apart. To his relief, Andreas was smiling. Day realised that the Greek rule of hospitality, filoxenia, which bound host and guest in the same code of warmth and generosity, had subtly changed the relationship between them. It was a rare officer who would put himself in the position that Nomikos had done when he had accepted Day's invitation to dinner.

"Well," said the policeman with a smile. "Here you are, in the shadow of Mount Zas, offering hospitality to travellers like mighty Zeus himself."

Day foraged in his memory for his long-ago classes in Greek mythology. "Oh, I see. Zeus was 'the friend of strangers', wasn't he?

You're very welcome, Andrea. Come through to the balcony. Would you like a drink?"

"Why not? I'm as off-duty as I ever am. Whatever you're having will be fine for me, thank you. Congratulations on your house, which I believe is quite a new acquisition? Living in the city, I really appreciate the quietness of island life, especially away from the coastal strip which is so busy in summer."

Andreas Nomikos sat down on the balcony admiring the view until Day joined him with the drinks and a bowl of the fresh olives bought that morning. The sun was strong again but after the cleansing storm the heat was enjoyable. Day was struck afresh by his unusual guest, a tall Greek with fair hair and light blue eyes, and a mastery of English.

"Do you enjoy living in Athens, Andrea?"

"Living in the capital is essential from the point of view of my career," the inspector answered judiciously. "I must spend a few more years there before making any move. It suits me well enough. How about you? Do you actually live in England or in Greece?"

"I don't have a home in England now. I have this house and a small apartment in Athens, so I'm nearly always in Greece. When I need to work in London, I usually stay with a friend. Do you remember Helen Aitchison?"

"Certainly. I could not forget such a lady. Is she well?"

"Very well, and I'm happy to say that she's now back here after a trip to London."

Andreas looked surprised and glanced into the house as if looking for Helen. She was nowhere to be seen. Day thought he had better get the bad part over with, or Helen would never appear.

"Ah. I suspect she's in her room, waiting till she knows whether you're going to arrest me or not."

Andreas leaned forward slightly in his chair, placing his gin and tonic gently on the table as if he thought Day was about to make a confession. Day raised a hand defensively.

"No, I just mean … I think you've spoken to Peppino Berducci today?"

"If you're referring to what Signor Berducci said with regard to a lady who was with Professor Childe the night before he was killed, he did tell me about that."

"I apologise, Andrea, I should have told you about her myself. I was trying to protect the lady, for Edward's sake. I wanted to find her and tell her about Edward's death before she heard it less sympathetically from the authorities."

"The police can be sensitive too, you know, Martin," said Andreas wryly. "Actually, your friend Signor Berducci explained it very well to me. Despite the short time I've known you, I must say I wasn't surprised at what you did. You can make up for it by telling me everything about this young woman and her relationship to the professor."

At this moment an inner door closed in the house and Helen appeared. She walked towards the balcony with a smile, ready to greet Andreas. She had heard every word they said through the open window of her bedroom.

Andreas Nomikos immediately stood and turned to Helen. Day was struck by the strange sense of role reversal again. Helen was now the host, whereas only a few months ago she had been interviewed by the police as a witness in a murder. To make matters more complicated for Andreas, Helen was wearing a flattering yellow dress, had clearly applied the make-up about which she had told Day he knew nothing, and was at her most relaxed. Day went into the kitchen to make her a drink and bring out some of the Santorini pistachios he had bought earlier. Andreas could handle this himself, he thought.

They chatted in the sunshine, making light conversation. Before long Day drifted off into his own thoughts. He wondered whether it would be better to get the police talk out of the way before dinner, or concentrate on being sociable until dinner was over. He really wanted to find out if Andreas had any new information about Edward's death. He was pretty sure Andreas would have phoned him if so, but as everyone seemed to be adept at keeping secrets he could not be certain.

Before long, Helen resolved his problem by asking what the inspector had discovered so far. Well, that was direct at least, Day thought. Andreas Nomikos was surprised too, but quickly gave a small smile of approval.

"Would you like me to give you a brief overview?" he teased. "I'm in touch with the British Embassy, normal procedure in these circumstances, and Professor Childe will be cremated in Greece and the ashes returned to the UK. His funeral is in the capable hands of his former colleagues. The Cambridge police have interviewed the professor's university associates, his solicitor, his publisher, his housekeeper, his neighbours … nothing new has emerged. I was interested in his valuable art collection, but his death has done nothing to enrich any individual, so I've been unable to see a link between it and his death."

"Can I ask how the coroner ruled, Inspector?" asked Helen.

"With pleasure, if you would call me Andrea."

"Then please call me Helen."

Andreas nodded and continued.

"The Coroner found that your friend Edward was in good health for a man of his age. The exception was his heart, for which he took prescribed medication daily, enabling him to live as comfortably as any man of his age. The toxicology report found nothing to suggest any kind of overdose. He had not even taken an alcoholic drink in the hours before he died."

"So there's no way this was suicide?" said Helen.

"Correct. Moreover, no indication of death by natural causes was found. His heart, for instance, had not deteriorated. No, I'm afraid the truth is quite different. The Coroner concluded death by suffocation. I'm sorry."

"So am I, although I never actually met Edward myself. From what Martin has told me, I would have liked him very much."

The policeman regarded her thoughtfully.

"We've questioned people who knew the professor at the British School of Archaeology and the National Archaeological Museum, but nobody was able to tell us anything helpful."

Day had been expecting that too. He took some nuts and peeled one meticulously before eating it and beginning to peel another. "That leaves the people here on Naxos, including Angelika Spetzou," he said.

"I've started by talking to the people at Kyrios Saris's workshop," continued Andreas. "Kyrios Saris telephoned his friend Markos Ioannakis, who came over from his shop in Halki."

Helen looked puzzled, so Day helped her out. "That's the man who owns the 'Blue and Gold Naxos' shops in Chora and Halki. He sells

Konstantinos's pottery, and some of his smaller marbles. He's always popping in to the atelier and he met Edward."

"That's right," confirmed Andreas. "I also learned about the two break-ins at the marble workshop. I understand you're involved in those too, Martin?"

"Involved in the sense of a concerned friend, Andrea!" laughed Day. "When I called to tell them about Edward it was the morning after the first break-in. I urged them to inform the police, but Konstantinos didn't want to. After the second incident Peppino called me and we persuaded Konstantinos to change his mind."

"Andrea, do you think there's a connection between the marble workshop break-ins and Edward's murder?" interrupted Helen, making a leap which Day himself had not yet considered.

"There already is one, Helen. Kyrios Saris is the obvious connection, and his friends at the workshop. There's also another person common to both, isn't there, Martin? Saris's granddaughter Angelika, who was with Professor Childe the day before he was killed."

Martin realised the time had come.

"When I talked to Angelika I discovered the historic connection between Edward and Konstantinos, which is that as young men they knew the same woman. Edward found it out from Angelika just before he died, but Konstantinos still doesn't know. Angelika wants to keep it from him, to save his feelings."

Andreas placed his empty glass on the table. "Forget what Peppino Berducci might have told me, Martin, and tell me everything you know about this. Try not to omit any details. Would you mind if I made a few notes as you talked?"

Helen slipped away to the kitchen to prepare the meal as Day began his narrative. She knew he would tell the story of Edward's youthful romance with all the flair at his disposal. She listened from the kitchen counter. The part that brought tears to her eyes was the moment when Edward knew he would meet the granddaughter of the young woman he had loved and lost in 1959.

***

Andreas Nomikos looked up from his notes. Day had told him Edward's story from first meeting Artemis in 1959 to the letter he had sent to Day just before he died. He was about to embark on the story of his own meeting with Angelika, when Nomikos interrupted him.

"Before you go on, Martin, I have a question. Tell me what you know about how Edward and Konstantinos met?"

"It was at an exhibition in Cambridge a few years ago. Konstantinos was there as an exhibitor, and a student of Edward's was an administrator of the event and introduced him to Konstantinos. They took an immediate interest in each other and went for dinner together the same night. Since then, Edward has been to stay with Konstantinos several times."

"When was that first meeting?"

"I'm not certain, but maybe 2013 was mentioned. You'll have to ask Konstantinos."

"When we spoke in Athens, Martin, you mentioned that you and Edward were planning to work together, is that so?"

"Yes, Edward was planning a series of programmes about Greek marble, past and present."

Rather a good title, Day thought with a little smile.

"Is it a coincidence that Konstantinos is a marble sculptor?"

"He and Edward shared a love of marble, it was the basis of their friendship. Edward wanted to involve him in the project to illustrate the modern marble tradition of Naxos."

"And did he want to involve Signor Berducci too?"

"No, Peppino arrived after Edward had left for Athens. They didn't meet."

"What can you tell me about the Niarchos Foundation project?"

Day told Andreas as much as he knew about the well-funded, three-year project. Andreas made detailed notes, before changing the subject again.

"Konstantinos told me that the Niarchos project would affect Markos Ioannakis, who would usually sell his work in his shops but will not be permitted to continue for three years. What do you think of this, Martin? Serious enough to be behind the break-ins?"

"Presumably you interviewed Markos yourself? I found him a likeable man who seemed to have a lot of respect for Konstantinos and a good bond with everyone at the atelier. Although Konstantinos asked me not to talk about the project in front of Markos, I don't see Markos in such a thuggish role, do you?"

"I have no pre-conceived ideas at this stage, I promise you, Martin. However, I have two investigations to consider now, the murder in Athens and the break-ins on Naxos, and although I'm not yet looking for a single perpetrator, the single undeniable link between them is Konstantinos Saris."

***

Helen returned to the balcony with a bottle of white wine from the Moraitis Winery on Paros, which Day had found on a recent foray to that island. She poured wine into each of three small glasses. They raised a toast to friendship in the traditional way.

"If you don't mind, Andrea," Helen said, "I'll take my wine inside. I'm just finishing preparations for dinner."

"Of course. I'm so sorry, I've come without a gift, I ran out of time today. I hope you will dine with me, both of you, on another occasion?"

Helen smiled and took her glass back into the house. Andreas turned back to Day.

"Shall we get all the work out of the way before dinner, Martin? Tell me what you learned from Angelika Spetzou."

Day complied, and the telling became easier as he sipped the cold white wine. It really was excellent. He made a mental note to share a bottle with Aristos, who was an enthusiast of Cycladic wine.

"OK," sighed Andreas finally, closing his notebook. "I spoke with Angelika Spetzou and her fiancé this afternoon, and what you say confirms my impression. Thank you for giving me your personal insights. I think now we can leave the police work on one side and enjoy our evening."

***

The old wooden table in the main room of Day's house now bore a magnificent centrepiece - a large old plate which Day had found in the larder when he moved into the house. On it lay a fish, a Mediterranean sea bass called a lavraki in Greece, grilled and dressed with oil, garlic, chilli, lemon and thyme. In another dish were shrimps in a tomato sauce with a little melted Feta cheese. A bowl of rocket, one of Day's favourite things, flanked a dish of traditional Greek salad or horiatiki. Everyone began with the shrimp dish, eating it with bread: Helen had found a suitable bread basket in one of Day's cupboards. She then slit the skin of the fish with a practised hand, eased the flesh from the bones, and invited everyone to help themselves.

"I thought we could have cheese on the balcony," she suggested when they were finished. She had prepared a platter of cheeses including not only local Mizithra but a piece of Long Clawson Stilton which she had smuggled out from London in her suitcase and which had miraculously survived the journey. Soon they were sitting with their plates and small glasses of red wine on the balcony, just in time for that precious moment of evening when the sun, having vanished behind the opposite hills but not below the distant horizon, attracted attention to itself with pulsations of amber and gold.

"This is a perfect setting. Thank you both for inviting me," said Andreas Nomikos, raising his glass to them. "I'm sorry I had to speak of police business."

"Much nicer to be questioned this way," murmured Helen. "Have you finished with Martin, Andrea?"

"Yes, thank you, but tomorrow the work continues. By the way, my colleague Inspector Cristopoulos sends you both his regards."

"That's very kind," said Helen, suspecting the regards came only from Andreas. "How often do you come to Naxos, Andrea?"

"Whenever I'm needed. My job takes me to many of the islands. It's good to escape the heat of the city in the summer. I believe you live in London, Helen?"

"Yes, I have a house in Hampstead. I used to live in Greece with my late husband, but we separated many years ago and I moved to Hampstead."

Andreas acknowledged the implications with a very small turn of his head.

"I've heard Hampstead is an attractive suburb," he said. "I was nearby last year meeting a friend at a wonderful Greek restaurant in Belsize Park, but unfortunately I didn't have time to visit your area."

"What a small world," said Helen, and continued with her usual directness. "Talking of which, Andrea, may I ask where your family originally comes from? You're a Greek man who has fair hair and blue eyes, which does rather make you stand out. I've heard that your colouring is characteristic of Greek from Macedonia, but I don't know if that's true."

"You've heard correctly, Helen, but I'm not from those parts. My father was Greek and my mother was from Norway. I've inherited her colouring."

"That's wonderful! You're a Greek Viking Policeman!"

Andreas smiled at her, again with the slight sideways inclination of the head. Day thought he might as well help himself to the cheese. Helen was not to be sidetracked.

"Do your parents live in Greece?"

"My mother returned to Norway when I was young. My father lives with my sister in Patras now."

His emotions heightened by the wine and the heady evening warmth, Day reflected that in Andreas's story there were elements of both his own life and Helen's. A broken marriage and the woman's return to her home country was also part of Helen's history. The loss of a mother at an impressionable age was, of course, the story of Day's own youth.

19

Day dedicated his Saturday morning to working in the Nikos Elias house going through Elias's early finds from an area of shoreline on the west coast of the island. He had read everything that Elias had written about them, but he wanted to handle the objects again himself, meticulously examining the more interesting ones and describing them in his own words, noting differences between his own observations and those of Elias.

He unlocked the archaeologist's former house and locked it behind him. It felt cool after the heat outside, cooler even than the air-conditioned interior of Day's car. The shutters were locked, the windows closed and a stale smell filled the downstairs rooms. Day never went upstairs. He felt that the ghosts of the house's former occupants remained there, and he wanted to avoid the melancholy that might overtake him if he dwelt on the building's recent past.

Throwing open the windows and shutters of the small room that he used as his office, Day let light into the place and into his mind. Around the walls were shelves full of files, and on the desk by the window were the papers he had been working on over a fortnight ago.

He connected his laptop to a power cable and booted up the machine.

By the time he had finished constantly moving between his desk and the Finds Room, making notes on his computer and downloading photographs from his camera, he was tired and hungry. He packed away, pleased at having completed what he had set out to do. It was time to go home. He took the fork in the road away from the sea and drove the familiar route to Filoti singing a snatch of Gilbert and Sullivan he knew from his childhood, unaware of why it had come into his mind.

He was still chuckling when got in and found Helen on the balcony snacking on some cheese and a peach, a book on her lap. Day made two cups of English Breakfast tea and put some cheese and ham on another plate for himself.

"Ah, tea!" said Helen, regarding him with surprise. She closed her book without marking the place. "Tea cures everything, in my case a rather disappointing book. Did you make headway with your friend Elias?"

"Yes, it was a productive morning. I've been bent over a laptop or working through a box of pottery sherds for hours and I feel extremely virtuous. I think I'll stretch out for half an hour and then carry on with work so I can go to Angelika's this evening with a clear conscience."

When he got to his room he realised that he had not asked Helen about her morning. He resolved to do so after his nap. He stretched out on the bed and slept well in the warm bedroom with the window ajar and the light curtain motionless in the still, hot afternoon.

He woke with a sense of happy anticipation. He was soon to meet Artemis's daughter, Sofia. He wondered about Sofia's depression and what had caused her to suffer from it. He realised he was quite ignorant about clinical depression and decided to read about it online before he did anything else. He opened his laptop and put a search into Google.

The internet provided both too little information and too much, and Day still didn't know what to expect that evening. Just then a new email arrived, the notification of which flashed on the screen. The sender was Cameron Maxwell. Day opened it quickly.

Martin,

I hope this finds you well. I know you will be relieved to hear that Edward's ashes are now in the safekeeping of the solicitor's office and I am making arrangements for an occasion in his honour at which friends and colleagues can be present to wish Edward a final farewell. I will send you an official invitation, but you may appreciate advance warning of the date, in case you can attend. In view of colleagues' various commitments at the start of the semester, the date will be Saturday 19th October. The venue will be in Cambridge.

I attach the list that you requested of Edward's art collection. I hope what you find therein proves useful.

If I can be of further service to you, please let me know.

Regards,

Cameron

Day glanced at the time. Regrettably he must postpone opening Maxwell's attachment until later. He switched on the iron and went for a shower. The hot water was invigorating despite the mere trickle that emanated from the shower head, and afterwards he dressed carefully, choosing a light pink shirt and navy trousers, adding a jacket that would provide a more formal note. He wanted to create a good impression on this family, an impression of which Edward would have approved.

He found Helen making supper for herself, including more vegetables than Day, personally, would ever have dreamed of using. A sliced yellow pepper, some courgette cut into thin strips and a grated carrot were already in readiness. Helen was chopping garlic and chilli, and a piece of chicken lay on a plate to the side of her chopping board.

"What are you making? Is this your dinner?"

"It will be, and I'll know what it is when I've made it," she said. "Is it time for you to go?"

"Yes, I'm leaving myself plenty of time to find the house. It's a case of parking outside the Kastro and walking through the lanes, and you know what a labyrinth it is. Have a good evening. I don't think I'll be late back."

Day remembered to take his gift of dark chocolate goodies from the fridge, but as he drove away from the house he realised what he had forgotten. He had not asked Helen whether her writing had gone well that day. Guiltily he acknowledged to himself that she put up with a lot from him.

***

Darkness had fallen by the time he parked in a public car park below the mound of old buildings that surrounded the town's Venetian castle, the Kastro. Below the Kastro itself, the houses of the Venetian townspeople had been built cheek by jowl, so close together it felt as if they had all joined into one. The alleyways of the higher Kastro were too narrow for vehicles, so only occasional small delivery vans and motorbikes passed him. Everything seemed to be painted white, lit sporadically by small lights over house doors and the occasional bulb along the lane. Day passed under several white-painted archways, walked along white-painted paths, up flights of shallow steps, and under tunnels created by the upper storeys of houses. Narrow staircases decorated with flowerpots led to doors on the level above the street. Many residents decorated their front doorways with painted flowerpots of geraniums, oleander, bougainvillea and jasmine, which Day could smell as he passed. Cats, probably fed by the residents and looking very healthy, darted away with feral glares as he approached. They lingered in the shadows, turning to watch him suspiciously.

Angelika's instructions proved to be good. Using the tourist signs that had been made to lead them to hidden restaurants, historic houses and a variety of accommodation, Day ventured uphill towards the more historic part of the Kastro. He had been walking for less than five minutes, but he was already touched by its magic. The stepped alleyways were filled with scents from wood-fired ovens, and though he passed few people he could hear voices raised in conversation over evening meals.

He reached Angelika's house and knocked on the door. Angelika herself opened the door and gave him the friendly two-kiss greeting. He followed her into the house. In the first reception room Day noticed the high ceilings, book-filled shelves and comfortable chairs. A record player stood on a table next to a collection of vinyl records. On the floor was a carpet which Day might have called Turkish, but not aloud. Angelika beckoned him into the next room.

This was a second reception room, the centre dominated by an antique wooden dining table. The walls of this room held Day's attention, covered as they were with striking paintings. This house was clearly more imposing than you would guess from the lane outside. Day also observed that the table was not set for dinner.

"I promise I'll bring you on a tour of the house later, Martin," said Angelika with a smile. "but for now, come and meet my mother."

They left the room and emerged outside into a little courtyard from which a wrought iron staircase led in a spiral up to the roof of the house. Angelika went first, warning Day to mind his step. At the top he found himself on a roof terrace with a pergola from which small lights had been draped. In the daylight there would have been an interesting view from this roof, he thought, but now the darkness of the Kastro beyond was intense, unspoiled by light pollution. He could hear muted conversation and laughter rising from other houses in the vicinity.

A lady seated at a central table stood up on seeing them approach. Day fixed a smile firmly on his face as a mask against the emotions he was feeling. This was Artemis's daughter, and clearly a woman who had experienced more than her fair share of difficulties in life. Sofia was quite short, shorter than Angelika, and rather too thin, but her straight Greek nose and bright eyes suggested she had been a beautiful girl. Her tanned Mediterranean complexion was full of lines, despite the fact that she could only have been about sixty, but they actually made her more attractive.

Day gave her the parcel of chocolates which Angelika had not accepted from him at the door. Sofia Spetzou's face opened in a smile of delight as he gave it to her. She thanked him, and sat down again, the gift resting under the hand on her lap. After a minute of smiling at Day, she carefully untied the silver and red ribbons, opened the box, and gave a little laugh of pleasure. She thanked him in Greek.

Making a sudden decision, Day spoke in Greek for the rest of the evening. Angelika said nothing, but she too changed to Greek. Day began to relax, realising that the meeting with Angelika's mother was, after all, going to be a success. He allowed himself to think of Edward, even to imagine Edward with them at the table. Was this

Edward's daughter? Day knew he would never find out. This beautiful woman, Angelika's mother, did indeed look a hundred per cent Greek. All the same, part of Day remained hopeful that in her and Angelika something of Edward lived on.

Angelika excused herself after a while, and went back down to the house. Day noticed that the table was laid for four, and soon voices came from the courtyard below, a man's voice talking with Angelika. The man concerned soon appeared at the top of the steps.

"Hello. You're Martin? I'm very pleased to meet you. I'm Loukas Veakis, Angelika's fiancé."

Loukas Veakis stepped closer and shook Day's hand before bending over Sofia and kissing her on both cheeks. He was a small man of slight build, with bright eyes behind black-framed glasses, a meticulously shaped moustache and a well-trimmed beard of the kind that the British would once have called a goatee.

Angelika poured a fruit drink from a jug on the table into glasses of ice and offered them round. She suggested that Loukas tell Day more about the history of the house, and excused herself to finish preparing the dinner. Day watched Sofia's face and listened politely to Loukas, while he was really enjoying the faint sound of a cicada from beyond the darkness. Loukas told a colourful story about how Konstantinos's father had bought the property from a family who could trace their ancestry back to the Venetians who built the Kastro.

Day found the story slightly less than convincing, and decided to divert Loukas onto subjects in which he was currently a great deal more interested.

"Angelika tells me that you live and work in Athens, Louka. What do you do?"

"I work for the GNTO, the Greek National Tourism Organisation," the younger man said with pride. "It's a government agency which is concerned with all aspects of promoting tourism in this country. As you know, tourism is a major source of national revenue for Greece. I myself work in the headquarters on Tsoha Street, not far from the National Archaeological Museum. I expect you know where that is?"

Day nodded, thinking how often he had worked in that particular building in the last fifteen or so years. He reflected that Loukas's office was not far from the police headquarters where he had visited Andreas Nomikos, and only a short walk from his own apartment in Dinokratous. What this told Day was that Loukas's office was very close to Edward's hotel. He wondered whether this was significant.

"Angelika and I met here on Naxos," Loukas was saying. "We were both born on this island and went to the same junior school, although we didn't meet until much later. I succeeded in getting away to the capital. There's no security in today's Greece unless you have a government job. Without it, I would not have proposed to Angelika, but my future looks secure now. We hope to be married very soon."

"Congratulations!" Day said, trying to sound sufficiently enthusiastic. He was not sure why this man was ruffling his feathers. "How often do you manage to see your fiancée, with such a demanding job?"

"I visit here at the weekend whenever I can, arriving on Friday night and leaving on Sunday. Angelika comes to Athens, when she can."

He glanced at Sofia, who seemed not to have picked up on this remark. Her eyes were turned to the dark, starry sky with the look of someone who found solace there. Day wondered whether she was losing herself in the vastness of the night sky as a preferable alternative to listening to Loukas Veakis.

"You've met Angelika's grandfather, I understand?" went on Loukas. Day confirmed that he had indeed met Konstantinos.

"I'm well aware that Konstantinos is not a great admirer of mine, but to be frank, Martin, nobody would be good enough for his darling granddaughter. That's understandable, of course. I believe that after we're married he will come round to me. As Sofia's husband is long gone, it will be useful for the old man to have a young son-in-law in the family, and he will surely have the blessing of great-grandchildren. Konstantinos is a very successful sculptor, as you know, but he isn't young any more. He pays for this house and for Angelika and her mother, and another income will be important as he gets older. Don't you agree?"

Day sipped his drink while nodding to save himself from having to speak. Much of this was common sense, but it was expressed with a note of self-regard which Day found quite objectionable. They were not the words of a man in love, as Day understood such things. He wished Angelika would return to the roof terrace.

Angelika soon appeared and, realising that Loukas was not going to help her to bring the dishes up to the terrace, Day insisted on doing so. Together they brought out plates and crockery, a basket of fresh bread, a traditional salad and a deep dish of chicken in a rich and chunky sauce of tomatoes, aubergine and potatoes. There was water and there were jugs of wine. As they helped themselves, Day talked to Sofia about the plants in her roof garden, life in the Kastro, and the friends who visited to play cards and drink coffee with her on a Wednesday morning. As Angelika had assured him, her mother was relaxed and happy, showing no signs of the affliction which was sometimes so severe. Day enjoyed himself. The older woman was charming and spoke with the clear, courteous Greek of an earlier era.

He became aware that, on the other side of the table, Loukas and Angelika were not talking. They ate quietly, Loukas helping himself to more wine occasionally without offering it round. Day felt embarrassed on Angelika's behalf.

"Tell me, what do you think of the amazing Niarchos Foundation project?" he asked them all, hoping to start a table-wide conversation. Loukas answered first.

"The old man has done very well for himself. There must have been hundreds of artists for the Foundation to choose between. It's a huge honour. I'm going to make sure that we, the GNTO, make the very most we can of the final exhibition in the Niarchos Centre. It's going to be a major opportunity to attract international visitors and raise the profile of modern art in Greece. I'm looking forward to it, actually. Between ourselves, I suspect it won't do my career any harm either. That's good for the whole family, no?"

Day smiled at Angelika, then at Sofia, and once again responded with a nod of the head. He later felt that this was the moment when he decided he really did not greatly like Loukas Veakis.

After the meal Angelika offered to show Day round the house before coffee. Loukas announced that he was going off to smoke a cigarette, his tone suggesting that he was not allowed to do so around the house. Once he had gone, Day stood up to follow Angelika, turning to make sure Sofia was content that they should all leave her. She was smiling, and gave a gracious wave as if wishing him enjoyment of her home.

Rather than taking him on a guided tour, Angelika took Day to a small room which had paintings on the walls and two upholstered armchairs, indicating they should sit.

"This is my sitting room," she explained. "We won't be disturbed here. I want to talk to you, Martin. Inspector Nomikos came to see me today, as you said he would, and he was very kind. I expect it was because you had explained to him my relationship to Edward. I'm so pleased that he's looking for whoever did this, and I do find I trust him. After we finished he spoke to Loukas briefly. I don't think I told him anything that he didn't already know."

"It doesn't matter. The police are building up a picture of the days before Edward's death. Andreas - that's Inspector Nomikos - also talked to your grandfather yesterday, to Fotis and Xanthe and even Markos Ioannakis. Then he spent the whole of the evening talking with me. He has a hard job ahead of him, I think."

"When he'd gone and I was thinking it all over, I had a feeling that the Inspector might suspect Loukas in some way. What do you think?"

"I think he simply has to look closely at everyone, Angelika."

"Loukas is … I've known him since we were young. He once told me that when he was about sixteen he knew that he was going to marry me. My mother and my grandfather aren't very happy about it, I think. But even though I became engaged to him, I keep telling him that I'm not ready to be married, because of Mama. I can't leave her, not when she still needs me. I'm rather upset with Loukas for pressurising me to get married and not understanding my feelings about it. Loukas wants me to move to Athens with him, you see, leaving my mother with grandfather at Kato Potamia. Anyway, nothing is going to change for now. Would you really like to see round the house?"

"I'd really like to. It can hardly be more lovely than this room. The paintings are beautiful."

Angelika smiled and offered to tell him about the pictures. She described each one by associating it with a person or an event in the family. Day was impressed to hear that they were all painted by Sofia. They showed Naxos in every light, describing its mountains, beaches and buildings, the sea and the boats, in a way that reminded Day of the French Impressionists. On a small table in the corner stood a statue about half a metre high that Day correctly guessed was made by Konstantinos. It was almost abstract, yet suggested a woman looking over her shoulder.

They moved round the house together talking about the paintings. In the two reception rooms were paintings which he could now identify as Sofia's, and some older pictures in wooden frames. Angelika had stopped talking, and Day realised she was giving him time to realise what he was looking at.

"These are by Artemis?" he asked. "This one? And these two?"

"That's right. She painted very few portraits, and they're nearly all in this room. That one over there is her portrait of my grandfather as a young man. And that one is of my mother when she was about fifteen."

"They're wonderful. I like them very much. Your mother's work too. Do you paint?"

"Yes, but I don't like to see them on the walls. I haven't painted very much recently because I don't make enough time for it. It's important that I spend my time with my mother. If I talk to her, it keeps her in better spirits. If she spends too much time alone, she feels worse. The medication helps, of course."

"I understand."

"Anyway, grandmother was a much better artist than I'll ever be! Has my grandfather told you that he's going to set up a fund in her name to support young Greek painters? Don't you think that's a wonderful idea? He's going to launch it once this Niarchos project is over. He's so proud of her, and it's making him very happy to do this in her memory. You must ask him about it."

"I will. May I ask you something? Where did you come across the box of Artemis's diaries where you found out about Edward?"

"Oh, that's easy. Grandfather gave it to me when my grandmother passed on. He said he wanted me to have something of hers. I put it away safely and forgot about it. So, shall we go back to my mother? Coffee?"

The transition was too sudden for Day, who was imagining the depth of Konstantinos's love for Artemis, and also for his granddaughter. "Thank you for showing me round, Angelika. And for being open with me. I'll do all I can to support you."

She looked at him as if she might laugh it off, but she didn't. Instead she gestured that he should precede her up the steps to the roof terrace. Sofia was still sitting there alone.

"Loukas will have taken a walk to the harbour for his evening smoke," said Angelika. "He won't be back for a long time. I'll bring our coffee up here, unless you're cold, Mama?"

For the next hour, Day, Sofia and Angelika chatted under the stars, the women draped in shawls, all warmed by the coffee and the effortless Greek hospitality.

20

"Morning!" said Day cheerfully on emerging from his room. He was showered, dressed and ready for the day ahead. The sun was barely visible above the hills, indicating that he was up far earlier than he normally entertained. Helen was having a cup of tea and a chunk of buttered crusty bread while answering her emails.

"Was it fun last night?" she asked without taking her eyes from the screen. "I went to bed early with my book but I heard you come in."

"Angelika and Sofia, her mother, were lovely, and we sat on their roof terrace all evening. The Kastro is magical at night, as you know. Their house is large and old, and hung with paintings by Artemis and Sofia."

"You must have been pleased to finally conclude what Edward started."

"Mmm. Yes, I mean, I certainly did have that feeling. It was very good to stand in front of paintings by Artemis. I felt Edward would have liked that. The slight downside to the evening was Angelika's fiancé, Loukas. She's far too good for him."

"You didn't like him, I'm guessing."

"Oh, he's OK, he just has a rather high opinion of himself. And he didn't seem to help Angelika or appreciate her. She actually told me privately that he wants them to get married soon, but she isn't ready and feels he's not sympathetic to her responsibilities towards her mother."

"I hope she's standing firm?" said Helen, who had married very young herself.

"I think so, and she mentioned having the support of Konstantinos. I was very impressed with her mother, Sofia. I'm not very good with illness, I never know what's best to do or say. Sofia was relaxed and happy, we talked and got on well. As Angelika said, Sofia has bad times but she loves having visitors."

"Will you go again?"

"Certainly, if I'm invited. Now, when you've finished that, would you like to look at the list of Edward's art collection with me? Cameron Maxwell sent it through yesterday."

Helen abandoned her emails and joined Day in front of his computer.

"Here goes," said Day, opening the attachment. "It's arranged alphabetically. My God!"

The list had been made on the headed paper of the solicitors Bland and Wilmott. Some names had stood out to Day immediately. Beside him, Helen said nothing.

Art Collection of Professor Edward J. Childe of King's College Cambridge Valuation by Sothebys of London Dated 2/2/95

(Two items removed. Amendments initialled by EJC and David Wilmott of Bland and Wilmott solicitors on 3rd July 1995).

Frederic Edwin Church	*Study of the Parthenon.* Watercolour sketch. (1869)
Henry R. Cook	*Landscape Ionian Islands.* Watercolour. (1853)
Thomas Hartley Cromek	*Temple of Olympian Zeus.* Pencil and watercolour (1845)
Edward Dodwell	*Temple at Sounion.* Three pencil sketches (partial) (1821?)
J. R. Crichton Helpmann	*Portara, Naxos.* Pencil sketch (1852)
Edward Lear	*Landscape near Thebes in storm.* (1848). Dedication: 'For Charles Church'.
Edward Lear	*Euboia.* Pencil sketch (1848?)
Edward Lear	*View of the Acropolis of Athens.* Watercolour. (circa 1845).
Henry Byam Martin	*Parthenon.* Watercolour sketch (1835)
Artemis Pantrakis	*Head of Artemis of Brauron.* Watercolour (1960) **(Removed 1995)**
Artemis Pantrakis	*Ruins at Bassae.* Two pencil sketches. (undated)
Artemis Pantrakis	*Kouros.* Pencil and ink. (1969)
Artemis Pantrakis	*Olympia.* Watercolour. (1972)
Artemis Pantrakis	*Girl with Hare, Brauron.* Pencil and ink. (1960) **(Removed 1995)**
Artemis Pantrakis	*Young man sleeping.* Pencil sketch. (1959)

"Six works by Artemis?" Helen's astonishment reflected his own.

"It can only mean one thing, can't it? Edward bought some of Artemis's work. He must have known about Artemis long before Angelika talked to him. When he spoke to me he told me he'd never managed to find any trace of Artemis after they broke up in 1959, but that clearly wasn't true. He'd been acquiring her work, and if he bought it anonymously or using an agent nobody would know he was the purchaser. Perhaps Edward even knew about her marriage to Konstantinos, and their daughter."

"Why do you think he lied to you?"

"I don't know. It could simply be that he was in the habit of keeping it a close secret and didn't want to share the whole story. You notice something about her pictures? Edward bought the paintings that Artemis made during the summer they were together, or inspired by it. He hasn't bought anything that she made later in life. I respect that. It seems honourable, as if he didn't want to intrude."

"Mmm. You see the amendments, Martin, where two works have been removed? They're both connected to Brauron."

"And they correspond to the paintings which were donated to the museum at Brauron, according to the retired director I spoke to. I assumed that Konstantinos or Artemis herself had given them to the museum. The truth would seem to be that it was Edward who sent them."

"Did you find out when they were donated to Brauron?"

"I think the lady said they were received before she took up her post. That would fit the date on the list showing their removal. I wonder why Edward decided in 1995 to give the paintings to Brauron rather than keep them. They must have held very precious memories for him. I don't suppose we'll ever know."

"Wouldn't you expect the solicitors to draw up a new list, with those pictures removed?"

"Maybe they were left for sentimental reasons."
Day suddenly pointed to the list again, the final item.

"See this? Edward told me that Artemis made a sketch of him asleep and left it for him when she went, a kind of goodbye present. I think this must be that drawing!"

***

They walked into Filoti for coffee at Cafe Ta Xromata. The road was busy with people on their way to work, and they were passed by the bus from Chora heading to Apeiranthos. To their relief the cafe was practically empty. Their coffees arrived with two small pieces of homemade cake on a saucer, gift of the owner.

Both pieces of cake would be for Helen, of course. She was quite content. After a while chatting about Edward's astonishing secrets, Day opened his mobile to check for new messages and was still scanning the phone when Helen had an idea.

"I think I know why Edward didn't tell you that he knew about Artemis's later life."

"Why?"

"Because you were about to meet Konstantinos. Edward also hoped you might work together on his marble programme. It would have made it awkward for Edward if you'd known the truth about Artemis, and it would have put you in an impossible position."

"I think you're right. You know something else? It puts Edward's story of how he and Konstantinos met in a whole new light. They didn't just 'hit it off'. Edward must have known almost at once that he had just met the man who had married his beloved Artemis. No wonder he wanted to see more of Konstantinos. No wonder they went to dinner together that same night."

"And Edward has visited Konstantinos regularly ever since. He must have learned immediately that Artemis was dead, but at least he has seen the place where she used to live. The only wonder is that he never met Angelika."

"He must have heard about her from Konstantinos, and probably longed to meet her, but didn't feel he had the right to initiate it. She wouldn't have known about him, and can never have met him otherwise she would have recognised him in Athens, and I don't think she's been hiding something like that. I expect they never met because Angelika spends all her time with her mother."

"Edward was a dark horse, was he not?" reflected Helen.

Day's phone emitted the noise that indicated the arrival of an email. Day picked it up and opened it.

"It's from Andreas. He's on the ferry back to Athens. He thanks us again for dinner, particularly you for your cooking and general charm! Then he says … mm … he's saying that he's afraid that there isn't much more he can do on Edward's case unless some new information turns up. He's going to do a back-check on Loukas Veakis and confirm his alibi for the night of the murder. Blah blah … no more leads … 'reducing the priority on the investigation'. He says he's satisfied that Angelika had nothing to do with the murder. And he says that he believes the same person is behind Edward's murder and the break-ins."

Day was still reading from the email when the mobile in his hand rang with an incoming call. He deftly pressed the answer button.

"Hi, Peppino. You OK?" He had already guessed that the answer would not be yes.

"Martin. I hope this isn't too early to phone. Konstantinos wants to see you. There's been a third break-in, and this time someone was hurt."

***

Day's drive to Saris EM was a grim one. It was very much in contrast to the happy anticipation he had felt when he driving to Paralia Votsala to meet Angelika three days ago. On that occasion, he had passed the entrance to Konstantinos's place with a smile on his face. Now his mind was clenched with alarm.

Peppino was standing at the gate with Dali the dog waiting for Day. The big Sicilian looked as if he had dressed in haste in the clothes he had taken off the night before. Across the courtyard in the shop the door stood open and Xanthe was using a broom to sweep up a pile of broken pieces.

"Thanks for coming, Martin. Konstantinos is waiting for you on the terrace."

"Who was hurt?" asked Day. He had feared it was Konstantinos himself.

"Fotis. He's going to be fine. They've taken him to the hospital in Chora as a precaution. I'll tell you everything when we're with Konstantinos."

On the terrace overlooking the valley of Potamia, staring not at the view but at Day and Peppino as they came towards him, Konstantinos was looking every bit his eighty years. He stretched his hand out to Day but didn't get up. Day took the proffered hand, but rather than shake it he clasped it in both his own before touching the old man lightly on the shoulder and sitting down next to him.

"Are you all right, Konstantine?" he asked, as if they had known each other for twenty years rather than a couple of weeks. The sculptor suddenly smiled, either at Day's kindness or because Dali had laid his head adoringly on his knee.

"It's so good of you to come, Martin. The police have just left. Poor Fotis. He's been taken to the hospital for a thorough check-up."

"What happened? How did Fotis get hurt?"

At a glance from Konstantinos, Peppino told the story.

"The intruder came again last night and broke everything in the shop. Normally there isn't anyone in the lower buildings at night because Fotis, Xanthe and I go home, and Konstantinos is up in the house with Dali. However, it was Saturday night and Fotis had brought in a few beers and been drinking quite a bit in the store. He decided not to drive home and went to sleep in the storeroom. I gather he does that from time to time and keeps some bedding there. Anyway, he was woken up in the night by the sound of things being smashed. He realised it was coming from the shop and went across the yard to see what was happening. There were no lights on, but there was moonlight and he could see someone wrecking the place. Fotis went in to stop him and was attacked with a piece of wood. He was beaten quite badly and lost consciousness, and didn't wake till about six this morning."

"I found him. We called the police and an ambulance," said Konstantinos, "and Xanthe got here first with some things to clean up Fotis's poor face. Fotis couldn't describe the man because he was dressed in black, including some kind of hat which hid his face, and it was too dark to see much anyway."

"Fotis was very brave and I hope he isn't badly hurt. Was there much damage? Was there any message like last time?"

Peppino answered. "A great deal of damage. Just about all the stock in the shop has been trashed, glass shelves destroyed, the computer thrown against a wall. No message this time. Perhaps Fotis interrupted the man before he had time to leave one."

"The police told me I should get some security, Martin," said Konstantinos. "They think the escalation of violence since the first break-in is something I should be worried about."

"Well, I'm worried too, Konstantine!" said Peppino. "I agree with the police, we should install a security system for you as soon as possible."

"That will take too long, Peppino," said Day. "You must find a security guard to be here overnight until the security system is in place. Look, Fotis interrupted the intruder, he may be frustrated and come back to finish what he started. I think you should move out, Konstantine, until this is all over. You're at risk alone here at night."

"I'll be fine in the house. Dali will take care of me."

"Well, make sure you lock and bolt yourself in at night and get that security guard for the workshop. If the intruder is angry at being disturbed last night he could return and do something even worse. Now, what can I do to help right now? I could collect Fotis from the hospital and bring him back, or take him home?"

Konstantinos looked grateful and Peppino said he would go with Day to the hospital, leaving Xanthe with Konstantinos. Day looked at Konstantinos, and felt guilty that he was keeping secrets from the old man, everything that he now knew about Edward and Artemis, and that he had met Sofia and Angelika. Through this muddled anxiety Day realised that Konstantinos looked almost happy. He couldn't resist asking why.

"What are you thinking, Konstantine?"

"There's one good thing to come out of this, Martin. I'm sure the police suspected Fotis of the break-in before. He had a key, he knew about the kiln, and people always suspect someone with a mental difficulty, don't they? I knew Fotis wouldn't hurt me, he would defend me to the best of his abilities. But now the police know it's not him. A man can't beat himself up."

***

Day and Peppino first went to the shop, where the devastation was appalling. Xanthe was leaning against the counter rubbing her eyes, taking a break from sweeping it into piles. She was happy to go and sit with Konstantinos, give him a cup of tea, some cake perhaps. She looked as if the break would do her as much good as her employer.

Day and Peppino got into Day's car and headed for the hospital. Peppino was quiet. At Chora Day drove round the peripheral road to the hospital, parked in the car park and prepared to get out. Peppino stopped him.

"I think you were right when you said that these break-ins happen at the weekend, so I've decided to stay overnight at the atelier next Friday though to Monday. I'll convince Konstantinos somehow and sleep in the workshop. I can handle myself, don't worry," he grinned, "I'm a Sicilian! I'll try to find a real security guard, but I want to be there myself anyway."

"As you prefer, but this man has shown he can be violent. You know what I'm saying?"

"Yes. I'll be prepared."

Day thought he detected a determination in Peppino's voice which convinced him to leave it there. This man did come, after all, from the home of the Mafia. Day didn't know how much to believe of what he had seen in films, but he guessed that Peppino's must have been a very different childhood from his own.

"You know," Day said, "I can't shake the feeling that all these break-ins are meant to confuse us as much as frighten us. It's a series of distractions."

This was too subtle for Peppino. "Distractions from what?"

"I don't know," muttered Day. "Something much worse."

21

The ringing of a telephone in the night rarely fails to cause a surge of adrenalin, and bad news seems inevitable. When Day reached for his phone on the bedside table and opened it, he was even more concerned to see the caller's name: Konstantinos Saris.

"He tried to kill Dali, Martin! He tried to poison my Dali!"

Konstantinos's voice was ragged. His heart beating too fast for thought, Day shelved his questions and told Konstantinos that he would come straight to the atelier. Making certain that Konstantinos was not alone, Day ended the call and swung his legs over the side of the bed.

It was not quite seven thirty. He dressed quickly, left a note for Helen and grabbed the car keys. He took the road to the marble workshop faster than usual. Only the previous afternoon he had driven home along the same road. Things were serious when less than twenty-four hours passed between incidents at the atelier.

He slowed down to drive through Halki. It gave him a chance to consider whether there might be something in what Andreas had texted yesterday. If Andreas believed that the same perpetrator was behind both Edward's murder and the break-ins, he might actually be right. Two friends, Edward and Konstantinos, both about eighty, both of whose lives revolved around marble, both of whom had loved the same girl, had astonishingly both become the object of somebody's hatred. Edward had been murdered, and Konstantinos was being targeted. What could have made some ruthless individual determined to harm them both?

On pressing the accelerator as he left Halki, Day realised that the hidden agenda he had sensed behind the break-ins might be the intended murder of Konstantinos.

***

Peppino and Fotis were approaching the gate as Day parked on the verge. Fotis had a seriously black eye, a dressing on his forehead and his left arm was in a sling, but he looked less shaken than he had on being collected from the hospital the previous afternoon.

"Let's go up to the house, Martin," said Peppino. "Thanks for coming."

"Tell me what's happened as we walk. I'd like to hear it from you first."

"As I understand it, Konstantinos came down from the house this morning with Dali, who started to bark and run about near the gate - around that big olive tree over there. Konstantinos followed him and found a dead animal next to some half-eaten mess and vomit. It's pretty clear that somebody put poisoned meat on the ground where it couldn't be seen from the courtyard. Dali would almost certainly have found it and eaten it, and that would have been the end of him, but he was up in the house all night and some poor stray mongrel ate the stuff instead. Konstantinos is very upset. It's a horrible sight over there…"

"And Konstantinos didn't hear anything during the night?"

"No, and nor did I. I slept in the workshop last night and I still didn't hear anything. I stayed awake as long as I could, and I sleep lightly. It looks like the guy's taken his revenge for Fotis interrupting him on Saturday night, doesn't it?"

"Either that, or this was always going to be the next incident. The break-ins have been more serious each time, and now it's gone from a decapitated statuette to an actual death. Between you and me, Peppino, the next escalation from the death of an animal is the death of a person. I'll make sure the police take this seriously."

They reached the big house and went in to find Konstantinos and his dog sitting together on the sofa. Konstantinos raised a smile for Day. If he had been emotional earlier, as Day had guessed from his voice on the phone, there was no sign of it now.

"I expect Peppino has told you what happened, Martin," he remarked astutely, continuing to stroke Dali's head. "This proves that these terrible things have nothing to do with Fotis or Xanthe or Markos - they all adore Dali. None of them would hurt him."

"Of course not. Look, we must take more precautions from now on, Konstantine. I'll get the police to provide protection overnight and I'll stay here myself with Peppino."

Konstantinos focussed on his dog's silky coat, and eventually looked up.

"I appreciate how you want to help, Martin, I really do. But I think I'll have to pull out of the Niarchos project. I'm sorry, Peppino. I'll ask them to allow you to take over instead. I can't go on like this. I'm going to do exactly what they said in the note."

"What note?"

Peppino raised a hand in apology.

"There was a note this time. We found it by the dead dog. This is it."

He brought a sheet of paper from his pocket and gave it to Day. The demand was clear: Konstantinos was to pull out of the Niarchos project and everything connected with it, and publish this decision in two of the main Greek newspapers, *Ta Nea* and *Kathimerini*, by Thursday 5th September, or face serious consequences.

"What could be more serious than killing my dog?" muttered Konstantinos. "What kind of wickedness was that?"

Day and Peppino left the question unanswered. Day looked at the note again.

"What does this mean about 'everything connected with the project'?"

Konstantinos bowed his head, and stroked Dali's neck behind his ear before answering.

"Perhaps it's the scholarship fund, Martin. I've been discussing it with my solicitor and the Niarchos Foundation, but nothing is finalised yet. My major pieces from the final Niarchos exhibition were to be sold and the money invested in a fund named after my wife to support young Greek painters who wished to study at the Athens School of Fine Arts. Even if only a handful of students a year could benefit, my Temi and I would be happy. I was about to write a new will to make this secure, but nothing would happen until the Niarchos project had finished. I suppose that's what the note refers to. Of course, Sofia and

Angelika wouldn't be affected. They inherit the house in the Kastro, the atelier and this house, and all my other work and possessions. There is financial provision for Sofia for life and for Angelika until she marries."

"I'm going to see the police," said Day, once he had digested the information and made noises of approval about the scholarship. "Keep Dali in here, because we need to leave the poisoned meat and the dead animal for the police. Peppino and I will spend every night here from now on. One of us will sleep in the workshop and the other with you up here. I don't think there's any danger during the day, so I think you'll be safe here while Peppino comes with me to the police station. When is Xanthe due?"

"Soon, and I have Fotis. Would you ask him to come up, please, as you leave? I'd like his company. And would you put the closed sign on the gate, Peppino?"

With that the old man gave them a wave and bent to stroke his dog.

***

Day and Peppino waited until Fotis arrived to stay with Konstantinos, then walked towards the gates where they met Xanthe arriving. Day explained what had happened as they put up the closed sign, and Xanthe went straight up to the main house to attend to Konstantinos.

"This is obviously serious now," began Peppino, squeezing himself again into the passenger seat of the Fiat with some difficulty due to his size. "Are you thinking what I'm thinking?"

"I'm thinking that Konstantinos's new will could be the key to all of this. It's not about an art exhibition. This is personal and much more sinister. I wish Konstantinos had told us before. I bet he didn't even think to tell Andreas."

217

"It looks like your friend Loukas, Angelika's fiancé, has all the required motivation. The new will doesn't provide for Angelika if she marries."

"I'm not sure, Peppino. Putting aside my personal dislike of the man, the will doesn't leave him badly off, even with the scholarship fund in place. It makes generous provision for Sofia, which means he wouldn't have to support her, and he'll be marrying a wealthy woman if he marries Angelika. Loukas is already earning well, if we believe what he says, so why risk everything to stop the new will? Once Konstantinos is gone, and Sofia provided for, there's nothing to stop him marrying Angelika and living very well between Naxos and Athens."

"Mmm. So you don't think he's connected with Edward's death either? I fancy him for both the murder and the break-ins."

"I'm not sure. He's the only person apart from Angelika who's connected to Konstantinos and also knew about Edward. Andreas Nomikos may be right and the two things are connected, but I'm not confident that Loukas is the man. Nor is Andreas."

They were approaching the final stretch of road to Chora. It was a very pleasant August morning, already warm, a perfect temperature for one of Day's beloved pastimes, coffee at a seafront taverna. However, nothing was further from his mind. There was just time to explain to Peppino how he knew Inspector Cristopoulos of the Naxos Police before they met.

"So you see, the events of last May led Cristopoulos to regard me with decidedly mixed feelings. I thought you ought to know before we go in and see him. On the one hand, I was useful. On the other, I deliberately misled him and that made him feel used. If the outcome had not been successful for him, I think he would have arrested me."

"What exactly did you do, for God's sake, Martin?"

"Long story. I went to talk to a man who had become a killer."

"Respect!" said Peppino, at his most mafioso-like. "You must enjoy living on the edge."

"Not me! I never believed it was a risk, or my strong sense of self-preservation would have kicked in. Cristopoulos never understood that."

"He's a policeman," Peppino said, as if that explained everything. "Where on earth are we going to park for the police station?"

"Ah, I have a secret place."

Day found his parking place and they walked the short distance to the Naxos police station. On the corner of a busy square, the white-painted building was typical of this part of town, but having been acquired by the police it now boasted a secure door and a prominent Greek flag.

"Good morning," Day said to the man on the desk, when they had been admitted. "My name's Martin Day. I need to speak to Inspector Cristopoulos, please."

Before the young officer could reply, a door behind him opened and a short, older man in civilian clothes emerged. He looked like some kind of academic, his jacket casual and unbuttoned, his shirt collar free of a tie. He stopped outside the door and looked hard at Martin.

"I thought I heard that name," he said unsmilingly. "I don't believe it, Professor Day. We meet again. Good morning, Signore Berducci. You'd better come through to my office, gentlemen."

Inspector Cristopoulos may have looked more like a friendly uncle than a senior policeman, but he kept his finger on the pulse of Naxos.

Day reminded him that he wasn't actually a professor, which provoked a wry smile. Day realised that the inspector had been provoking him.

Nothing, of course, had changed in the slightest in the inspector's office in the three months since Day had last been there. Seating himself behind his oversized desk, Cristopoulos peered at them between his two computer screens. He picked up a pair of reading glasses and played with the arms as he waited.

"We're here about Konstantinos Saris," Day said. "Since you were at the workshop yesterday, Inspector, there's been another incident. Someone put down poisoned meat, and it looks like he intended to kill Konstantinos's dog. A stray dog was killed instead. This happened twenty-four hours after the previous break-in when a member of staff was injured, so it seems an escalation of violence with Konstantinos the ultimate intended victim."

Cristopoulos summoned a junior officer to take notes, asked them to give him the details, and listened carefully. He read the demand note which Peppino gave him.

"I'll arrange for the poisoned meat and the dead animal to be removed," he began. "In the context of recent events, and in view of the threatening letter, we will escalate the investigation. Can Kyrios Saris stay elsewhere for the time being, somewhere where he can be concealed and protected?"

"He won't go, Inspector," said Peppino. "He's a stubborn old man of eighty. Can you provide an overnight guard, maybe? Or a visible presence during the day, to deter whoever's doing this?"

"I can and I will, although that will only defer the problem until we remove the guard," answered Cristopoulos. "Leave it with us, Mr Day, I shall give it my urgent attention."

Outside the station, Day turned to the Sicilian.

"Shall we find a cafe? I need a coffee, and we need to make a plan," he said.

"If you hadn't said that, I would have!"

They found a cafe where a row of tables sat up against the sea wall. Here they would benefit from the slight breeze off the sea as well as the excellent coffee served by the taverna. Day ordered his usual frappé, and Peppino ordered a double espresso and a ham omelette.

"I don't work well on an empty stomach," he explained.

By tacit agreement they said nothing of importance until supplied with coffee and omelette. Peppino finished his breakfast with relish and wiped the plate with bread. He waved to the waitress and ordered another coffee; Day was still only halfway down his frappé.

"So, we're going to set a trap."

It was a statement from Peppino. Day found it alarming, not because of its call to action, nor because of the determination in the Sicilian's voice, but because he had been planning exactly the same thing.

22

"So, the attacker gave a deadline of Tuesday 10th, which is a week tomorrow. By that time Konstantinos must have quit the Niarchos project, pulled out of changing his will, and put an announcement in the national newspapers. First question, can we be certain that there won't be another attack before then?"

"I don't think we can rely on it," answered Peppino. "Agreed?"

"I agree. Since you and I will be sleeping in the workshop, and the police involved, I suppose Konstantinos and the atelier will be safe, but I'd feel better if Konstantinos would move in with Angelika and Sofia."

Peppino pulled his mouth into a grimace. "I still think Loukas could be the man behind this, Martin, and if so Konstantinos would be more at risk there than in his own house under our protection."

"OK, let's keep Konstantinos with us. Anyway, we don't want to put Angelika and her mother in danger. So we have to catch this man in the act of breaking in. It's the only way to stop all this."

The waitress appeared at their table and Peppino insisted on paying. When she returned to the bar they continued to sit where they were, formulating their plan.

"Let's consider what we know for a fact," said Day. "The incidents are becoming more threatening, more aggressive, and more frequent. After being interrupted by Fotis, the attacker returned with the poison and the demand note within twenty-four hours. That could mean he was simply frustrated, or it could mean he's up against a deadline. My guess is that the deadline is Konstantinos changing his will."

"Before we assume that, are we sure that the issue isn't the Niarchos project, Martin? The latest demand and the red paint on the wall both specifically mentioned it."

"I can't see what anyone would gain by the Niarchos project being cancelled. I still have a feeling that there's more behind this."

"I don't know, Martin, I don't go in for intuition when it comes to this kind of problem. But I do agree this man is dangerous. We need to bring him out into the open and put a stop to him."

"Spoken like a Sicilian!" said Day. "What do you suggest?"

Peppino sat back in his chair and crossed his arms over his broad chest.

"I spent some time last night thinking this over. First, it must look like Konstantinos is going to do what he's been told, which will buy us time. The intruder must believe that Konstantinos is going to Athens to withdraw from the Niarchos project and tell his solicitor he's changed his mind about the new will. He must really book his ferry tickets, make actual appointments with the solicitor and the director of the Niarchos project, everything must look right. We can even spread the word that I'm going to carry on the Niarchos project from Sicily, although that could be awkward if it reached the ears of the Foundation! That should satisfy the attacker and he should leave Konstantinos alone for now. Then, the day before Konstantinos is due to go to Athens, the day the announcement has to appear in the newspapers, he lets it be known that he's changed his mind. He's now planning to *reaffirm* his participation in the project, *reaffirm* the Artemis bequest, and sign his new will the following day. That will force the attacker's hand, but give him only one specific night on which to act, to prevent Konstantinos leaving for Athens. We will have the police ready, you and I will be ready, trap set!"

"My God, have you done this kind of thing before?" said Day in admiration.

"Not exactly…" Peppino rubbed the side of his nose, the mannerism Day had noticed once or twice already. Day grinned.

"Well, I like it. How do we make sure all this reaches the ears of the attacker when we don't know who he is?"

"We just tell everybody we know, starting with everyone at the atelier and the family, and encourage those we trust to spread the word. Whoever he is, the attacker is close. I could put something on my social media. I'm sure the attacker will have his ear to the ground."

Day smiled to himself at the Sicilian's use of colloquial English. "OK, so our first job is to speak to Andreas Nomikos. He can then tell Cristopoulos for us, and organise the police side of it."

"You think your friend Nomikos will help us, Martin?"

"He'd better. I don't know what else we can do to sort this out."

***

Day drove Peppino back to Saris EM, promising to phone Andreas Nomikos and join Peppino later for the night vigil. A police car was parked outside the gate of the atelier, deliberately visible from the road, and two officers stood talking to Xanthe. Inside the courtyard, the poisoned meat and its unfortunate victim were being removed. Cristopoulos had acted quickly.

As Day drove on to Filoti he thought about his forthcoming conversation with Andreas Nomikos. He was far less confident of convincing Andreas than he had told Peppino. It was fair to assume that the police were not enthusiastic about civilian plans to take the law into their own hands, especially one designed to provoke a criminal attack. Day realised that he was heaving sighs repeatedly, and made an effort to unclench his fingers from the steering wheel.

He decided to have some lunch before phoning Andreas. He chewed bread and ham without thinking what he was eating. He couldn't begin to tell Helen what had been happening. It wasn't really that he wanted to hide it from her, he told himself, it was simply that he felt too weary. He was suddenly so very tired. He'd explain everything to her later.

After a while, he told her that he needed to get an hour of sleep and went to his room. He put on an eye mask, actually got under the sheet and within minutes had fallen asleep. Two and a half hours later he surfaced from a deep slumber and wandered to the shower. He felt very far from recovered but it was nearly four o'clock and he must call Andreas Nomikos. He took out his phone, sat in the chair in his room, and dialled Andreas's mobile. It went to answerphone, on which Day left a very short message.

Andreas returned the call twenty minutes later. Day told him everything clearly and directly, but when he finished there was no response from the other end. Day had to ask what the policeman thought.

"I think this is now a very serious situation, Martin, as I understand you do too. I still think we are looking for the same perpetrator for the break-ins and the murder in Kolonaki. That means, in case I need to say it, that I too believe there is a threat to the life of Konstantinos Saris. I don't know why, any more than you do. Believe me I do understand why you and Berducci have come up with this plan to lure the person responsible into the open, but you won't get my colleague Cristopoulos to agree to it, and I can't condone it either. You must know that. We are the police, you are civilians. The police exist to protect civilians and not allow them to put themselves in danger, at least that's what I've always believed. Agreed? So I am telling you officially NOT to go ahead with this scheme of yours, but to leave it to the police to protect Kyrios Saris and his property."

Day said nothing. He had a feeling that Andreas had not finished yet.

"I am going to give you some very firm instructions now, Martin. I hope you're listening?"

"I'm listening."

"You are to encourage Kyrios Saris to make appointments with his solicitor in Athens and the director of the Niarchos project for, let's see, this coming Friday. He must buy his ferry tickets, and reserve a hotel room in Athens for the night of Friday 6th September, because a man of his age would not travel there and back on the same day. However, Kyrios Saris must not take the ferry, nor keep the appointments, because he might be in danger if he does. You must keep him safely protected, and indeed hidden from view inside his own house for the entire period, and particularly the night of Thursday 5th."

He paused, as if to let his instructions sink in. Day felt the need to prompt him.

"Yes?"

"You must be with Kyrios Saris at all times. Not a moment should you leave him unattended. Do you understand?"

"Yes."

"Signor Berducci can stay with you if he wishes. If you suspect anything at all is taking place on or near the property, you must immediately call me on this number."

"How will that help us, Andrea?"

"I will come to Naxos discreetly in the next day or so. I will take Cristopoulos into my confidence, of course, which is official courtesy anyway. If anything happens - preferably before it happens - you must call me. Understand?"

Day tried to make sure that the smile on his face could not be heard in his voice as he confirmed that he had, indeed, understood. Andreas Nomikos had just agreed to their trap, and moreover agreed to take care of the police end of the arrangement.

"One more thing, Martin. You and I both consider Angelika Spetzou to be a sensible young woman and we are both confident that she's not connected with either crime, so I suggest you take her into your confidence and enlist her help very specifically. She must understand that she must only say exactly what you instruct her to say, when you tell her to say it. She should tell her mother and fiancé *tomorrow morning* of her grandfather's plan to go to Athens on Friday, adding that her grandfather is going to give in to the threats made by the unknown assailant. Then, on Thursday morning, *and absolutely not before*, she must let it be known that she is now worried because her grandfather now intends to confirm the bequest in the name of his late wife and make a new will accordingly."

At his end of the phone Day was nodding. "OK, Andrea. I'm happy to involve Angelika and Peppino. I still need your help with something."

"With what?"

"There's now a police guard up at Saris EM, which I asked Cristopoulos to put in place. I think it will deter the intruder and unless he takes the bait we won't catch him."

Nomikos sighed audibly, as if regretting the abandonment of his coded instructions.

"I think you'll find that the police are unable to supply the guard after today."

"Thank you, Andrea. Peppino and I will be spending the nights at the workshop from tonight onwards, but I'll also let it be known that we can't be there on Thursday night. And I'll take care that Konstantinos's dog is elsewhere that evening too."

"We understand each other then. Goodbye for now, Martin. I'll see you soon."

He rang off. Day had another call to make, and he had to handle it carefully. He needed to explain to Angelika her role in the plan to protect her grandfather.

He need not have worried. Angelika listened intelligently and agreed to do as Day asked. He rang off and sat thinking for a while. He was surprised that Angelika had not queried why he wanted her to pass false information to Loukas. Had she not realised the implications of his instructions?

It would soon be time for him to return to the atelier for the night's vigil with Peppino. When he got there he would have to tell Konstantinos about the plan. He hoped Konstantinos would not protest. He found a bag and filled it with warm clothing for the night, his phone charger and laptop cable. He threw his pillow and a blanket on top and left everything by the front door. At least he would be warm enough and have something to do during the long night.

"Hi. Feeling any better now?" asked Helen, letting herself into the house after a walk.

"Yes, quite a bit better, thanks. Sorry about earlier, I just had to get some sleep. I had a bit of a reaction to the whole situation with Konstantinos. Coffee or tea? I'll make it and bring you up to date."

He carried the drinks out to the balcony, where he found that the heat of August had mellowed into September without him noticing. They sat together in their usual quiet, companionable way while Day marshalled his thoughts. He decided he could simply tell Helen everything. That was a relief - it would keep things simple.

He told her about the poisoning of the dog, Konstantinos's new will and the proposed bequest in Artemis's name. Then he told her of the plan he and Peppino had made, Nomikos's clever endorsement of it and Angelika's acquiescence. Throughout it all, Helen just listened.

"Here we go again, Martin Day," she said when he'd finished, and he knew he was in trouble. "Just like last time, you're diving in like some adventurer and taking needless risks. Believe me, you're an academic, not an action man! Peppino and Andreas have even less sense than you do."

Day smiled. He knew she was not going to make any serious objection after all. She might actually be a little proud of him, but he'd better not assume that. He would be unwise to let her think he even suspected it.

"I won't be alone," he said instead. "Peppino will be there, and what's more, the police will be close by, I'm sure of it. I'll have three sleepless nights, which is a worse prospect at the moment than the thought of an encounter with whoever's responsible. I'm sorry, you're going to have a lot of time alone here between now and next weekend."

"That's not a problem. I'm happy with my own company, as you know. Just keep me informed. Now, you should have something to eat before you go tonight. How long till you need to leave?"

"I'll go soon. I need to get Konstantinos to agree to the plan, and he might need some convincing."

"I'll make something hot for us to eat quickly. It won't be very special, but it'll keep you going."

***

"What are the chances of a break-in tonight, do you think, Martin?" asked Peppino in a low voice.

He and Day were sitting in Konstantinos's living room while Konstantinos made them coffee in the adjacent kitchen. Day shook his head.

"I'd guess he'll wait to see whether his instructions are followed, so nothing will happen tonight. Tomorrow he'll hear the rumour that Konstantinos is going to give in to his demands, and ..."

Day cut himself short as Konstantinos returned with a tray of coffee, but the old man had heard enough.

"What do you mean, Martin, that I'm going to give in?"

The thrust of his chin and the sparkle in his eyes reminded Day of the Konstantinos he had first met with Edward, a witty, feisty old sculptor still at the top of his form. Day hadn't seen that man since. He got up and took the tray from Konstantinos, placing it on the table and handing round the coffee.

"So, you've changed your mind about giving in to the demands, have you, Konstantine? Good, because you're only going to *pretend* to give in, and we're going to catch whoever is doing this. Peppino and I have a plan, and the police are supporting us. It means that by the weekend, all this will be over."

"Well, that would be nice," said the old man, giving nothing away.

Day explained the details to Konstantinos. Nobody apart from present company was to know the truth of the entire plan, not even Xanthe or Fotis. Tomorrow Konstantinos was to ask Xanthe to book him a return ferry ticket to Athens, leaving on the morning of Friday and returning the next day. She must also book him a room in his usual Athens hotel for Friday night, an appointment with the solicitor, and one with the Niarchos Foundation. Fotis too must be aware of these things.

Konstantinos questioned the necessity of lying to Xanthe and Fotis. Day had expected this, and answered that it was important that the news spread so that it reached the man they needed to catch, and it was better that Fotis and Xanthe believed what they were saying than asking them to lie. This appeared to satisfy Konstantinos.

Day went on to explain the rest of the plan. On Thursday morning a very different story was to be given out, which was that Konstantinos had decided not to capitulate after all, and was going ahead with both the Niarchos project and the scholarship fund. He would also be signing his new will.

"The reason for all this, Konstantine," said Peppino in support of Day, "is to provoke whoever is behind the attacks into acting rashly on a specific evening when we will be ready to catch him."

"Oh, that's very exciting," said Konstantinos, to Day's surprise. "I like that. Well done, both of you!"

Konstantinos had clearly recovered his resilience. Day was encouraged, and continued.

"I'm going to get Angelika to help us, but she won't be in any danger."

Day flushed, remembering too late that he hadn't told Konstantinos that he even knew Angelika. He hastened to explain.

"I spoke to your granddaughter, I thought she should know what's going on. I think she should take Dali to her house on Thursday morning to support the idea that you'll be away for a night. She's expecting your call to ask her, and will come and collect him. It's important because we don't want Dali frightening off our intruder before the police can catch him!"

"Agreed."

"So, tonight Peppino and I will stay here. Peppino, why don't you be here in the house, and I'll take the workshop? Tomorrow morning, Konstantinos will start to make the travel arrangements and phone calls. If anyone asks, we're helping him with his difficult decision. Both of us will be here throughout the night every night till this is over, although we'll let it be known that unfortunately neither of us are able to be here on Thursday night."

"I'll be here during the daytime too," said Peppino. "I've brought my stuff."

"What about the police? If they're here, you really don't need to spend all your time babysitting me, Peppino," protested Konstantinos.

"I don't think the police presence will be here after today," murmured Day.

"I see," said the old man. "You mean, they have to go away so your little trap will work."

There's really no fooling Konstantinos Saris, Day concluded. He hoped, however, that the old artist had not understood that his life was now in considerable danger.

23

Day settled himself uncomfortably in a dark corner of the workshop and worked on his laptop until the eyestrain had reached an intolerable level. He closed the laptop, as it was getting late and the glow might be visible from the courtyard. The night was mild, but he was still glad to have the blanket with him, and the pillow went some way towards softening the hard chair in which he was propped. Two in the morning came and went, and there was no sign of an intruder. He moved to the floor and stretched out on some flat-pack cartons, cursing that he hadn't brought something better to lie on. He slept fitfully for the rest of the night, waking every time he turned over, which was as infrequently as possible.

He woke for the final time with the dawn and sat to the side of the window watching the light strengthen until he thought he could reasonably appear at the big house and beg for coffee. He washed his hands and face in the sink by the workbench and ran his hands through his hair. He felt better as soon as he was outside, and made a circuit of the other buildings to make sure everything was undisturbed. The atelier was peaceful, and the morning air was fragrant with late jasmine. Dali barked only when Day knocked on the door, confirming the solidity and soundproofing of the house.

From the look of Peppino he had not spent the night asleep in the spare bed. However, there was a smell of coffee in the air and the Sicilian looked cheerful.

"Konstantinos is getting dressed," said Peppino. "I take it nothing happened down there?"

"Nothing. Just a hundred owls hooting, and I heard most of them. No wonder they're the national bird of Greece. So, our man didn't visit last night. That's good: one night down, only four to go. Let's hope the next three are as uneventful as this one."

"And that the fourth is a riot!" said Peppino under his breath.

Konstantinos came in and proposed coffee in the garden. He unlatched the door that led from his kitchen to a terrace which overlooked the private garden behind the house. A well-made slatted roof supported by stone pillars sheltered a modern table and six chairs draped with hand-woven throws. The garden was full of shrubs and flowers: bright bougainvillea in every colour, giant red-edged succulents, stocky slow-growing pines, and creeping scarlet-flowered geraniums which overflowed from terracotta pots. Day leaned against a low wall and gazed at the beauty of the garden. He noticed a rectangular stone pond to his right, its walls about a metre high, in which water lilies with carmine petals and gold stamens shone in the morning sun.

"This is beautiful, Konstantine," he said, unable to find any more imaginative words. He was still noticing things in the garden: the deep blue of the water between the lily pads, reflecting the pure azure of the sky; huge spiked cacti that had clearly been growing in the garden for decades; a solitary tree, some kind of conifer with gracefully upturned branches; and an elegant, weathered statue of a woman partially hidden by foliage.

"The garden was one of Artemis's passions. Fotis looks after it now," said Konstantinos.

"I hope you slept well?" Day asked, turning to examine Konstantinos's face for signs of stress.

"As well as usual, thank you, Martin. I don't need many hours' sleep at my age. I'm always up early, usually around the dawn. That's when I have my briki of Greek coffee with Dali. It's a routine of ours."

The old man sipped his Greek coffee with pleasure and satisfaction as he spoke. Day was not a fan of Greek coffee, and took his first swallow of the filter coffee made by Peppino with relish and relief, starting to think through what needed to be done that morning.

"So, this morning we must start to put the plan into action. Konstantine, your first job is to go and see Xanthe, and ask her to make your ferry and hotel reservations. Make sure you explain that you're going to tell the Niarchos office that you're pulling out, and your solicitor that you want to keep your existing will and forget the scholarship. You must look very sad, like you believe it. Xanthe must be made to feel really sorry for you, because we want her to spread the word. If Fotis isn't there when you speak to Xanthe, find him and give him instructions for the days you'll be away from the atelier. Make sure both of them know the details of your trip and feel happy to discuss them with other people. Remember, we need this to reach the person behind the incidents."

"I understand, Martin. There's no need to lecture," said Konstantinos mildly, replacing his coffee cup delicately on the table.

"Sorry," smiled Day. "I'll call Angelika and confirm that she'll be hearing from you, Konstantine, to ask her to collect Dali on Thursday morning. So when you speak to her she'll know that you aren't actually going to leave at all and you won't have to lie to her. When you've spoken to Xanthe and Fotis, call Angelika from the shop, it will sound natural and you'll be overheard."

"I'll also ask Xanthe to make me appointments with my solicitor and the Niarchos office," Konstantinos said sternly. "I have a good memory, you know."

"I think you're rather enjoying this, Konstantine," said Day. "Right, I think Xanthe will have arrived by now, so I'll go and chat to her. I can drop in some remarks that will support what you tell her when you arrive. Then I'll come back and call Angelika. See you later. Thanks for the coffee."

***

Day was saddened when he saw the state of the shop. The room, which had been bright and full of tempting items for sale when he had first visited, was no longer impressive. The breakages had been cleared away, but the walls were damaged where shelves had been smashed, it needed completely redecorating. The counter where the computer had stood was empty, only Xanthe herself sat behind it, looking at what Day assumed was her personal laptop. Very few items were on display. They chatted about the expense of the repairs and how much business would be lost during what remained of the tourist season.

"Konstantinos doesn't seem to want to get the shop repaired," said Xanthe sadly.

"He's upset, and who can blame him? What did the police have to say yesterday?"

"They don't say much. They haven't arrived yet this morning either. Were you and Peppino here all night?"

"Yes, and we'll be here tomorrow night too, but after that, well, we can't sleep rough indefinitely."

"No, of course not. At least Konstantinos has Dali. I don't know why he won't go and stay with his daughter."

Through the window Day spotted Konstantinos making his way over the courtyard to the shop. Dali was running in excited circles round him with his little stone. The dog at least was not feeling any stress. Day said goodbye to Xanthe and went in search of Fotis, winking at Konstantinos as he passed him.

Fotis was in the storage building where he spent most of his time, sitting at a table in the window drinking coffee. He stood up awkwardly when he saw Day come in. They had a brief conversation, mostly on Day's side, but Fotis gained in confidence when Day asked to see the various pieces of marble that had arrived for the two sculptors. Fotis also pointed out the containers of different types of clay which Konstantinos used. This gave Day the chance to talk about how Konstantinos was anxious about the break-ins and worried about what he should do.

Leaving Fotis before Konstantinos could arrive, Day returned to the house and called Angelika. When she answered, Day made sure she was on her own and would not be overheard.

"I'm sorry to be so secretive, but as I explained last night we have to be careful at the moment."

"I've thought about what you said last night, Martin. Can I ask a question? Please answer me truthfully."

Day agreed, knowing what she was about to ask.

"You told me last night not to tell Loukas about the real plan, but to make sure he heard the lie about my grandfather going to Athens. You think Loukas is involved in the attacks on my grandfather, don't you?"

"It's complicated, Angelika. I don't know. What's important is that we spread the message, the bait if you like, as widely as we can, not only to Loukas but to everyone connected to your grandfather. Nothing would please me more than to catch somebody outside the family circle in our trap and know for certain that Loukas isn't involved."

Even as he said this, Day knew it was untrue. Day was trying to prevent his antipathy to the man from clouding his judgement, but the more he considered it, the more suspicious of Loukas he became. He was biassed, of course. He didn't want to see Angelika married to Loukas, not because he was attracted to her himself but because she deserved someone better.

Angelika was quiet on the other end of the line. Day forged on.

"I assume Loukas is in Athens at the moment, as it's Tuesday?"

"That's right. He's coming back on Friday for the weekend."

"So, are you ready to start with the first part of the plan? You should make sure that Loukas, Markos Ioannakis, and everybody close to Konstantinos hear about it today. Your grandfather will be calling you soon about Dali, but he'll probably have people with him and not be able to speak freely."

"I always have Dali when grandfather needs to go away," she said. "I suppose you need Dali away from the house to leave the way clear for the intruder? Are you sure grandfather will be safe?"

"I'm sure. Peppino and I will be there, and the police too. Your grandfather is really quite a man, isn't he? He seems to be relishing all this, now that he can see that there's an end in sight."

Day could almost hear the smile on Angelika's face as she said goodbye.

***

Peppino and Day met at lunchtime and reviewed how things had gone during the morning. Konstantinos had put on a superb act and it was clear that Xanthe and Fotis completely believed his decision to give in to the demands. Day decided to go home and return in the evening, while Peppino spent the rest of the day at the atelier working on new designs. If all went well, he said, he and Konstantinos would soon have a lot of work to do to catch up with their schedule for Niarchos.

Before leaving the atelier Day texted Helen to propose lunch at Thanasis's. He had a real need for comfort food and good company. When he reached the house she was waiting at the door, and they took the car to the taverna in case Day needed to get back to the atelier in a hurry. They parked at the side of the road and took the table in the window.

"No wine for me," said Day, "but don't let me stop you."

"No, I'll keep a clear head for work this afternoon. What happened last night?"

"Nothing. Peppino stayed in the house with Konstantinos, and I slept on the floor of the workshop. It was an uneventful night. We had coffee with Konstantinos this morning in a stunning little garden behind the house, and then set the first part of the plan into action."

"What does that involve again?"

"We let the guy think he's won, and that Konstantinos is going to pull out of the marble project. Everything is set up as if he's going to Athens on Friday morning, including the ferry tickets and a hotel booking, and a real appointment with the solicitor. Angelika is working with us: she's going to collect the dog so that it's not in the house on the night of the trap, but it will also confirm the impression that Konstantinos is really going away."

"Clever. Hang on, let's order our food, shall we? What do you want for lunch?"

"Chips," said Day without pausing for thought. "And something filling. I think I'll have a good old moussaka."

Helen smiled at the lunchtime waitress who came to take their order. There was no sign of Thanasis or any of his family.

"Hello. We'd like a moussaka, a yemista, a portion of fried potatoes and a Greek salad, please," she said.

"For the yemista, would you like stuffed tomatoes, stuffed peppers, or one each?" the waitress asked.

"One of each," said Helen, without consulting Day. "Thank you."

They feasted on the dishes, which they shared between them, as if they hadn't seen food for a week. They even finished the basket of sliced crusty bread and almost the entire litre bottle of mineral water.

"That's so much better!" Day sighed.

"You looked absolutely drained when you got back, Martin. Do you have some time to relax before you need to be back at Konstantinos's?"

"Yes, hours! Some of that is going to be spent thinking, and the rest catching up with sleep."

***

After his filling lunch, Day decided to begin with the sleep and do his thinking, such as it might be, when he woke. He lay on his bed with the window open, enjoying the warm, clean air that cooled his right cheek and the faint scent of herbs and grasses. Just as he thought sleep would never come, it did. He woke feeling better, and lay listening to the silence. No sound from the rest of the house. He concluded Helen was either also resting or working quietly in her room. He checked his phone.

There was a message from Peppino reassuring him that everything was calm at the atelier, and a formal invitation from Dr Maxwell to the event in celebration of Edward in Cambridge in a few week's time. Maurice had emailed to ask for an update on the biography of Nikos Elias, which caused a pang of guilt when Day considered how little time he wanted to give it. Maurice followed this with a kind enquiry into his health, by which Day understood him to mean emotional health, and a reassurance that a delay in producing the work would not be the end of the world. Lastly, did Day intend to take on Edward's Greek Marble series, Maurice wanted to know. If so, with whom would he want to work? A couple of names were mentioned for Day's consideration, academics who would be more than capable of co-writing the programmes which Day would present.

Day closed his phone; he couldn't think of all that now. Some things were more important than work. Quietly, caught unawares, he thought of Deppi on the yacht, looking proudly at her son. Day sighed, and put the image of her aside.

He showered, dressed and re-packed his overnight things. He made a cup of tea for Helen and a coffee for himself, and Helen joined him on hearing the kettle. She took her tea back to her room to continue working, and Day felt guilty, knowing he had time to work on the Elias chapters but a strong disinclination to do so. He emptied the contents of a box of Nikos Elias's papers onto the table, opened his laptop and spent a couple of hours stoically working on the biography. The next chapter would concern Elias's earliest references to the Mycenaean tomb which he had not lived to excavate. Before long, despite his preoccupations, Day was completely absorbed.

When it was nearly time to go to the atelier for the night, Day ate a few things from the fridge, drank some mineral water, and made sure he had anything he might need. Saying goodbye to Helen, he took the road yet again for Kato Potamia.

***

Day and Peppino prepared to stay awake for a second night. It was Peppino's turn to take the workshop, and they didn't spend much time talking before Peppino took himself off for his lonely vigil and a few hours working on his designs. Day settled himself in an armchair in the living room with his laptop, while Konstantinos, Dali by his side, watched the television.

At eleven o'clock Konstantinos switched off the television and fetched a glass of water for himself and one for Day.

"I really am grateful to you and Peppino, Martin," he said. "You're very good friends to me. I'm sorry you're getting so little sleep. You're very welcome to use the spare room …"

"That's OK, I'll be fine in here, and I don't want to get too comfortable in case I nod off. Could you tell me one thing? Where will you be sleeping?"

"Oh, my room is through there and on the right. Let me show you round the house. You should know the layout."

Konstantinos gave him a tour. The house had been well modernised with quality materials and good taste. Day tried to memorise it so he could find his way round in the dark if necessary.

One of the last doors Konstantinos opened was to his study. Day knew what he would see on the wall: Artemis's portrait of Angelika, the picture that Peppino had photographed and sent to him. The actual picture, its brush marks as powerful as if carved on the canvas, made a strong impact on Day. He stifled a comment on what a good likeness it was, as he had not told Konstantinos that he had met Angelika. He settled for expressing his genuine admiration.

Konstantinos was gratified, and told Day that the portrait had been painted by his late wife. After a short pause the old man added that Angelika would have been about twenty when the portrait was made. The picture was a fine work, and the woman in it was as lovely as Day had found her in person.

"I'm extremely proud of my granddaughter. She looks after her mother, who has been quite ill for some years and needs almost constant care. Both of them, my daughter and my granddaughter, are also painters. My wife taught and encouraged them both."

"Your late wife was an exceptional artist," Day said, feeling deceitful because he meant to get as much from Konstantinos as possible about the mysterious Artemis. "This painting is outstanding."

"She gained quite a reputation but she preferred to avoid publicity. She only sold through one gallery in Athens, and the people who bought her work were asked to respect her wish for privacy. They seemed to keep their word. One or two collectors repeatedly bought her paintings, but I have her best work, believe me. One day I'll hold an exhibition."

"What was your wife's name, Konstantine?"

"As an artist she used her maiden name, Artemis Pantrakis. She didn't use Saris professionally so that our lives would remain private. She must seem to you a very secretive person, but in reality she was just the opposite. There were no secrets between us, Martin, you see. I'll tell you something about Temi - that's what I called her. I met her in 1959, after she'd been travelling round Greece alone, determined to improve her skills as a painter and making many wonderful sketches, pencil drawings and watercolours of the ancient sites around Greece. She loved marble and was interested in trying to draw and paint marble sculptures and marble temples." He chuckled. "I think Temi loved me because I worked with marble before she ever loved me for myself. I fell deeply in love with her, Martin, probably more deeply than she with me. The French have a good saying: 'In love there is always one who kisses and one who is kissed'.

"I was the one who kisses, but Temi was very fair to me. When she understood how I felt about her, she told me that she had just ended a relationship and was expecting a baby. She thought it would scare me away, I expect. It didn't. We married soon afterwards, and it was the best thing I've ever done."

"What a love story," said Day quietly. His head was spinning. "A perfect outcome for you both."

Konstantinos looked at him sharply, but not in any way critically. It was the look of a teacher towards an intelligent child who has simply misunderstood the question and arrived at the wrong answer.

"In every way but one, it was a perfect outcome. We had a very blessed life together. We both loved that baby before he was even born, but he didn't survive to grow up. He lived only two days after first taking a breath. Temi and I were heartbroken, but it brought us even closer. We decided to try for another baby as soon as she could safely be pregnant again. Our lovely Sofia was born a year later."

"I hope for your sake that Sofia's illness was not from birth?"

"No, thank God no. It began when her husband left her when Angelika was small. He was not a good man, and Temi and I weren't sorry to see him go, but things were hard for Sofia. We told everyone that her husband had died. Sofia's problems worsened when we lost Temi, as you can imagine. Temi's death affected the whole family, but Sofia the most."

Day could find nothing to say. Konstantinos closed the door to the study and walked with Day back to the living room. Picking up his glass of water again, Konstantinos turned to face Day.

"My granddaughter is engaged to be married, Martin. She has agreed to marry a boy she's known for years, but I don't think she loves him. It's not up to me, of course. I'm just worried because of what happened to Sofia when she married the wrong man. All may yet be well. My granddaughter is not naming the wedding day because she wants to look after her mother, and that's not something most young men have in mind, is it? I pray that it all ends well. I couldn't bear to see Angelika suffer as Sofia did."

24

The Tuesday night vigil was also undisturbed. Day spent the following morning analysing everything he knew about Edward's murder and the break-ins, then considered Edward and Konstantinos themselves, looking for any good reason why someone would commit an apparently motiveless murder or series of attacks against an inoffensive old man. This was the kind of thinking that Day was good at, although he was hampered now by lack of sleep. He ended up feeling he was missing something obvious.

That evening, Wednesday, Peppino took his turn in the big house again and Day was back in the workshop. Day expected another appalling night, but that was not what eventually happened. In the small hours of Thursday morning, when Athena's owls were hooting in the darkness and Day lay listening on the workshop floor, his mind cleared and with astonishing clarity he realised that the answer was quite simple. He knew who was responsible for the break-ins and who to expect the following night. Within minutes he fell asleep knowing nothing would occur to disturb him. The disturbance would take place on Thursday night as they had planned, a night during which he would not get any rest. If he was right, the perpetrator had very serious intentions.

***

Day joined Konstantinos and Peppino at eight o'clock the next morning for coffee in the garden as before. He may have looked rough, but Day was feeling elated. He decided not to share his breakthrough with Konstantinos, and he had no opportunity to speak to Peppino alone.

Just after nine they went down to the atelier to stage the second act of the trap. Fotis and Xanthe had arrived, and Angelika's car was slowly climbing the gravel road to the gate. Dali bounded to greet her, wagging his tail and dropping his pebble repeatedly at her feet when she came in. Konstantinos was clearly delighted to see his granddaughter. They had a long hug before releasing each other and turning to Day and Peppino.

Angelika greeted Peppino and Day as if she hardly knew them. Day imagined that, like him, she hated deceiving Konstantinos. Peppino, who really was meeting her for the first time, covered the moment with a display of Italian good manners.

Angelika had come to collect the dog and was not in a rush to get home because her mother's 'Wednesday morning friends' were with her. She linked arms with her grandfather and they walked slowly towards the terrace, Angelika kicking Dali's pebble from time to time. Xanthe came out of the shop to embrace her, and Fotis emerged from his storeroom to kiss her on both cheeks. Day watched him do this with interest. It was the first time he had seen Fotis lose his shyness.

As sparky as a magpie after a good night's sleep, Konstantinos took his chance to initiate the final phase of the trap. He had chosen a good moment, when everyone was present.

"Angelika, my dear," he said without preamble, as if the news was so exciting that he could not contain himself a moment longer. "I've had a change of heart! I'm an old man but not, I hope, a coward. I shall not give in to the threats we've been receiving, and I shall not be dissuaded from my original intention of fulfilling the Niarchos project. I'm going to Athens as planned, but to confirm my intentions, and put all the arrangements in place! I feel so much better now I've made my decision. I know this is the right thing to do. And I'm going to get the solicitor to go ahead with the scholarship fund!" The old man opened his arms in a gesture that included them all. "My friends! My wonderful family! Thank you for your love and support. Doing the right thing is the surest way to combat the forces of evil. Don't you agree?"

There was a group exclamation of approval and Angelika, who knew this to be part of Day's plan, added how glad she was to see Konstantinos looking happy again. Day knew that her words concealed reservations, and that she was placing her faith in him to protect her grandfather. He caught a sharp glance from her before she turned back to Konstantinos and listened as he talked enthusiastically. In Xanthe and Fotis, Day saw only delight and respect.

A clenching in his stomach told Day that he was relishing this, including the threat of danger and violence. The trap had been set.

***

Angelika gathered up Dali and his paraphernalia, and took him away for his mini-break in Chora. Konstantinos walked over to the shop with Xanthe to listen to her suggestions for refurbishment, and Day heard him asking Xanthe to telephone Markos Ioannakis and ask him to call the following Monday. He had, he said, something good to tell Markos, something he would be confirming while in Athens.

Thus Konstantinos ensured that word would reach Ioannakis too. Day admired the old man's grasp of the situation. The sculptor ambled back to Day and Peppino looking pleased with himself. He was clearly enjoying this, except for one thing.

"I don't like deceiving my granddaughter," he observed. "I shall apologise to her when this is all over."

"So shall I," said Day.

"Is there any chance that something will happen during the daylight hours, do you think? Should we be on our guard?" went on Konstantinos.

"I don't think the intruder will hear of your decision to confirm a new will until later today, so he's not likely to act till tonight. He's desperate, but so far he's been careful not to risk getting caught. We mustn't be complacent, though. One of us will stay here with you all the time."

"Thank you, Martin. I'll go and prepare some items for Markos, I think. See you both later."

He pushed himself up again from his chair and walked to the workshop, where he left the door open for fresh air and could be heard humming to himself. Day and Peppino agreed that the plan was going very well.

Day's mobile emitted a beep to indicate the arrival of a text.

"This is from Angelika," he told Peppino. "She says that she's sent a message to Loukas and included her grandfather's change of plan. She's chatted about it with her mother, although she doesn't think her mother will speak to anyone, and she's about to go to see Markos Ioannakis in his Chora shop where she will let him know too. She says that both her mother and her fiancé seemed pleased. She also told them that you and I won't be here at the atelier tonight. Will you make sure Fotis and Xanthe are aware?"

"Of course. What about the police?"

"I'll text Andreas now to find out his plans."

He sent a message to Andreas, and they waited for a reply. Nothing came through.

"Odd," said Day. "Maybe he'll get back to me later."

"We can handle it, Martin," said Peppino, grinning. "I'm rather looking forward to catching the bastard."

"Let me tell you what I've been thinking," said Day, echoing the Sicilian's enthusiasm and preparing to explain the result of his nocturnal reflections.

***

That afternoon Konstantinos asked Fotis to kindly get out a small suitcase for him, as he was about to pack for his trip. He asked Xanthe for confirmation of his ferry bookings and the times of his appointments in Athens, all the phone numbers he might need, and the details of his overnight hotel booking. As he did so he laughed at himself, saying his memory wasn't all that good any more and he liked to have everything written down.

When Fotis brought his case, Konstantinos actually packed. Everyone heard Peppino offering to collect him and take him to the ferry at nine o'clock. Nobody could be in doubt that Konstantinos was leaving for Athens the next morning.

There was still no reply from Andreas Nomikos, but Day decided against calling Cristopoulos instead. Andreas would not let them down, he was certain of that.

Konstantinos told Fotis and Xanthe to go home at four o'clock as there was no work to do, and Day and Peppino made a show of leaving at the same time. For half an hour Konstantinos remained at the atelier alone. Neither Xanthe nor Fotis had been happy to leave him, but the old man had stubbornly dismissed their protests, saying he would lock himself in the house and if he heard anything suspicious he would call the police.

Once Fotis and Xanthe had really gone, Day returned in the Fiat with Peppino. They hid Day's car in Konstantinos's garage, joined Konstantinos in the house, locked the door and closed the shutters.

"Do you think we should both stay here with Konstantinos tonight, or should one of us be in the workshop?" asked Peppino.

"There's a chance that he won't come directly to the house," said Day, avoiding using the name of their expected visitor. "And we don't know what he might be planning to do. He could decide to start a fire in one of the lower buildings, for instance. One of us needs to be down there, the other up here. OK? We'll text to alert each other if anything happens."

"I'll take the workshop then, Martin. If I hide myself by the window I should see anyone coming up from the road before you do up here."

"OK, I'll take the house. God, I wish I'd thought to bring some food," grumbled Day. Inexperienced at this kind of thing, Day had not eaten enough and been attacked by a ravenous hunger. In the films he had seen there was never a point at which the hero needed to eat.

"I have enough for us all," said Konstantinos. "And I have plenty of coffee to keep you boys awake!"

After the meal Konstantinos put on the television and washed up as he would normally do. Peppino went straight to the courtyard, discreetly checked the various buildings, then created himself a lookout in the workshop from which he could observe the access road, the gate, the courtyard, the shop and the storeroom. He checked his torch and ensured his mobile was on silent.

In the house, Day too checked his mobile. He knew it was on silent, but he hoped to find a response from Andreas. There wasn't one. Day began to be concerned. He sent Andreas another message, saying that Peppino and he were in position. That too failed to bring a reply. If there was a signal problem, Day thought, this was going to be a disaster.

Day went round the house for a final time, checking that doors and shutters were securely locked, but removing the keys from the keyholes and ensuring the bolts on the main door weren't fastened. He knew the intruder had a key and he wanted him to get in because it was the only way to catch him. Satisfied, Day concealed himself in the study, the room that gave him the quickest access to Konstantinos during the night. If the intruder got past Peppino, Day expected him to enter the house by the main door and make directly for the old man's bedroom, where only Day stood between Konstantinos and harm.

If Day was right in guessing the attacker's identity and motive, the man intended to kill Konstantinos to achieve what he wanted. In fact, as Day had sensed from the start, the series of break-ins, demands and threats had been a smoke screen to conceal the attacker's actual intention from the start: the murder of Konstantinos Saris.

Waiting silently in the study beneath Artemis's portrait of Angelika, Day heard the television being switched off and Konstantinos's voice quietly saying good night as he walked past the study door. Day's mobile phone lay open on the desk ready for a call to Andreas or Peppino, and a large torch was within easy reach. Konstantinos's bedroom door closed quietly on the other side of the corridor, and Day resigned himself to many hours of wakefulness, cramp, and something more unusual. An unaccustomed amount of adrenalin. This was not something that Martin Day the archaeologist, Martin Day the TV presenter, Martin Day the writer, had ever expected to be doing.

***

Two o'clock in the morning. Day flexed his hands for the hundredth time and extended his legs. He wondered what was happening in the atelier below. He was not in the least afraid of falling asleep. He had heard every owl that hooted, every car that passed along the road below the atelier, though they had been few. No car had slowed, much less stopped. He wondered where the police were, but all he could do now was trust Andreas. He was relying primarily on Peppino and on himself. He wondered whether Konstantinos was actually asleep, his little bag packed in the corner of the bedroom, no Dali to keep him company. He imagined the man he suspected of planning to kill the sculptor even now driving towards the atelier. Where would he leave his car? Would Peppino hear it? Day didn't expect to hear any car through the solid house walls. What would be his first indication that their expected intruder had taken the bait?

If, that is, the bait was taken.

Day quietly stood up to stretch. The study door was open just a crack, and now he opened it a little further so that he could hear the smallest noise from within the house. He listened for a while but there was nothing. Then he heard something, a slight scratching sound. His stomach dropped violently as adrenalin surged through him. He stepped quietly back to the desk, lifted his mobile, flicked to the message he had already prepared, and sent it to Peppino and Andreas. He knew now what the sound had been: a key being introduced to a lock in the darkness, the scratching sound as it found the place and entered a keyhole that was nearly invisible, and the rasp as it was quietly turned.

Day prepared himself. The noise had not come from the main door but from the outer kitchen door, the one leading from the kitchen to the garden. The kitchen door had no bolt. Their intruder knew the house well, and possessed a set of keys. Another noise, really faint, told Day that the outer kitchen door had been closed again, and the intruder was now inside the kitchen. Day braced himself to intercept the man as he came towards Konstantinos's bedroom. A small bronze sculpture on the desk would make a handy weapon if he needed one.

Nothing happened. The kitchen door remained closed, and Day thought he might have imagined it all until he heard small noises from within the kitchen. What the hell was the guy doing? Making coffee?

Day picked up his torch but didn't switch it on. He padded to the front door and opened it silently. Peppino was standing there in the moonlight, a threatening silhouette with broad shoulders and wild black hair. He edged in past Day, who shut the door behind him noiselessly. Day pointed towards the kitchen. Peppino nodded. Silently they walked towards the closed kitchen door, fearing to make a noise and alert the intruder. Something salty trickled into Day's right eye.

Whoever was in the kitchen must now be standing stock still, making no noise. Had they been heard? He caught a glance from Peppino, but if it was an instruction it was lost on Day. A second later the Sicilian had put his shoulder to the kitchen door and burst through. Day followed close behind and hit the light switch hard with his hand. In the sudden glaring light he saw a truly frightening Sicilian with one huge arm round the intruder's neck, his other hand pinning his right arm behind him. Day thought it was over, but it was not.

Loukas Veakis was not surprised for long. Shouting with rage he crouched and twisted, loosening Peppino's hold on him. As he twisted round to attack the big man he grabbed a kitchen knife from the rack on the counter. Instinctively Day grabbed the marble ashtray from the centre of the kitchen table and brought it down hard on Loukas's shoulder, making him drop the knife. This was all Peppino needed to retake control, and he quickly had his victim immobilised. Loukas let out a stream of abuse in the fastest Greek that Day had ever heard, none of which was like anything he had ever been taught at school.

"Call the police," Peppino shouted above the noise. "I've got him."

***

Several police cars arrived noisily within minutes, responding to Day's original text from the study. Clearly they had been nearby already. Day had switched on all the exterior lights and beckoned them up from the courtyard. He could see Nomikos's mane of fair hair among the first of them.

Konstantinos peered out of his bedroom door and came into the living room, still fully dressed. He stared open-mouthed at the man who had wanted to marry his granddaughter resisting Peppino's hold and shouting abuse. The police ran into the house, took Loukas from Peppino, handcuffed him and made him sit on a kitchen chair. A young officer guided Konstantinos to the sofa despite his protestations.

Day looked over at Peppino to check he had not been hurt. The Sicilian gave him a thumbs up. The kitchen knife lay on the floor where Loukas had dropped it. Loukas was now silent, staring at Day with loathing.

"Empty his pockets," Andreas ordered one of the policemen, "and bag the knife. Then take him to the station and charge him. Illegal entry, criminal damage, actual bodily harm and intent to commit murder."

The officer searched Loukas and placed what they found on the kitchen table in front of Nomikos. Loukas was then pulled to his feet and taken out. The front door closed behind them.

"Martin, talk to me," demanded Andreas.

Day obeyed. He succinctly described everything from hearing the key in the lock to the knife attack on Peppino, not forgetting his own use of the marble ashtray.

"I don't get it, Andrea," concluded Day, speaking quietly so Konstantinos would not hear. "What was he doing in the kitchen? Why not go for Konstantinos?"

Andreas did not answer directly. He glanced into the living room at the old man, who was clearly straining to hear what was being said. He gently closed the door and pulled on plastic gloves. He turned to the items on the table which his officer had taken from Loukas.

"Let's see," he said, carefully moving the objects around and isolating a small set of keys. "Angelika's spare keys, I suspect. She told me she had a set in case of emergency, but they were safely in her possession. Veakis must have made copies. This one is probably the front door key, kitchen door here, and these could be to the shop and workshop. This is how he could get in each time."

"I should have thought of that," muttered Day crossly. "Of course she would have had a spare set of keys."

"Veakis didn't bring a weapon," observed Andreas, "which is surprising, although he improvised with the kitchen knife. Ah, what's this?"

He had opened Loukas's wallet and extracted a small plastic bag. Peppino leaned in for a closer look. There were traces of white powder still in the bag.

"Drugs?" Peppino asked.

"Possibly," said Andreas, replacing the bag. "We'll get it analysed. Have you noticed the coffee pots?"

Day looked. Konstantinos kept two coffee containers by the stove, ceramic pots of his own making fitted with airtight seals. Day had noticed similar ones in the shop. One of the pots, the white one, was in the middle of the counter as if it had just been used, and its lid was off.

Andreas instructed his officer to call the scene of crime officer to come at once. "Stay here and make sure he takes those coffee pots and the knife. The ashtray too."

He picked up the set of keys, put them in an evidence bag from his pocket, and opened the door to the living room. Konstantinos looked up at them expectantly. His eyes darted from face to face as his living room filled with people.

"Inspector Andreas Nomikos of the Athens Police, we met recently. Have you been hurt?"

Konstantinos looked impatient. "I'm absolutely fine, thank you. No need to fuss. I slept through the whole thing!"

"Excellent," said Andreas. "Do you feel able to answer a few questions? Firstly, did you recognise the intruder?"

"Naturally. My granddaughter's fiancé, Loukas Veakis."

"Does your granddaughter keep a set of your house keys?"

"Yes, she does. She tells me that's in case she has to rescue me."

"A sensible precaution. Do these look like your keys?" He produced the set of keys from his pocket and showed them to Konstantinos.

"Yes, I'd say so."

"Tell me about the two coffee containers in your kitchen."

"What about them, Inspector? I keep my coffee in them. One is for filter coffee, which I keep for visitors such as Peppino because I know he prefers it. The other is for Greek coffee, which I prefer. I drink some every morning when I first get up, and another in the evening after dinner."

"And which pot contains that?"

"The white one."

"Mmm. Last question. Why might Loukas Veakis want to prevent you from going ahead with the Niarchos project?"

"I can't think of any reason at all. The Niarchos project would have brought kudos on the whole family, and it would have been good for Loukas in his work with the National Tourist Office. Oh dear! When the break-ins began and it seemed the intruder wanted me to quit the project, the only person I thought of was poor Markos, my good friend… Oh, I must apologise to him…"

"Then perhaps the Niarchos project was never what most interested Veakis," said Andreas. "I believe you were about to go to Athens and visit your solicitor? You intended to discuss a change to your will, I believe? How would that have affected Veakis?"

Konstantinos did not answer immediately and everyone waited. At first he appeared not to answer the inspector's question.

"The main reason that I intended to change my will was to fulfil an ambition which my late wife and I discussed before she died. We wanted to make financial provision, as far as we could, for the education of talented young Greek painters who were without the means to study at a good art school. I've been setting this up for some time, and was about to confirm it with my solicitor, together with an appropriately revised will. To fund the scholarships, my personal sculptures from the Niarchos project would be sold after the final exhibition, and the money invested. The scholarships would be funded by the income from the investment."

"Very admirable, Kyrie. I don't understand how it would affect Loukas Veakis."

"I was about to explain. I would never stop my granddaughter from making her own free choice of husband, but I didn't like Loukas Veakis. Angelika and Sofia are my only family. The man who marries Angelika will be very wealthy after my death. There are the two properties and my personal assets, and my larger pieces fetch quite remarkable amounts of money on the international market. I still own many of them. I suspected Loukas of being less interested in the lady than in her inheritance.

"As a result of the scholarship fund, however, the major pieces I create during the next three years would not form part of Angelika's inheritance. That is one thing that may have angered Loukas Veakis, Inspector, but it is perhaps not the worst thing. My revised will contains a clause very relevant to him.

"A fund for my daughter Sofia is to be administered by the solicitors, providing money for her lifetime to which Loukas would not have had access. The same for Angelika, but only for as long as she remained unmarried. In my opinion, when a woman marries, her husband is the bread-winner. On her marriage, all the money intended for Angelika would go immediately into a trust for any children she may have, money which they alone could access upon reaching the age of eighteen. If Angelika were to have no children, and if she remained married, the money would go into the scholarship fund after her death. If the marriage were to end in divorce or separation, the solicitors were instructed to administer the money for the benefit of Angelika only."

Day and Peppino exchanged glances. Day nodded to himself. Although these details were new to him, he had sensed Loukas Veakis's greed, his desperate desire to secure himself a fortune. Greece could be a hard country in which to be poor, but Loukas had not simply wanted security from poverty. Loukas had seen the chance to become extremely wealthy. Day guessed that Angelika would have told Loukas about her grandfather's new will, encouraged perhaps by Konstantinos himself in order to test the young man. At that point, from anticipating a fortune on which he had counted for many years, Loukas had realised he was looking at a comfortable but unexceptional future as Angelika's husband. That is, if they married after Konstantinos had signed his revised will.

Angelika herself had not been enough for Loukas Veakis. Day wondered whether Loukas had intended only to terrify Konstantinos into a change of mind or had decided on a more permanent solution. It would be up to Andreas to find out.

Andreas had heard all he needed for the time being. He thanked Konstantinos and stood up to take his leave. He explained that his officer would remain in the house until the scene of crime people had finished, and asked Day to go to the police station in Chora to make a statement before midday. They walked together to the door.

"Well, Martin, once again your unconventional intervention has been successful. A very serious situation has been averted." Andreas crossed his arms and looked at Day directly. "I may be the only policeman in Greece who would have allowed you to do what you have done. You haven't let me down. Cristopoulos will take over the case now, and I shall return to Athens. I'll be on Naxos for another couple of days, though, and I'd be grateful if we could meet. We can make the arrangement by text."

"Thanks, Andrea. Of course."

"Goodbye, Martin. Get some rest."

Day went straight to the study to call Angelika. It was not yet dawn, but he wanted to call right away. He did not relish the prospect of the news he had to give her about her fiancé, but he knew she wouldn't have slept much for worrying about Konstantinos.

"Angelika? It's Martin. Your grandfather's fine, and you can come and see him any time you want. The intruder did arrive tonight and the police have arrested him. I'm sorry, Angelika, I'd better just tell you straight away. It was Loukas."

25

Day returned to the living room where Konstantinos and Peppino were sitting at the dining table. The dawn light was feeble and the room felt cheerless, like a house where someone had died. Lack of sleep made Day feel cold, and the aftermath of the adrenalin was worse than a hangover.

"Is it all over now?" Konstantinos's voice sounded older and more weary now that the police had gone and he was among friends.

"I believe so," said Day. "Loukas will face charges for tonight and for the other break-ins. I'm sure Angelika won't have anything more to do with him, and I doubt you'll see him again."

"I didn't hear him at all from the workshop, Martin," interrupted Peppino, still working through the events of the night.

"He must have parked and walked the last few metres. The police will find the car."

"*Minkia!*" exclaimed the Sicilian, the expression needing no translation for Day. "I need some sleep! I'm going to get my head down in the spare room for a few hours. If that's all right with you, Konstantine?"

"Of course, Peppino, go ahead."

The door closed after him, and Konstantinos stretched with a sigh. Day suggested that he too should get some rest, but the old man shook his head.

"Xanthe and Fotis will arrive in a few hours and they'll be worried if they don't see me. You don't need to stay with me, Martin, you should go home and rest."

"I'm fine. I've just spoken to Angelika and she said to tell you she'll be here as soon as she can get a friend to stay with her mother."

"Poor Angelika, what a shock for her. I can't say I'm surprised, now I've thought about it. I always had a feeling that Loukas was one man on the outside and another on the inside. I'm relieved we've discovered his true nature before Angelika was tied to him. But I'm so sorry for her."

"It will be hard at first," said Day, "but I think she knew that Loukas wasn't the right one."

"Well, she'll talk to me about it when she's ready," said Konstantinos. He looked at Day as if considering whether to tell him something else. "Angelika is like her grandmother, Martin, and Temi was completely open and honest. I told you that she was expecting a baby when I met her, didn't I? She was quite open about it with me. You may be surprised at what I'm going to tell you now, but I think it's right that you know the rest, as a friend of Edward's.

"Temi not only told me that she was pregnant, she told me about the baby's father. That was Edward, of course. I suspect you may have guessed. She told me that she'd left Edward because she didn't want him to be trapped into marrying her. She left in the night while he was asleep because she knew he'd try to stop her, and she would have found that too hard. She adored Edward. She wrote to him some time afterwards, and I was with her when she wrote the letter. She sent it to his Cambridge college. In the letter she told him that she'd met me and we were going to get married. She didn't give my name or our address, and she didn't mention the baby. She begged Edward not to try to find her. I don't know if Edward received the letter, because we never heard from him. I like to think he was respecting her wishes."

"She didn't tell Edward that she was carrying his child?"

Konstantinos winced, but shook his head. So, twenty-year-old Artemis had decided on a clean break with Edward, willing to accept that her English boyfriend would consider her to be the kind of girl who flitted carelessly from one man to another. She had pretended not to care for him, which must have hurt both of them very much.

Day had no idea what to say. He studied Konstantinos like he would an ancient text that had suddenly revealed its true meaning, unguessed, surpassing expectation. As his understanding grew, the sweep of time presented itself to Day. The two old men had known about each other for decades. When they had met by chance in old age, they had seen no reason to speak of it, maintaining the secret of the past sixty years. And they had become friends.

"I'm glad to have had the opportunity to share this with you, Martin," said Konstantinos. "You were a good friend to Edward despite knowing him so short a time, and I owe him more than you can imagine. I've always felt the weight of how much I owe him. I never spoke to him honestly."

Day realised it was time for some honesty of his own.

"There's something I think Edward would want me to tell you now, Konstantine. In fact, I know he would. And as for me, I'll feel better once I'm no longer concealing anything from you.

"Edward and I had quite a lot to drink one evening and started to talk of personal things. Edward told me a story about meeting a beautiful girl in Greece when he was a student, and falling in love with her. He didn't give many details, except that she was a wonderful artist and that he never told her how much he loved her. He said that one morning he woke up to find her gone. He completely blamed himself for not having told her how he felt. He said nothing to me about a baby or a letter, but he did tell me that he didn't know how or where to find her. He said he hadn't found anyone else he wanted to spend his life with, but he didn't sound regretful about that. Quite the opposite, he said he had never looked for anyone else.

"I didn't realise that he was talking about your wife, Konstantine. Edward only used her first name, and you rarely spoke of your wife and I don't think you mentioned her name to me for a long time. Edward was very discreet in what he shared with me, and I truly believe I was the only person to whom he'd ever told the story."

The next thing that Day had to confess was more difficult.

"There came a time recently, though, when I began to understand the truth, and for several reasons I chose not to speak to you about it. I discovered that Edward must have known about Artemis for some years, because he owned several works painted by her. I discovered this only when I asked to see the list of his art collection. Only then did I connect Edward's Artemis with your wife. With that realisation, other things became clear. Edward had always known how to find Artemis, and must have known who you were all this time, but he never tried to contact her and never said anything to you.

"Although I realised this, I thought you knew nothing about Edward other than your recent friendship. I thought it wasn't my place to say anything.

"In my opinion Edward probably did receive your wife's letter, and I think he probably guessed that she was pregnant, although I have nothing to support that guess. He did as she requested and didn't make contact with either of you afterwards. I don't think he can have known, though, that the baby didn't survive. When Angelika asked to meet him, he had some reason to think that he might be meeting his granddaughter."

Konstantinos was staring at him when Day found the courage to meet his eyes.

"I consider Edward to have been the most unselfish of men," said Konstantinos in a small voice, "and he must have loved Temi very much."

"Yes."

"Do you remember that afternoon on the terrace when he told us that he was going to meet the granddaughter of the love of his life? He was so excited. That was Angelika he was talking about, I assume?"

"Yes. Did you guess, at the time?"

"Of course. I knew that Edward was Temi's Edward. I don't think I gave myself away, did I, Martin?"

"You fooled me, Konstantine. But why? Why didn't you ever want to talk to Edward properly?"

"I suppose it was easier that way. I had no heart for an emotional scene. I did want Angelika to know about her grandmother, though, that's why I gave her Temi's box of diaries when she died. I knew Temi's account of that summer was inside. I found it too hard to tell Angelika myself, but it was right that she should know. Then I realised Angelika hadn't opened the box. Perhaps she felt it was invasive to read the diaries, or perhaps she was just too busy with Sofia. When I heard Edward say he was meeting her, I assumed she had read the diary and contacted him. She'd said nothing to me…"

Day nodded thoughtfully, knowing exactly why Angelika had not told her grandfather. It was time he backed away from this family maelstrom. Angelika would have to tell Konstantinos herself.

"Does anyone else know about Edward and Artemis?" Day asked.

"No, only Fotis," replied Konstantinos. "I felt a bit low after you and Edward left that evening, knowing Angelika and Edward were to meet. I'm guilty of using Fotis now and again to get things off my chest. He's a simple soul and I knew he wouldn't repeat what I told him to anyone."

With that, Konstantinos excused himself and went to his bedroom to shower and dress in fresh clothes.

***

The sun was well above the rim of the horizon by the time Konstantinos returned, waking Day from a doze on the sofa when he entered. Konstantinos looked much better, once again the man Day had first met, the renowned sculptor with a dry wit and twinkle in his eye. Day suggested that Konstantinos should return with Angelika to Chora, because for the rest of the day his house would be full of police. No sooner had Konstantinos agreed than Angelika arrived. She had clearly been crying, but that was behind her now as she fussed over her grandfather, over Day, then her grandfather again. She demanded to know everything that had happened, which Day explained as Konstantinos went to pack an overnight bag, for real this time.

There was no sign yet of the police. Konstantinos wanted to wait for them and also to speak to Xanthe and Fotis before leaving with Angelika, so they went to sit outside in the early morning sun.

"I'm very sorry, Pappou," said Angelika, "I know you never liked Loukas, and because of me he could have hurt you. I should have sorted him out a long time ago."

"None of this is your fault, agapi mou," said Konstantinos fondly. "You were always going to make the right decision, I knew that. You're a person who makes good choices." He nodded and reached for her hand, holding it as he spoke. "I think you decided to read your grandmother's diary, didn't you? It's what I wanted you to do. I'm sorry, I should have had the courage to talk to you myself."

Angelika flushed.

"Yes, I read it, and I decided to find him, this Edward. I wrote to him and he replied, and I even met him in Athens not long ago. It was the day before he was killed. You know, don't you, Pappou? Did Martin tell you?"

"No, agapi mou, in a way it was Edward himself who told me. He said he was meeting the granddaughter of someone he had loved, and that was enough for me to work it out for myself."

Day struggled to know what to say, what secrets to keep and what to share. His face must have shown his confusion. The old man's sombre expression suddenly opened into a fit of laughter that brought on a series of helpless coughs.

"Everyone has been keeping secrets from everyone else," he said, wiping his eyes with the back of his hand. Tears were streaming down Angelika's cheeks, though Day could only guess what confusion of emotions had caused them. "Everyone except Artemis, who alone was always honest. Oh, don't be upset, Angelika, I know you were trying to protect me. You too, Martin. I expect Edward was doing the same. What else haven't you told me, both of you?"

"I took Peppino into my confidence, so he knows a lot of the story," admitted Day. "I trusted him because he was the only outsider in all this. He was determined to help you, Konstantine, and in fact he's the one who devised the plan…" He held back the end of the sentence, because whatever he chose to say would probably upset Angelika.

Konstantinos said he liked Peppino and was very grateful to him. He looked around briefly, as if expecting to see him, or Dali perhaps. Instead he reached for his granddaughter's hand again and held it.

"Angelika, my dear, I believe there's one more thing I should tell you. Edward was a dear man, and he and your grandmother were very much attached. But he was not your grandfather. No, don't cry, agapi mou, just let me tell you the story. Temi was expecting a baby when we met. The father was Edward, and Temi was very honest about her pregnancy, not wanting me to commit myself to her without knowing. It was not a problem to me, I found: I was very happy to take on both mother and child. Temi and I married, and we looked forward to the birth of our baby. We chose names, we told our families, everyone was full of joy. A little boy was born. He was beautiful. But he had a difficult birth and sadly he only lived for one day. Temi and I were heartbroken. We talked about it and we both wanted to try for another child as soon as possible. Your dear mother was the result. I don't think Edward knew anything about this."

He glanced at Day and pretended not to see Angelika's continuing tears.

"In 2013, two years after Temi died, I went to Cambridge for a conference and bumped into an interesting man from the university's ancient history department, and we talked about marble for a long time before we introduced ourselves. Of course, I recognised his name at once. Perhaps he had been in my mind at some level since I'd arrived in Cambridge, but I was completely shocked. I'd never thought I'd meet him, Temi's Edward. While I was blindly considering how I felt, Edward suggested we have dinner together. I agreed; why not? I liked him, and it didn't matter what had happened all those years before. Half a century before. We were two old men with similar interests and tastes. He had a great sense of humour. I remember we talked and laughed all night.

"From what Martin was telling me before you arrived, agapi mou, I think Edward also knew who I was that night, and also chose not to speak about it. Really, we were very alike."

Angelika leaned across and kissed her grandfather on the cheek. She smiled at last, and gently wiped his cheek which was damp from her tears.

"I'm glad you told me, Pappou, and I'm glad you're my grandfather. Even if you'd told me a different story, you'd always be my real grandfather."

They chatted for a while, leaving Day to watch the rising sun across the garden and wallow in his own thoughts. He was glad that Konstantinos had the love and support of a woman like Angelika, especially in view of the further shock which, in Day's opinion, he would soon have to face.

The sound of cars arriving at the gates alerted them to the return of the police. Angelika went to greet them, while Day and Konstantinos watched from the elevation of the garden. Watching the real world from this distance made Day more than usually reflective, and he decided to share it with his companion.

"I've been thinking a great deal about Edward," he said. "Edward remained single all his life, keeping his love for Artemis alive, collecting her paintings, no doubt thinking of her, but not trying to find her. For some people that would be enough, I know, but Edward wasn't an introverted man, he was intelligent, gregarious, worldly. I wondered why you thought he chose to live like that, and didn't ever move on?"

"Well, Martin, of course Artemis was a special woman, one whom a man couldn't easily forget. But I don't think that quite answers your question. Edward was a very intelligent person, you're right, and he was content with his life. We are all different. Some men love women, some men love other men, we understand that these days. I think there are also some men whose sexual preference is neither for women nor for men, but for unrequited love, regardless of gender. It has a perfection, and a safety. I think Edward may have belonged to the last group. It did him no harm, did it? I think he rather enjoyed it. You know what they say? 'A heart that loves is always young'.

***

Day arrived back in Filoti around half past nine that morning. Helen was in her dressing gown, looking as if she hadn't had much sleep. She looked both relieved and annoyed. He realised he should have called her hours ago but he hadn't thought. He took preemptive action.

"I'm really sorry, Helen, I know I should have called you. It was thoughtless of me. It all worked out as we planned and nobody was hurt."

"I'm sure you had your hands full, Martin. I'm pleased that everybody's all right. You'd better tell me what happened."

"The intruder was Loukas, Angelika's fiancé. He showed up in the middle of the night. Peppino was keeping watch down in the workshop and I was in the study in the house. The first we knew about the intruder was when I heard a key turning in the outside kitchen door. Peppino ran up from the workshop and we both burst into the kitchen. Loukas was in there, and Peppino managed to grab him. Andreas and the police got there quickly and Loukas was arrested."

"So he didn't have time to attack Konstantinos before you stopped him?"

"No. I expected the intruder to go to Konstantinos's bedroom, but he actually made no attempt to find him. Andreas thinks Loukas was putting some powder in Konstantinos's coffee pot."

Day suddenly felt extremely weary and full of burdens and sadness. He could barely speak. He wanted to say more to Helen but found he had nothing left.

"I'm sorry, Helen, I can't do this now. I didn't sleep at all and I feel truly awful. I really will tell you all about it in detail after I've had a bit of sleep. Oh, but I've got to call Andreas. Unfortunately this isn't over yet."

Through his scratchy eyes he saw enough of Helen to realise she understood, and went to his bedroom to call Andreas from a horizontal position.

***

Nomikos answered his mobile immediately, although judging by the background noise he was at the Naxos Police Station.

"Martin. What can I do for you?"

His tone suggested he meant 'What do you want now?'

"I know we'll meet later, Andrea, but I need to speak to you at once. If you're charging Loukas for the murder of Edward, I think you're mistaken. I believe we have two criminals here, each targeting a different old man. No, hear me out, Andrea! Why would Loukas kill Edward? The only motive I can see is if Loukas saw a problem with Angelika's inheritance if Edward was found to be her actual grandfather. But knowing Konstantinos there wasn't much danger of him disinheriting her. Also, whoever killed Edward took an enormous personal risk, and that's not in Loukas's character. No, I think somebody else killed Edward: Fotis Vassos."

Day listened patiently as Andreas expostulated on the other end of the line.

"Let me tell you why I think Fotis killed Edward, Andrea. This morning I learned that Konstantinos has always known about Edward, because his wife had told him everything from the start. When they met in Cambridge in 2013, Konstantinos realised who Edward was but found it didn't matter about the past. They became friends, and Konstantinos didn't tell Edward what he knew.

"Konstantinos never found the courage to tell Angelika about Edward and Artemis, but he believed it was her right to know the story and so gave her the box containing Artemis's diary, so that Angelika could discover the truth for herself. As we know, she did this. She kept it from Konstantinos to protect him, but sought out Edward.

"Edward, meanwhile, had known who Konstantinos was all along. He'd been careful to keep the secret all his life, but for some reason he blurted out one day that he was going to meet the granddaughter of a lost love. I was there, Konstantinos was there, Fotis was there. We all heard Edward say that the meeting would be in Athens in a few days' time. Konstantinos knew then that Angelika had arranged to meet Edward, but he said nothing at the time.

"Konstantinos told me this morning that he's in the habit of letting out his feelings to Fotis, believing that the man wouldn't really understand the significance of what he was hearing. I think he's always underestimated Fotis's abilities. Fotis is certainly damaged, but he's far from stupid or insensitive. Konstantinos vented his feelings in private to Fotis after hearing that Edward and Angelika were to meet. This told Fotis when and where Angelika and Edward were to meet, and how much his adoptive father, Konstantinos, hated the whole idea.

"Do you remember that Fotis lost his parents in an accident when he was young? Not only has he regarded Artemis and Konstantinos as parents since they took him in, I believe he has a very special feeling for Angelika. He seems to adore her. I think he wanted to stop Edward from meeting Angelika, to protect Artemis, Konstantinos, or Angelika herself. Fotis is clearly very affected by his traumatic childhood, and you can understand why, but he may not be the gentle giant he seems. I think he went to Athens in order to stop Edward from meeting Angelika. He may have meant to kill Edward, or it may have been a disastrous mistake, but Edward would have opened his door to Fotis, and I think Fotis killed him. Oh, and I know Fotis saw Edward take his heart pills and knew what they were. Even if the killing was unpremeditated, Fotis knew about the pills and used them to make the murder look like suicide."

"OK, you realise this is all completely circumstantial, Martin?" protested Andreas patiently.

"Certainly. I could go and talk to him, make him confess."

"Absolutely not. You are forbidden to do any such thing, Martin. Do you hear me? The correct procedure is to find evidence, check the ferry passenger lists, show his photograph to the hotel staff in Athens, many things, good thorough police work. Then we'll bring him in for questioning. Leave this to me now. OK?"

"OK," said Day, only half reluctantly. "I'll be sleeping if you need me...."

"Don't forget to come in and make your statement, Martin," was Nomikos's parting demand.

26

It was quiet at Taverna Ta Votsala. The building occupied a tranquil situation at the far end of the bay of Paralia Votsala, nestling between higher ground behind and a wide stretch of the Aegean. Day settled back into a cushioned sofa, stirring his frappé gently. Opposite him sat his friend Vasilios, the owner of the taverna, whom Day had not made time to meet for several months. Their conversation had lapsed into a comfortable pause. Day watched an expensive yacht make its way south towards Chora or Paros, and a small white fishing boat chug northwards towards the headland through the glitter of the morning sun's dance on the surface of the sea.

His friend's voice recalled Day from his enjoyment of the beauties of the Cyclades.

"I was afraid we were in for a summer of bad luck, Martin, but fortunately I was proved wrong. From what you've just told me, poor Kyrios Saris suffered all the ill fortune. Do you think his problems are over now?"

"I think so. The culprit has been arrested and things will get back to normal again. Konstantinos is busy now with the work for the Niarchos project with Peppino Berducci, which will clear his mind of his recent troubles, I hope. As for me, I have time to finally get finish the Nikos Elias book."

"Are you anywhere near finishing it?" The implication was clear: Day had been working on the book for many months.

"No, these things really do take a long time, Vasili. At least I'm close to having done enough to keep my agent happy. He's quite impatient now, of course; I should have sent him something a month ago. Hopefully he'll get the completed draft soon and then we have to lick it into shape for a publisher. Publishing takes for ever, Vasili!"

"Well, at least your time is your own, Martin. To me it sounds a wonderful life."

Day had to acknowledge the truth of this, and nodded with a small smile. He drained the last of his frappé.

"Right, Vasili, thanks for coffee, it's been good to see you. I'm going to spend a couple of hours over at the Elias house now, then I'll be locking it up for a while. I probably won't need to work there again. You might notice some strangers at the house because the lawyers want to do an inspection as part of the transfer to my ownership. I'll let you know when they're coming."

Vasilios walked with Day to his car. He had already expressed his pleasure that Day would soon be the new proprietor of the Elias House, having been gifted it by its former owner. Day remembered a favour he wanted to ask.

"Once I own the house legally, Vasili, I wonder if you would have time to oversee it for me? I'd pay you, of course. I'm planning to open it eventually as a study retreat, there will be paying guests, and hopefully your business here will benefit from that too. What do you think?"

"Of course, Martin, of course!" said Vasilios, and gave him a very firm shake of the hand.

***

Several hours later, Day locked up the Elias house and prepared to drive home. The sun was high and the Fiat 500 had become a small oven. He opened all the windows to enjoy the breeze on his face. He smiled as he drove, going slowly to savour the colours of the landscape. The grass was many shades of cream and yellow now, exhausted by the summer drought, and the higher slopes were grey and orange with lichen-covered rocks and crisp, half-dead scrub. Day sang aloud, with more gusto than accuracy, another joyful excerpt from Gilbert and Sullivan. His work at the Elias house was finished: he had gleaned all the information he required about the man's life and work, and much of it had been written up. He was at a stage of the project he knew well, feeling torn between satisfaction and a pressing need for something new. He didn't know what his next work would be, but for some reason he suspected that it would not be Edward's marble project.

Helen was working on her laptop, a familiar sight at the big dining table that dominated the living room of the Filoti house. They made some lunch from what they could find in the fridge: cucumber, tomato, onion, and a little cheese that had been around rather a long time. They would have to visit the supermarket again, something both of them put off.

"We're celebrating today, Helen!" said Day. "I finished at the Elias house. I can soon send what I've done to Maurice, and the pressure's off for a couple of weeks."

"Congratulations! I suspect you'll be pleased to put Nikos Elias out of your mind for a while."

"I think so. Have you been making good headway with your book?"

"Not really," she answered. "I've been a little distracted."

This surprised Day, who had been working at the Elias house for the last four or five days and had not asked Helen about herself in all that time. He raised a quizzical eyebrow.

"Yes, I've been out rather a lot."

"Out?" There was only one car, and Day had used the Fiat to go to Paralia Votsala every day. "Walking?"

Helen looked at him and gave a short laugh.

"No, Martin. I was collected in a smart hire car and driven off to lovely tavernas overlooking beautiful scenery, and treated to many interesting accounts of life as a police inspector in Athens."

"What?" Day said before he could stop himself. "Andreas? And you?"

Helen chose not to respond. As she picked up her plate and moved towards the kitchen, she called back over her shoulder.

"Andreas called earlier, by the way, while you were out. He's invited us to have dinner with him this evening in Chora, a restaurant called Astakos. It's about three hundred metres from the police station, apparently, in the direction of the Kastro. Eight o'clock. All right? He says he has news for you."

"Fine," called Day.

Day did not know which astonished him more - that Helen had any interest at all in a relationship, since her disastrous ex-husband Zissis seemed to have put an end to all that, or that Andreas had room in his mind or schedule for anything other than crime. He thought about the invitation. A three-some meal promised to be awkward, he thought, but he hoped that Andreas also had news of the investigation into Fotis Vassos.

***

O Astakos, or The Lobster, was a restaurant set off the beaten track in the quiet back streets of Chora. It had a modest frontage and the only indication that it was a restaurant was an arched gateway, a menu board and a pathway lit with small lights. The dining area was concealed within a walled terrace at the back of the house, surrounded by white walls topped with wooden trellis and adorned with flowering climbers. The place was expertly lit with warm lights which picked out romantic features such as small statuettes, curiously twisted young olive trees, and, in the centre of the courtyard, a pair of old wine barrels topped with a display of bottles and glasses. No intrusive sounds reached this inner sanctum; only a murmur of voices rose from the three or four occupied tables.

Day and Helen were shown to a table against the far wall, above which rose a pale pink bougainvillea. The table was laid with a white linen tablecloth and napkins, a range of cutlery and glasses, and a bottle of water in a slender thermal container. Andreas Nomikos, who was already waiting for them, rose and extended his hand. There was no meaningful greeting for Helen, Day noted. He suspected Andreas was on his best behaviour.

"Good to see you both. What would you like for an aperitif?" said Andreas.

Day asked for a G&T, hoping it would raise his spirits. Andreas decided to have the same, and Helen chose a glass of Kir. Day leaned back in his chair and watched the pleasantries being exchanged. There was, he thought, an extra warmth in Andreas's blue Viking eyes.

"I thought we should combine business with pleasure again tonight," began Nomikos. "I'm definitely in your debt after the special evening you gave me in Filoti. Shall we begin with the business, then we can enjoy the rest of our evening in peace?"

Their drinks arrived and Day took a sip of the neat gin through the ice cubes and sliced lemon. The spirit warmed his throat, then his chest, and then began to have some effect on his mood. A second sip confirmed this phenomenon. Day added the tonic to his glass.

"First," said Andreas, "I'll update you regarding Loukas Veakis. The traces of powder in his wallet were a strong anticoagulant drug, an illegal copycat product not unlike the prescription medicine Warfarin. He had bought it online; we got into his computer and found proof of the transaction. He had also bought a strong poison identical to that which killed the dog, a type of rat poison.

"When you caught him, Martin, Veakis was mixing the lethal powder into your friend Konstantinos's ground Greek coffee in a quantity which would have been deadly. He knew his future father-in-law drank Greek coffee from that container every morning without fail. I doubt the poison would have been noticeable through the flavour of the coffee, and of course it would have been invisible. We think Veakis intended to get the early boat back to Athens in time to go straight into work the next morning, thus establishing an alibi if he should need one. He probably hoped that Kyrios Saris's death would be thought accidental, because Kyrios Saris takes Warfarin on prescription. Veakis must have been aware of this.

"So, he's been charged with the attempted murder of Konstantinos Saris. Veakis has also admitted to the other break-ins, claiming that he only meant to alarm Kyrios Saris into changing his plans. The prosecutor has sanctioned additional charges of illegally entering a property, malicious damage, assault (on Fotis Vassos), and misuse of a hazardous substance (the rat poison).

"Veakis had obviously planned all this for a while. You were right, Martin, when you sensed a more serious threat behind the break-ins. Veakis meant to give the impression that somebody wanted to stop the Niarchos project, but his intention was always to kill Konstantinos Saris, who was an obstacle between him and a fortune."

Day nodded and forced a smile. "How did he get to and from the atelier every time without being heard or noticed?"

"We found a motorcycle concealed in a gully a few hundred metres from the property. Nobody notices a motorbike, do they? There are so many on the island. His fiancée was unaware that he even owned one, so we believe he bought it deliberately for the break-ins and kept it hidden somewhere."

"Did he really think that Angelika would marry him?" Helen said with disbelief. "From what I've heard she's an intelligent young woman. She knew of her grandfather's opposition to her marriage."

"Veakis wouldn't agree with you, Helen. He's spitting mad at what he thinks is the ruination of his brilliant plan by a couple of outsiders. Criminals don't think in the same way as you."

Helen shrugged and sipped her Kir.

"I assume you've questioned Loukas about the murder of Edward?" asked Day.

"Yes. Ah, I'll come back to that. It looks like this lady is coming to speak to us."

An elegant Greek woman in a long satin evening dress walked up to their table with a welcoming smile. She greeted them with all the grace and charm of a duchess, and introduced herself as Penelope. Her natural poise was enough to captivate all three of them. Helen said afterwards that the restaurant hardly needed to spend money on advertising when word got round about its owner.

Day's considered opinion, after seeing Penelope and falling in love with the entire restaurant, was that the meal was likely to be expensive. It was a remarkable place, and its owner matched it very well.

Penelope apologised unnecessarily that there were several other tables occupied that evening, but assured them of her personal attention. She handed them small, hand-written menus bearing the date of that particular evening, and invited them to take a look while she brought them some things to try while they made their choice.

She swept away, and Andreas took the opportunity to insist that the evening was to be entirely his treat.

Penelope returned followed by a young man who placed three small oval plates of food on the table. Penelope introduced the dishes, for which Day was grateful. Two of the dishes were completely new to him.

"Here you have a little taste of the smoked tuna from Alonissos, a very special delicacy. On this dish are fresh *kidonia*, the small local clams. We eat them like oysters, raw with a little lemon juice. And these of course are crispy fried tomato balls. I hope you enjoy them!"

They decided to try the delicacies one at a time. The kidonia first, split open already and needing only a few drops of fresh lemon juice, were cool and smooth and, like oysters, tasted salty and rich. Then they moved on to try the smoked tuna, which Andreas explained was only produced in one place, as far as he knew, which was an island in the Northern Sporades. As most of his work in the Aegean had so far been in the Cyclades, Day had forgotten that the small island of Alonissos specialised in tuna. Finally they ate the tasty little balls of fried tomato, which had a lovely crisp texture and simple flavour.

The gin had worked its magic on Day, who was not a man to sulk for long. As he drained his aperitif he realised that the fault was entirely his. Helen had not kept anything from him, it was he who had not asked. Moreover, she had every right to see whomever she pleased. She had good taste, too. He liked Andreas Nomikos.

Penelope appeared at the table and placed in front of each of them a small liqueur glass containing something creamy.

"This is a small mousse to prepare your palette. I hope you like it. It's made with lemon. Would you like to order some wine?"

Andreas and Penelope discussed the choice of wine in depth. Day's absolute favourite Greek wine was an Agiorgitiko from Nemea in the Peloponnese, but he usually drank local wine 'from the barrel', not least for reasons of economy. He was more than content when Andreas chose an Agiorgitiko from Northern Greece at Penelope's recommendation.

In the same way as Andreas chose the wine, he effectively chose the food too. Day was hardly going to object to this display of Greek filoxenia, the hospitality which Andreas exemplified. The two dishes he ordered were mussels steamed with garlic, followed by a lobster dish which Penelope recommended to them, a speciality of her chef. At her suggestion, they ordered nothing more.

"This is wonderful, Andrea," said Helen, finishing her tiny lemon mousse. "This is a very special place. How did you find it?"

"I asked one of the lawyers in the town, a man I worked with some years ago; we try to have a coffee together when I'm on Naxos. You like it?"

"It's sensational, and absolutely beautiful."

Andreas looked as if he would have liked to respond with a matching compliment to his guest, but he refrained. Day glanced at Helen. The warm lights of the courtyard brought out the golden colour of her hair and suntanned arms, which looked even more pronounced against her cream-coloured sleeveless dress.

"So, I imagine you questioned Loukas about Edward's death?" he asked, turning back to Andreas.

"At length. He was contemptuous, I think that's the right word. He absolutely denied having anything to do with Edward. More importantly, he has a solid alibi which is corroborated by several of his colleagues. He was at an event for the Department of Tourism in Thessaloniki, which was why he didn't spend the weekend at Angelika's house on Naxos. He left Athens for Thessaloniki early on the Saturday morning, more or less at the same time that Angelika left to come home to Naxos. We've traced him on the internal flight. He couldn't have been in Athens when Edward was killed in the middle of Saturday night."

"Well, that sorts that out," said Day, trying to hide his satisfaction.

He was interrupted by the arrival of their wine, its uncorking and its ceremonial tasting. Day was not disappointed when he sipped his glass.

"Unfortunately," Andreas resumed, any chagrin about his prime suspect's alibi softened by his pleasure in the wine, "we can't trace Fotis Vassos to Athens that weekend either. His name doesn't appear on the passenger register of any ferries, his vehicle wasn't seen in the port, and the hotel staff at the Lykavittos Comfort don't remember seeing him. We asked in Kato Potamia, among his neighbours and in the local shops, but they had nothing to tell us. Fotis Vassos, as we know, is a very withdrawn person, so nobody missed him that weekend; they simply wouldn't expect to see him around. No, I'm afraid I don't think that line of enquiry is leading anywhere."

That clearly brought business to an end as far as Andreas was concerned. When their food arrived at the table there could be no further thought of murder. The mussels were perfectly cooked, and the lobster dish was one of the best Day had ever tasted, although the amount of expensive lobster dishes he had eaten could be counted in the time it took to heave a sigh. Tender pieces of lobster meat had been prepared with tomato, garlic and herbs, and served with pasta, but with a finesse which Day would have found it impossible to describe.

Day's mood had improved considerably, not only as a result of the good meal, the wine and the beautiful setting. Not even his new regard for Andreas, or the glow he perceived around Helen, accounted for it entirely. He had decided some time ago to get justice for Edward, and that's what he still intended to do. He now saw no reason not to go and speak to Fotis Vassos as he originally intended, since the police no longer regarded him as a suspect.

He was not going to let Edward's killer go unpunished.

27

At seven thirty the next morning Day left the house quietly and drove to the atelier. He had deliberately avoided Helen. She would try to stop him, and for once he didn't want her opinion, or any other voice of common sense. He knew very well it was stupid, but this was something he was going to do for Edward.

Peppino was waiting for him at the gate of Saris EM, which he opened to let Day through.

"Thanks for coming, Peppino," Day said quietly.

"What's this about, Martin?"

"I'm going to have a chat with Fotis when he arrives. I'll explain later. Would you go up and stay with Konstantinos? Keep him in the house. And could you unlock the store for me?"

"OK," said Peppino, rubbing the side of his nose with his index finger. "Don't you want my help?"

"Not this time. Thanks for the offer."

Peppino unlocked the silent store building with his personal key and walked reluctantly away. Day scanned the courtyard before going inside. His small Fiat was as unmissable as the Temple of Olympian Zeus, but Day didn't need to take anyone by surprise. He thought Fotis was probably expecting him anyway. He reckoned he had about half an hour to search Fotis's personal sanctuary before the man arrived for work.

A single-storey barn built of brick and timber, the store housed all the deliveries for the atelier from marble to packing boxes. Day's eyes struggled with the gloom inside until he opened a pair of shutters. In the darker recesses of the store he saw the crates and boxes methodically stacked, and what looked like a makeshift bed with dishevelled blankets in a corner. Empty beer cans overflowed from a plastic bin.

Satisfied that he was alone, Day started to look round. He felt a brief pang of guilt, like an intruder. He was drawn to the table by the window, which was piled with papers held down by a chunk of green marble, delivery notes mostly. Concealed underneath them was a closed notebook with a biro between the leaves to mark a place.

Day lifted the notebook and opened it. It was some kind of private journal. He closed the book and put it down, then, shaking his head and pursing his lips, he picked it up again, sat in the chair, and began to read. The handwriting was childish.

My Private Journal - 34th Birthday

I'm 34 today. I'm not sure I'd have got to this age without Artemis. I didn't have the best start, did I? I never talked about it till I started this journal. I write whatever I like here. So here I am again, writing for myself.

I've been thinking about Zas recently. He was my own dog, a little brown one. He was a stray puppy and dad said I could keep him if I looked after him. I never let that dog out of my sight. I loved that dog.

Zas was still a puppy when my parents went off in the van one day to sell their vegetables at the market. I was allowed to stay at home with Zas as long as I promised to be good. I felt very proud and grown up. They said they'd be back for dinner. They weren't telling the truth. I never saw them again. I told people they'd had a car accident, but really they just went away and left me. They didn't love me. I know they thought I was stupid. That was when I was fourteen.

I went to live on a farm further down the valley. I tricked the farmer into taking me on as a labourer. I told him I had some family on the mainland who would give him lots of money for taking me in. So of course the farmer did. He gave me a bed in the outbuilding, and on Fridays I worked at the market. My job was to carry the boxes of vegetables from the van to the stall, and carry back what didn't sell. I could keep Zas with me at the farm, that was the best thing.

Then one day a kind lady came to the market, one of the farmer's customers. She talked to me, and I told her about my dog. Next market day she came back again and asked where my parents were and where I lived. I wanted to live with her rather than with the farmer, so I cried a bit and told her my parents had died in a car crash. I don't know what happened after that, but I ended up living with her. That was Artemis. She said I could call her mum, and I did sometimes, just to please her. I was always a bit afraid of Konstantinos then. Artemis told me I could stay with them always. She just wanted me to help out around the place, especially as she and Konstantinos were getting on a bit.

My dog Zas died in the end. That's when Konstantinos got Dali. I think Artemis told him to get a dog so I felt better about losing Zas. I love Dali. Dali is even nicer than Zas.

Then Artemis died. That was the second worst day of my life. Everyone cried. Afterwards Konstantinos talked to me a lot more. I think he really likes me now. He gets me to do jobs for him, but everyone has a job, don't they, and I don't mind doing things for Konstantinos. He's famous. And he makes plenty of money, and he takes care of me. I feel safe here.

He has a pretty granddaughter called Angelika. Angelika's mother is ill, I haven't seen her for years, she doesn't come here now. Angelika and I have both lost our mothers, in a way. She's my special sister, although she doesn't know it. She smiles and is nice to me, but I don't think she knows she's my sister. Anyway, it doesn't matter. What does matter is that I'm always going to look after Konstantinos - I've been calling him Dad recently - and my sister Angelika. I'm a nobody, and I like that, I like being on my own. But if anyone tries to hurt my family, they'll have to get past me.

So, it's my 34th birthday. It's been an ordinary year since I wrote in here last birthday. My mum Artemis has been gone now for a long time. In another journal, one that's already full up, I've written about the year she died, but I don't want to read it again. What about this year, then? I ought to write something in my journal about it.

Konstantinos won a big prize, and he told me there will be a lot more pretty marble delivered to us soon. I look after his marble. And a big man has come to work with Dad because of the prize. He's nice enough to me, I suppose. Dad has two more new friends. The younger one is OK, he's about my age. He's got a funny name like Mar Tin, and he speaks with a funny accent, but he's friendly and Dad likes him. Then there's the old man who's been before, Ed Wood. He's as old as Dad, and he speaks funny too. Dad told me Ed Wood used to love mum, and its a big secret from everybody except me. Dad said he doesn't want to tell Angelika, but he can tell me because he trusts me. He just doesn't want Angelika to know.

The other day Ed Wood said that he's going to meet Angelika in Athens. Or maybe it was Dad that told me. Dad was upset. But he's too old to do anything about it. Then he told me he's really happy with Angelika finding out. I don't understand, why did he say he was happy if he was so upset? I don't think Dad's telling the truth when he says he's happy with Angelika talking to Edward about mum. I think he wants me to help him. That's what he was trying to tell me. He doesn't want things to change around here, and I don't either.

Because it's my birthday I can write about how I feel, can't I? I feel like Zas when he growled at people because he was guarding me. He would growl and bark and show his teeth, and he would have bitten someone hard if they tried to hurt me. I feel like biting hard. Someone is trying to hurt Dad, and Angelika, and my mum would be unhappy about that. I'm going to be like Zas, I'm going to protect them.

"You mustn't read that. It's private," said a voice behind him. Day had not heard anyone come in. He got up and turned to face the voice.

"Hello, Foti. I'm glad you're here, I came to speak to you."

Startled, Day faced Fotis Vassos, trying to hide his alarm and assert some kind of authority into his voice and his stance. Fotis was between him and the only door, and Day believed he was looking at Edward's killer. He stood completely still, facing Fotis without speaking. The light from the window behind Day was in Fotis's eyes, so Day must be little more than a silhouette.

Fotis didn't look a formidable opponent. He was slight, his build weak and gangly, with thinning hair and an untidy beard. He was wearing work overalls and dusty boots, and he looked a mess, but Day noticed his hands, held loosely at his sides, which were long-fingered and strong.

Day struggled to remember what he had planned to say.

"I came to speak to you about my friend Edward. You remember him? Little man, old, he was here a few weeks ago."

Fotis remained silent and immobile, forcing Day to continue.

"Edward was like a father to me, like you feel about Konstantinos. I know you've been worried about Konstantinos."

Day was relieved to see a small nod, and carried on.

"Edward was a very kind man and when he died I was sad. Since he died, I've been thinking about Edward a lot. That's why I've come to talk to you."

He waited. Fotis shook his head minutely, his features immobile. Only his eyes betrayed that his mind was working on what Day had said.

"You're a sensitive kind of man, Foti. You'd want to know what happened to Konstantinos if someone killed him. I want to find out what happened to Edward. I'll never see him again …"

Day brought his hand up to his forehead and lowered his head. He hated taking his eyes off Fotis, but when he looked up again, pretending to recover from an emotional moment, Fotis had not moved. His fingers had not even clenched. Day found this inactivity almost as worrying as an attack.

Day spoke as slowly as he could manage. "I know you can tell me exactly what happened to Edward. I want you to talk to me. You don't like it when people don't tell the truth, like when your parents said they were coming back and never did. Like when Konstantinos didn't tell you the truth when he said he was happy for Angelika to meet Edward."

Blood rushed to Fotis's face and his eyes shone.

"You don't know what you're talking about! It's my job to look after Konstantinos. He doesn't have anyone else. That's what Mum would want me to do. Keep things happy here."

"I understand that, Foti, your responsibility to your family. I understand that's why you went to Athens to find Edward."

"I had to talk to him and stop him seeing my sister. He was going to ruin everything and hurt everyone. He had no right doing that."

"I get it. How did you know where to find Edward?"

"I didn't, not at first. I got his number from Xanthe's phone and I called him."

"You called him?"

"That's right, I called him and said, could I come and talk to him about Artemis? I knew he would say yes, and he did, and he told me which hotel, what room, what time to get there on Sunday. But I got there the night before, when he wasn't expecting me, and nobody saw me go upstairs to his room."

"I see. And he let you in. And did you talk?"

"Yes, he opened the door, I think he thought there was a fire, but when he saw it was me he let me in. He was in his pyjamas. He tried to tell me that he'd been protecting Artemis and Konstantinos for years and years by not going to see them, because he didn't want to make them unhappy. But now, he said, now that Mum was dead and Angelika wanted to know about him, he'd changed his mind. I told him, that will make people unhappy. He didn't agree. He just wouldn't agree."

Day remained silent.

"Don't look at me like that. It was all his fault. If he'd only gone away… I had to protect my family. They always protected me, now I had to protect them. You see? They don't have anyone else, it's my job."

Still Day said nothing; there was no need now.

"I don't remember what happened. I tried to stop him talking, stop him saying it would be fine and that this was what he'd wanted all his life, and stuff like that. Next thing I know I'm holding him down on the bed with the pillow over his face to stop him talking."

"And then you realised he was dead. What did you do then?"

"His tablets were right there on the table. With a glass of water. I flushed the pills down the toilet and left the empty bottles next to the glass. Then I came straight home. Nobody was going to hurt my dad or my sister now."

Day tensed, watching Fotis choose between fight or flight. Fotis glared at Day, then turned and ran from the building, leaving the door swinging. Day let him go, leaning against the edge of the table and remembering to breathe. He heard Fotis's running steps cross the courtyard, heading towards the house. Day picked up the notebook and put it in his jacket pocket, moved over to the door and looked out cautiously. There was no sign of anyone. Then he saw Fotis behind the workshop, running up the slope towards Konstantinos's house. Day tore after him.

The front door was open when Day reached the house, and he could see Fotis and Konstantinos inside. There was no sign of Peppino. Konstantinos and Fotis were just releasing each other from a hug, and Konstantinos was encouraging Fotis to sit down with him at the dining table. He had Fotis firmly by the hand. He saw Day and instructed him to come inside with a jerk of the head which Fotis appeared not to notice. Day took a hard chair near the door and remained silent, ready to move fast if he had to. Fotis had eyes only for Konstantinos, who waited silently for the breathless young man to talk.

Fotis talked. He told Konstantinos what he had done to Edward, filling in the details which he had omitted when talking to Day. Day clamped his hand over his mouth, appalled. When he had explained himself, Fotis begged Konstantinos to help him. Konstantinos lifted Fotis's hand in his own and held it as if it were very precious.

"Things are what they are, Foti mou, and you and I always do the right thing if we can, don't we? I know you won't let me down. You need to tell the police everything you've told me. I understand why you did what you did. And I'll stand by you, I won't leave you."

Day got up and slipped out of the house, confident Konstantinos was in no danger. He leaned against the house wall in the morning sun, his mouth dry. He couldn't hear anything now from inside. He took out his mobile and dialled Andreas.

Suddenly the back door of the house crashed open and Fotis hared over the rough land behind the house, heading uphill away from the road, flailing his arms to keep balance on the rough terrain, often stumbling among the rocks and scrub. Then a large figure careered after him, emerging from the house only seconds later. Peppino Berducci.

***

Within twenty minutes the courtyard of Saris EM was filled with police once again. Peppino had caught up with Fotis and had brought him back to the atelier, where Konstantinos had joined them to wait for the police. Day watched Konstantinos's face as Fotis was handcuffed and put in the back of a police car. He felt his chest constrict with regret that he had been proved right. He stood aside as Konstantinos walked past him without a word or glance.

Andreas Nomikos waited for the convoy of police vehicles to leave, then turned to find Day. Even from a distance, Day could tell he was angry. Day had been expecting it. The inspector took the steps two at a time towards him.

"What the hell did you think you were doing?" shouted Andreas, more out of control than Day had ever seen him. "I specifically told you not to see Vassos alone. Thank God nobody was hurt, but how dare you? Do you have *any* evidence of *any* kind, Martin? I could arrest you on so many charges - jeopardising a police investigation, endangering the life of a civilian, disobeying police instructions …"

"Last night you said you believed he had nothing to do with the murder, Andrea," Day protested, not taking kindly to this extended rebuke, "and you didn't intend to consider him any more. I think I was within my rights to talk to him. As for evidence, he confessed everything to Konstantinos, and I witnessed it."

Day's earlier tension had turned swiftly into fury, and he deliberately left the incriminating journal in his jacket pocket.

"You're a liability. I was wrong to trust you," snapped Andreas Nomikos, and pushed past Day towards the house.

His heart beating savagely, Day strode to the gate, got into the Fiat and slammed the door. He forbade himself to think about anything but the bends in the road until he parked outside his own front door.

***

Day let himself into the house to find it silent and Helen sitting on the sofa reading a book. The sight of her calmed him considerably. He even offered to make coffee, to which she agreed without much enthusiasm. From the galley kitchen at the far side of the room, Day regarded her.

"Sorry I didn't see you before I went out this morning. You OK?"

"Yes. I slept in a bit. Where did you go?"

Day told her in detail. He told her as he prepared the coffee, brought it over to her, sat down, sipped his own, and finally reached the part where Andreas Nomikos lost his temper.

"So, your hunch about Fotis was right after all," she conceded, a steely tone in her voice. "You know what you did was bloody stupid, Martin? Andreas was right to be furious. And I can see why you left without talking to me this morning."

"Sorry," said Day again. "I knew what you'd say. This time I couldn't afford to hear it. I had to see this through to the end, I owed it to Edward."

"I see it now. Last night, at the restaurant, when Andreas told you he wasn't interested in Fotis any longer for Edward's murder, you decided you'd go and see him yourself today."

"Pretty much."

Helen was silent. Day knew she was hurt that he could have talked to her of his plans the previous night and had chosen not to. She was also angry at him for taking the risk. He could think of nothing to say. For the first time that he could remember, he and Helen sat in a silence that was not in the least companionable.

"Andreas and I won't be seeing anything more of each other," she said finally. "At least you and he won't have to meet socially again."

Day stared at her. "I'm sorry to hear that. He's mad to pass up somebody like you."

"He didn't. I rang him this morning to thank him for last night and tell him that I don't want a relationship at the moment. I couldn't have put it any more kindly, I really couldn't."

"You were the one that ended it? No wonder he was in a bad mood today."

"No, Martin. He was furious with you, not with me."

"Of course. Sorry. Why did you do it, though? Last night it looked as if all was going well. You looked really happy."

"I just told you. Actually, Andreas completely understood."

"Does that mean … that you're happy now, Helen?"

"Ask me later, Martin, hey?"

28

The seventeenth-century Bazeos Tower on the road between Chora and Halki was a beautiful venue for an art exhibition. Naxos, an island which valued the arts extremely highly, had transformed many of its ancient and atmospheric buildings into cultural centres, none more stunning than this one. The Bazeos Tower, a square castle made of stone, had once been a monastery, had become a feudal stronghold, and was currently a prestigious and beautiful exhibition venue.

It was opening night, and the place was crowded. Konstantinos Saris, who jointly with Markos Ioannakis was organising the current exhibition, had had no difficulty in obtaining the agreement of the owner to use the venue. Day and Helen, each holding a glass in one hand and a small guide to the paintings in the other, were chatting to Aristos and Rania Iraklidis. Across the room, Day noticed Deppi Kiloziglou and her Greek-Australian husband Nick laughing together as they watched the other people in the room. Konstantinos, Peppino and Xanthe stood together, with another man. Day guessed this was Xanthe's husband. There was no sign of Angelika.

Somebody at the back of the room tapped a spoon against a glass to request silence. Konstantinos excused himself from his group and joined Markos Ioannakis on some steps where they could be seen by everyone. Day thought he had not seen Konstantinos look so radiant. The last time Day had seen him was at Fotis's arrest, when Konstantinos had looked straight through him.

Markos welcomed everyone and then introduced Konstantinos. It was a formality; Konstantinos needed no introduction to this gathering.

"Good evening Ladies and Gentlemen," he began, "and welcome to the Bazeos Tower. I'd like to thank you all very much for coming tonight, and wish you a wonderful evening. My thanks are particularly due to Kyrios Bazeos for his kind permission to hold the exhibition in this magnificent historical building, and for the hospitality which we are all currently enjoying. I owe a special debt to Kyrios Markos Ioannakis, on my right here, not only for his skill in creating the exhibition, but for his years of support to me and my family, which can never be sufficiently repaid. Thank you, Marko.

"The paintings on display tonight are the work of three generations of my family. Their work has never been exhibited together before. My late wife, Artemis Pantrakis, will be known to many of you. She achieved a modest success beyond this island during her lifetime, and her paintings appeared in Athens at the Greece Re-Explored Gallery, whose current owner, Kyrios Alekos Georgiades, is with us this evening. Welcome, Kyrie Georgiades.

"Our daughter, Sofia Spetzou, is unable to be with us this evening due to ill health, but her work is represented in the second room. Sofia benefited from her mother's skill and encouragement, of course, but her style is completely her own. She was self-taught, and had a natural flair. Her expressive depictions of our beloved island of Naxos have something of the French Impressionists about them, I think. I invite you to decide for yourselves.

"The third artist represented here this evening is my granddaughter, Angelika Spetzou, who has never before permitted me to exhibit her work, so this evening is a very important one for me personally. Angelika studied at the Athens School of Fine Arts before returning to Naxos for family reasons. Her paintings show a truly modern approach to both portraiture and landscape, which perfectly draws the artistic line of the Saris family into the twenty-first century. I hope Angelika will be able to join us later in the evening.

"I have a couple more people to thank before Markos and I leave you to explore the exhibition.

"Some years ago, a very precious family friend, Edward Childe, bought two of my late wife's paintings. He subsequently donated them to the Museum of Brauron, where he had met my wife when she was making the original sketches for the works. Edward is sadly no longer with us, but I thank him sincerely for this expression of love and respect. One of the 'Brauron paintings' depicts the marble columns of the Temple of Artemis, and the other shows a small girl with a hare, inspired by a votive statue owned by the museum. Thanks to the generous gesture of two very kind friends, those paintings are here in the exhibition. Dr Martin Day and Mrs Helen Aitchison persuaded Brauron to lend us the paintings, and went to collect them in person last week. Martin, Helen, I thank you very much.

"I must keep you no longer from the exhibition, my friends. Markos and I wish you a very enjoyable evening. It is a great pleasure to offer you a little piece of Saris family history tonight. Thank you once again for joining us."

The guests applauded, and Konstantinos and Markos stepped down. Casting a last glance at Deppi over his shoulder, Day followed Helen into the exhibition.

***

An hour or so later, having seen every work on display in the atmospheric setting of the refurbished tower, Day and Helen sauntered out into the gravelled courtyard. People were starting to emerge from the tower to enjoy a glass of wine there in the balmy evening. Day looked up at the looming stone facade of the tower, which was artfully illuminated by hidden golden uplighting. At the top of the facade was a semi-circular opening, through which the feudal landlords would have gazed down on their estate. Above it, at the very top of the building, a small bell tower recalled the original monastery. Day was rather ashamed that his knowledge of Venetian architecture was non-existent, and vowed to read up about this wonderful old place.

Helen accepted a fresh glass of wine from a man bearing a tray, and Day followed her example.

"That was one of the most enjoyable exhibitions I've seen for a long time," said Helen. "I think my favourite paintings were Artemis's 'Girl with a Hare', and Sofia's seascapes of Naxos. Is Angelika here yet?"

"I haven't seen her. I hoped you'd get to meet her."

"I had a chat with Peppino. What a nice man. He's quite a character, isn't he?"

"He certainly is. We must see more of him in the next few months. He's an excellent drinker, you'll like him."

"Don't be naughty, Martin." Helen sipped her wine and looked round at the tower admiringly. "This really is a stunning place, it makes a remarkable venue. Did you see any paintings that you didn't see on your visit to Angelika?"

"Actually, most of them were new to me. Artemis's self-portrait as a young woman is stunning, and seeing it gave me a jolt because that must be how she looked when Edward met her. I also love Angelika's portrait of Artemis as an old lady, which I hadn't seen before. Konstantinos told me that Angelika didn't want him to put it in the exhibition. He was right, though, wasn't he? Artemis is at the heart of everything. From Edward to Loukas and Fotis, everything that has happened was connected to Artemis."

"People felt strongly about that woman. Both Edward and Konstantinos spent their lives in love with her."

"Mmm. Fotis, too, acted as he did because of Artemis, even after her death."

Helen nodded and followed Day's glance round the people talking in the courtyard.

"This exhibition, you know, is Konstantinos's way of apologising to Markos Ioannakis, his friend from the art shops," said Day. "He suspected Markos of the break-ins, and wants to make it up to him. Markos will get some good publicity during the week of the exhibition."

"Is it all over now, Martin, the business with Loukas and Fotis?" asked Helen.

"I'm certainly finished with it! The law will take its course with the two of them. I feel very sorry for Konstantinos, because Fotis meant a lot to him. Actually, I have some sympathy for Fotis too. OK, I'm not excusing what he did to Edward. It's just that he was treated appallingly as a small child, and his mental limitations are indisputable. I think he's a victim too. I've been wondering what would be the right thing to do with Fotis's private journal. I didn't give it to the police at the time, and now that they have Fotis's confession I don't intend to. It doesn't seem right. I've been thinking of giving it to Konstantinos."

"If you think that would be the right thing to do, but definitely not tonight, Martin. Agreed?"

He glanced at her, glaring at him with her eyebrows imperiously raised. Her instincts were always spot on, he thought. The journal felt heavy in his pocket. He thought of what he had read in its pages, that night in the store and since. The lies Fotis had told about his parents' car accident, his manipulation of Artemis, his reservations about Konstantinos, his questionable feelings towards Angelika. He decided that no one else, after all, should ever see the journal.

As he took a final swallow of his wine, he caught sight of Deppi over Helen's shoulder. Her small frame and dark hair was backlit by the orange glow of the tower walls. She smiled at him then turned away to greet the group of people she had been about to join. Day adjusted his focal length back to Helen, who was looking particularly English, her hair turned a toffee colour by the floodlights, her white dress catching the golden glow off the Bazeos Tower.

Day smiled at her and took her empty wineglass, placing their glasses together on a small white table.

"Let's go, shall we?" he said. "Enough culture for one night. It's early yet, and Thanasis will have chips."

Printed in Great Britain
by Amazon

19713209R00180